Degrees of
Connection

JON CLEARY

Degrees of Connection

HarperCollins*Publishers*

HarperCollins*Publishers*

First published in Australia in 2003
This edition published in 2004
by HarperCollins*Publishers* Pty Limited
ABN 36 009 913 517
A member of the HarperCollins*Publishers* (Australia) Pty Limited Group
www.harpercollins.com.au

HarperCollins*Publishers*
25 Ryde Road, Pymble, Sydney, NSW 2073, Australia
31 View Road, Glenfield, Auckland 10, New Zealand
77–85 Fulham Palace Road, London, W6 8JB, United Kingdom
2 Bloor Street East, 20th floor, Toronto, Ontario M4W 1A8, Canada
10 East 53rd Street, New York NY 10022, USA

National Library of Australia Cataloguing-in-Publication data:

Cleary, Jon, 1917– .
  Degrees of connection.
  ISBN 0 7322 7631 4.
  1. Malone, Scobie (Fictitious character) – Fiction.
  2. Murder – Investigation – Fiction. I. Title.
A823.3

Typeset in Sabon 11/14 Times by HarperCollins
Printed and bound in Australia by Griffin Press on 50gsm Bulky News

5 4 3 2   04 05 06 07

FOR JOY
(1922–2003)

Chapter One

❧

1

"She's had more facelifts than the Strand Arcade," said Clements. "*And* she's a ball-breaker."

"You're a misogynist," said Malone.

"Wait till you meet her. You'll join the club."

They were on their way to see Natalie Shipwood. She lived at Sylvania Waters, a southern suburb that had been put on the map some years before by a TV documentary on a family that had aired and beaten its secrets as if they were carpets hung on a line. More secrets, Clements had warned, were to be hung on Mrs Shipwood's Hills hoist.

He had come across to Crime Agency's offices yesterday. Crime Agency and Homicide were housed on the same floor in the same building at Strawberry Hills, well away from the shadow of Police Headquarters, which was further uptown. Working police, like soldiers, work better the farther they are away from the generals.

"The Hyx murder," Clements had said, settling into a chair across the desk from Malone, moving his backside as if testing the seat; he had been across here only once since Malone had been promoted to superintendent. "The woman from Orlando Development —"

It had been no more than a three-line item in the newspapers and not mentioned at all on radio and television. Other, bigger things were happening on the other side of the world and another death, even by murder, could be ignored.

Malone waited. He had been here in his new job only two weeks; like Clements', his bum was still testing the new chair.

He had been welcomed by the other Crime Agency officers, but this was a new neighbourhood, though within shouting distance of his old office. Homicide had been like a hometown and he was missing it, an expatriate who would go on missing it for months to come.

"At first it looked like a break-and-enter that had gone wrong," said Clements. "A few things were missing from her house, the sorta things they take — some jewellery, her wallet, things like that. She'd been stabbed in the chest twice, but they couldn't find any weapon. Blacktown didn't call us in till two days ago. Then we started to find things —" He paused.

"You're getting tongue-tied, mate."

"I know. And before this is over, I may be hogtied. The fan is starting to whirr, mate, the shit is ready to be thrown —"

"Poetic, too. I miss you, Russ —"

Clements grinned, but he was not in good humour. "Nothing is gunna be poetic about this, unless it's justice. And we're a long way from that —" Another pause. "Forensic found a key to a strong-box. Gail Lee went down to the Commonwealth Bank in Martin Place, had a look at the strong-box. It was full of stuff that makes Orlando look a pretty sick company."

Malone was not a man who followed the business pages in his morning newspaper; his son, Tom, with an investment bank, was embarrassed by his father's ignorance of the *real* world. "I know nothing about Orlando. Is it big money?"

"It's not in the same league as Lend Lease and a coupla other biggies. But it's big enough and was thought to be growing. It was on its way up. Then I got John Kagal to follow up what was in the strong-box. Orlando is down the gurgler and so far nobody knows."

"Nobody but who? Somebody always knows."

"Okay. The woman who started the company would know, she's the executive chairman. Chairwoman, chairperson, whatever." Clements, like Malone, belonged to a derelict school where politically correct was looked upon as foul language. "Mrs Natalie Shipwood."

"I've heard of her. Who else?"

"The other directors, probably. And some of the senior executives."

"You're holding something back."

Clements nodded, held another pause before he said, "Derek Sweden. He's on the board, the deputy chairman."

Malone looked out the window. "While we're being poetic, how about bubbles in still waters, whispers on the wind?"

"You can be as poetic as you like, I'm heading for Tibooburra." The furthest outpost of the New South Wales Police Service, where no developer had ever trod.

Derek Sweden had been the Police Minister in State parliament some years ago; Malone and Clements had had dealings with him when his party had been in power. He had left politics when his party had been voted out, but he still had political clout, which he wielded like a master. His son, described by those who knew him as an unmitigated jerk and a scoundrel, had been murdered and Malone and Clements had conducted the investigation. Sweden had never appreciated their efforts and they knew their names were in the little black book he was said to carry like an unholy picture. He himself was suspected of dirty deeds, insider trading and other jokes that honest men never laughed at, and Malone knew the pressure that Sweden could bring.

Malone looked out the window again. The early spring sky was cloudless; if there were any whispers on the wind, the wind was too high for them to be heard.

Over the past few weeks the world, slowly at first, then with terrible swiftness, had been turned upside down. There had been political upheaval here at home as xenophobia, always latent in the national blood, had taken over and a mere 400 refugees had found themselves the centre of a crisis. Then, to put things into perspective, "reality" TV had turned too real as terrorists destroyed the world's financial centre. Pictures came out of New York that no-one could believe, filling living rooms where the very walls no longer seemed safe. Another week, another disaster, smaller this time and with no deaths, hit the headlines when the nation's second largest airline, overweighted with debt, crash-landed and tens of thousands of jobs were suddenly in jeopardy. Then a major mining company had fallen down a bottomless hole; crisis became a state of mind. And now Orlando . . .

"It's one thing after another," said Clements as if he, too, had been running the events through his mind. "But this is the one that's in *our* lap."

"Righto, I'll talk to Greg. We're not jumping into this head-first or even arse-first. Maybe you won't have to go any further than treating it as another homicide."

"Not a chance. I can already hear those whispers you mentioned."

Half an hour later Chief Superintendent Greg Random, Malone's immediate superior, had heard the whispers: "I was talking to Fraud. They'd heard rumours about Orlando, but decided there would be no criminal charges, not on what they've discovered so far. They passed what they'd heard over to the Securities Commission. That's what commissions are for. The too-hard basket."

"Did you know Derek Sweden was one of the directors?"

Random's long lean face had shown no surprise since his farmer father had taught him, when he was five, what bulls did to cows. All he did now was raise an eyebrow. "You don't say." No exclamation mark, just a flat statement. "Well then, you'd better stay with it, see things don't get out of hand. Use your Irish diplomacy."

"Don't start quoting any of your Welsh poets at me —"

"*Rage, rage, against the dying of the light* ... Get outa here. Keep me informed. I'll be hiding in the trenches, head well down."

So now Malone and Clements were on their way to talk to Natalie Shipwood. "Have you met her?"

"No. I went to a seminar she held, I thought I might put some money into Orlando, but she didn't convince me. She's imposing."

"How?"

"From a distance she looks like Elizabeth Taylor, big hair and all."

"How distant?"

"The other side of the street, maybe a bit more."

Sylvania Waters lies about 20 kilometres south of Sydney's CBD. It was once no more than a shallow bay with swamplands and oyster-claires. It had been part of a huge estate owned by a wealthy colonial politician who knew the difference between a bargain and a rort; he had bought it from a bankrupt fellow politician. He had built himself a mansion and, because the land was too poor for crops, had tried to run sheep and cattle on the property. No luck: in one year late in the 1860s, 13,000 sheep died of footrot. Subsequent human residents have managed to avoid the disease, though foot-in-mouth was prevalent while the TV documentary makers were the shepherds.

In the early 1960s the bay and its surroundings were taken over for private development. The swamplands were reclaimed with two million cubic metres of shell-strewn sand. And other fill: once residents moved in and began to dig to build swimming pools they dug up car bodies, refrigerators and other artefacts. The shallow bay was turned into a private waterway for permanent dwellers. Today there are six-bedroom mansions on twenty-metre lots; in some streets taste was just a statement to be made. The colour schemes ranged from stark white through several shades of blue, beige and brown to bright yellow with purple trim. It is, as battlers in territory several kilometres west refer to it, another country.

The Shipwood mansion was at the end of a dead-end street, spread over two large waterfront lots. It was another Tuscan villa; Tuscany was now so represented around Sydney that one kept awaiting for the arrival of expatriate British and American authors. Eight Roman pines, four on either side, led up the short driveway to the house. Malone looked for armless marble statues, but there was none. Just a grey-haired man in a T-shirt, shorts and old-style sandshoes washing a green Bentley.

"Morning," said Malone as he and Clements came up the mosaic-paved driveway. "You work for Mrs Shipwood?"

"You might say that." Behind him was a wide-fronted garage; inside there were three other cars. "I'm her husband."

He had a long thin face, further elongated by a spade beard; he looked like a gardener who had turned into one of his own tools. But he seemed friendly enough, as if he had dug into himself for some seeds of community.

"You from the Securities Commission?"

"No, police." Malone introduced himself and Clements and showed his badge. "Homicide."

Shipwood's equanimity was a little too studied.

He gave a final wipe of the Bentley with a chamois. "We're putting it up for sale, only a year old. You wouldn't care to make a bid?"

"I'll trade you a five-year-old Volvo for it," said Clements.

Malone leaned his backside against the polished green surface of the mudguard. It was a fine sunny day, everything was still and peaceful: just the day for a chat. "Do you work for Orlando, Mr Shipwood?"

"No, I'm retired. It took me sixty-seven years to find out what I do best."

"What's that?"

"Nothing."

"Inspector Clements and I still have to find out what we do best. In the meantime we're at home in Homicide. Did you know Mrs Hyx, who worked for Orlando?"

Even in the relaxed atmosphere it was a swipe at the chin. But Shipwood didn't duck or rear back. He wrung out the chamois, put it away in the boot of the car. "She was my wife's private secretary. A nice woman. But you've come to talk to my wife, right?" He led the way to the front doors, two of them, each with a brass head on it, bearded men with no welcoming smile. "Gog and Magog. They frighten door-to-door salesmen."

"But not cops," said Malone.

Shipwood smiled at them. "No, I shouldn't think they would."

He led the way into the house. A wide hall led right through to glass doors that looked out on lawns sweeping down to the water. The colour scheme was white, almost blindingly so; one would not have been surprised to find moths hovering around in daylight. Natalie Shipwood, all in white, stood on the bottom step of a curving staircase that led to the upper floor.

"Sweetheart," said Shipwood, but there was no endearment in it. "The police."

"Yes?" The two detectives might have been two Orlando office boys.

"May we sit down, Mrs Shipwood?" said Malone, and introduced himself and Clements. "This may take some time."

She studied him, as if checking his credentials. Then, without replying, she led the way across the wide hall and into a huge living room. Shipwood had taken off his sandshoes and, carrying them, went up the thickly carpeted, all-white stairs. Halfway up he paused and smiled down at Malone and Clements, but it was impossible to tell what the smile meant.

The living room was all white, except for three Australian landscapes on the walls: a Roberts, a Streeton and a Jackson. They looked as out of place in the ultra-modern room as a Francis Bacon on a convent wall. Natalie Shipwood sat down and Malone and Clements, as if directed, took chairs opposite her. They had the martial sense to sit on chairs and not on the wide lounge that would have put them on a lower level than her.

She looked at the gold watch, bigger than the usual woman's watch, on her wrist. "I can give you ten minutes."

Malone sat quiet while Clements said, "Mrs Shipwood, we police make our own time, especially when we're conducting a murder enquiry."

That didn't seem to disturb her. Malone sat relaxed, took stock of her. She was in her sixties, he guessed, and he had seen enough facelifting to recognise the tightness in certain parts of her face. If there was any grey in her hair it had disappeared in a black rinse; her figure was full and the white trouser-suit hid any sag; only her hands gave her away. Clements had been right: she did indeed look a little like Elizabeth Taylor. From a distance.

She turned to Malone: "You introduced yourself as Superintendent. Why am I being questioned by your junior officer?"

Malone laughed; he couldn't help it. "Mrs Shipwood, come down off your perch."

She stared at him, then, unexpectedly, smiled. It was a pleasant smile, full of expensive teeth, but practised: a politician's smile in a nursery at election time. "It's a business habit, Superintendent." She looked back at Clements. "Murder, Inspector? Marilyn Hyx?"

"Yes." Clements looked uncomfortable on the chair on which he sat, as if the seat was too small for his backside. "She was your secretary, as chairwoman of Orlando? Had she been with you long?"

"Fifteen years. Ever since I started Orlando. Why anyone would —" She stopped and Malone waited for the tiny handkerchief to the tearful eye; but Natalie Shipwood was a good actress, Elizabeth Taylor would have been proud of her. She sat for a moment, gazing out the big French doors at the end of the room. Then she turned back to Clements: "I don't think she ever harmed anyone in her life."

"We think she was planning to harm Orlando," said Clements. "She had a strong-box full of documents she had obviously copied. Had she made any attempt to blackmail you?"

Natalie Shipwood's hands were not *aged*; they just did not complement the manufactured bloom of her face. Whether as disguise or distraction, her fingers were on display: diamonds winked, gold shone. There were five rings on the fingers, a thick gold bracelet on one wrist, the gold watch on the other wrist. In bright sunlight she would be an airport beacon.

The hands folded into one another. "That's a shameful thing to say about her."

"About her or about you?"

Good one, Russ, thought Malone: a real beanball.

Mrs Shipwood ducked without moving her

head, as if from long practice. "That's insulting. To both Mrs Hyx and me."

"It's a practical question, Mrs Shipwood," said Malone, taking over the bowling from Clements. "We're investigating a murder here. We usually find in murder investigations we have to ask a lot of questions. Was Mrs Hyx trying to blackmail you?"

"Are you suspecting me of murdering her?" Her gaze was direct.

Malone looked at Clements. "Are we?"

The two of them could have been day-old recruits to the Service. "Oh, I don't think so. Not yet," said Clements, and resumed the bowling. "But we have to start somewhere, Mrs Shipwood, and we're starting with those who knew her best. We understand Mrs Hyx was a widow —"

"No." She shook her head, but there was not a tremor in the black hair. *She's lacquered from head to foot*, thought Malone, *and inside, too*. "Everyone thought she was a widow, but I knew her best. There was a husband, but he disappeared before she came to work for me. She never spoke of him, not after she had told me when she first applied for the job. I wanted someone who would be on call whenever I wanted her. Not a wife or a mother. I paid her well and she appreciated it."

"What sort of woman was she?" asked Malone.

She looked at him, then at Clements, then back at him. It was an old police trick to keep the questions coming from different angles, but she was not put off balance by them. Malone could imagine her running a board of directors like a circus dog-trainer. "She was capable, very capable. And loyal."

"If she was so loyal," said Clements, "why did she have the documents in the strong-box? Copies of letters, computer print-outs, a balance sheet, notes from a board meeting? Even copies of bank transfers overseas?"

Natalie Shipwood took her time, the hands still folded into each other. "I have no idea. It was against her character —"

"Mrs Shipwood," said Malone, "did she tell you what was in the strong-box?"

"No." Flat as a cough.

"She must have told someone about what was in the box."

"Why?"

"Because we think whoever she spoke to," said Clements, "was the one who killed her."

"You'd better tell them, sweetheart."

Harry Shipwood stood in the hallway door; in shirt, jeans and loafers now. He looked neater, more than the gardener or the handyman. Malone and Clements waited while Natalie Shipwood stared at her husband as if he were a stranger who had interrupted them. Then she turned back to Malone.

"There are problems with Orlando. We are trying to straighten things out before they become public. We don't want a recurrence of what happened with —" She named an insurance company and an IT company that had collapsed.

"It may be public very soon," said Clements. "The Securities Commission have what we found in the box. We passed it on to them."

For the first time Natalie Shipwood lost her composure. Her head jerked up as if she had been hit under the chin; the hands suddenly clawed at each other. "You had no right —"

"Mrs Shipwood," said Malone, "don't tell us our rights."

Shipwood had not moved from the doorway. He stood there like a spectator, offering no comfort. Then he said, "Shouldn't you be warning us about our rights? That we should call our lawyers?"

"Only if Mrs Shipwood feels she can give us information about Mrs Hyx's murder. We're not here to represent the Securities Commission."

"No, we don't need our lawyer." Natalie Shipwood had recovered; the head and hands were still. "I know nothing about the death of Marilyn. We were friends." She stood up. "Now I have to go. I have a board meeting."

The two detectives stood up, Clements twitching his hips as if getting circulation back into his backside. The two of them never minded being dismissed; it gave them an excuse to come back. Malone couldn't resist it, the tongue flapped as it had so often: "Give my regards to Mr Sweden."

"You know him?" She looked surprised, as if he had stepped up a class or two.

"Old workmates. He was once the Police Minister."

Shipwood, still in the doorway, was smiling; he looked untroubled, still a spectator. "It's a small world . . . I'll see the gentlemen out, sweetheart."

But Natalie Shipwood had turned away, staring out the French doors. Down beyond the wide lawn, a large motor cruiser was moored to a jetty. A young man lolled in the well of the boat, a straw hat propped over his eyes. Abruptly Natalie Shipwood walked to the doors, opened them and went down towards the boat.

"Our son," said Harry Shipwood. "B.J. Brandon Jurgen."

"He's your son?" said Malone. "*That* Shipwood?"

B.J. Shipwood was a rugby league footballer who had gained some notoriety by claiming a magazine's Bachelor of the Year contest had rejected him because his IQ was in double figures. The outcome was that football opponents of single digit IQ tackled him with vicious force and the magazine had labelled him a misogynist.

"The same. He's the darling of older women, they think he's Marlon Brando, or whoever their favourite was. Well, maybe not Brando — one forgets he's now ancient." He began to lead them out of the room. "He brings them home, the older women, and I look on them as stepping-stones across the generation gap. But I'd never tell 'em so. My mother taught me never to criticise older women … Ah, hullo, darling —"

They were out in the wide hallway. Malone looked up the stairs, expecting to see an older woman, maybe Shipwood's very old mother. But a tall, slim, dark-haired girl in a white silk dressing-gown was coming down the stairs.

"Our daughter, Chloe," said Shipwood. "These gentlemen are from the police."

"Really?" she said and went by without a glance and out towards the back of the house.

Shipwood appeared unembarrassed. "The young," he said, as if to himself. "Adores her mother, wants to be as successful as her."

"What does she do?" asked Malone.

"Nothing. Twenty-three-years-old and not even in the starting blocks yet. Do you have kids?"

"I have three, all out of the starting blocks, all sure they know more than me. Inspector Clements has one."

"Five, going on six," said Clements. "She wants to be an opera star. Could be worse, she could want to be Britney Spears."

"Lucky men," said Shipwood and opened the front doors. He stood between Gog and Magog, who glared at the two detectives. "Let us know if you're coming again. We'll invite our lawyer."

"An older woman?" Malone was beginning to like the man.

"Who else?"

As they turned away Malone said, "Your wife reminds me of someone."

"It's possible," said Shipwood and closed the doors.

The two detectives walked down the short driveway. "I don't think he sees his wife as Elizabeth Taylor."

"He thought you meant Michael Jackson," said Clements.

2

"I'd like to see the scene of the crime," said Malone.

"Which one? The homicide or the Orlando rort?"

"The homicide. Rooty Hill, wasn't it? If I'm going to be on this case, I think I should start at the beginning." He stood beside their car and looked back at the Bentley and the big house. "Is all that, the house, the cars, the boat, going to go down the gurgler?"

"I wouldn't bet on it," said Clements. "Mrs Shipwood will be looking out for Number One, right down the line."

"Ain't it the way," said Malone, thinking of

recent captains of industry whose feet were still dry after their ships had sunk out of sight.

They got into the unmarked police car and headed out of Sylvania Waters for the scene of the crime. Rooty Hill lies some thirty-five kilometres west of the city, on the plain that slopes towards the Blue Mountains. It, like so much of the original colony, began as a land grant. What distinguished it from other land grants was that it was given to an ex-convict, a jovial 140-kilo giant who had been condemned to the gallows in London for stealing £20 from his employer, but had the sentence commuted to deportation to Sydney, a lesser Hell. Since then, of course, Sydney has rewarded many criminals, but Lumpy Dean was one of the first. The area took a long time to prosper, always just "out there" on the fringes of the city and the awareness of the State politicians. It is not a suburb of statement, just content in its sense of community.

They had pulled off the Western Freeway when Malone said, "Have you got a key to Mrs Hyx's house?"

Clements shook his head at his own stupidity. "I forgot. The crime scene is closed down ... Is there a sledgehammer in the boot?"

"No. But maybe we could call up one of those private eyes from TV, the blokes who open locks with credit cards."

"You ever tried that? All you get is a bent credit card. We'll go to the local station —"

"No, forget it. Let's go home."

"We're almost there."

Clements turned the car into a side street that stretched down to a bank of tall eucalypts, like a windbreak, at the far end. They had come through rows of small timber and fibro cottages, all squatting neatly on their neat twelve-metre lots, and now were approaching a row of new houses: two-storeyed, brick, even a couple of Tuscan villas. Gardens were just being established, this obviously was a new end of town, developers, like explorers, moving west.

"That's it," said Clements and pulled the car in before an apricot-brick house. It was as new-looking as its neighbours, except for the gnarled jacaranda that hid one half of the house like a purple sunburst. "She moved in here only three months ago."

"The front door's open," said Malone and got out of the car.

"Could be an estate agent. They're on to deceased estates like vultures." Police, possibly because of their low esteem in the eyes of certain sections of the public, have their own prejudices. "Let's look like a coupla prospective buyers."

But when they knocked on the front door the man who came through the short hallway was in T-shirt, shorts and thongs: not estate agent's gear. "Yeah? I help you?"

"Police," said Malone. "We'd like to take another look at Mrs Hyx's house —"

"Mr Malone? Sergeant Clements? Well, waddya know!"

He was short and lean, with a dark complexion, gouged with deep lines, and a shock of greying curly hair. Malone squinted at him, running a projection of the gallery of rogues that every policeman keeps in the files of his mind. "Nigger? Nigger Brown?"

"Never forget a face, you blokes, do you? Same with me. Howyagoing, you two?"

"Staying alive," said Clements. "What are you doing here?"

"Feeding Marilyn's budgie. Mrs Hyx — I'm her next-door neighbour. The poor bloody bird's pining for her, I think. Hasn't chirped since she was done in. Bloody awful, that was. A good woman."

"You knew her well?" said Malone as he and Clements followed Brown into a living room off the hallway.

"Not that well. She only moved in here about three months ago. We met her down at the church, me and the missus, the local Catholic church."

"You're a born-again Christian?" said Clements.

"Twice." Brown's smile was a bright white feather in the nest of dark wrinkles. "The missus dragged me back in. Sometimes I have me doubts, but that's what religion's for, ain't it? Doubters."

Malone got the conversation back on course: "Mrs Hyx?"

"Oh, yeah. We got on well, the three of us, though she liked to keep to herself. Sometimes she'd have a bite to eat with us. Nobody should of done her in, not the way they did."

"What are you doing these days?" *Still in the same old game?* But Malone didn't voice the second question. Nigger Brown had been what the law calls a petty criminal, a term that was highly offensive to the more sensitive petty ones. He had been a burglar, a small-time conman, a forger: anything that earned a dishonest quid or two. He had never been a grievous-bodily-harm man.

"I got me own tow-truck business, three trucks. I been in it ten years now, got started back in the bad old days. Jesus, it was rough, them days. Some of the bastards would run you off the road, racing you to an accident. One of my blokes, they held a sawn-off piece to his head and threatened to blow his face off. I always carried a piece meself in them days — well, you don't wanna know about that."

"No, we don't, Nig — do they still call you Nigger, these racially correct days?"

Brown smiled again; he looked like a man who had been in good humour all his life. But Malone knew that couldn't have been. Behind the dark smiling eyes there was pain in the skull.

"I been called it fifty years, it started when I first went to school. You remember the old boot polish, nigger brown? With me name and me Abo mum, what else were they gunna call me? I got three kids, not a trace of the tar-brush in any of 'em, and they get a bit narky when they hear their dad called Nigger. I tell 'em forget it, it don't mean nothing, not to me. The narky label now is 'Middle Eastern appearance'. That's a laugh … Well, this is the room where I found her."

He gestured around him. It was a neat room, with beige leather couch and chairs, a marble coffee table and beige wall-to-wall carpet. There was a bookcase holding book club editions, a television set and a small sideboard with some bottles on a silver tray. There were three framed prints on the walls: an English village, a Rocky Mountains peak, a river somewhere in Europe. Marilyn Hyx had either travelled or dreamed of travel.

"How come *you* found her?" asked Clements.

"The wife noticed Marilyn hadn't brought in her papers — she got the *Herald* and the *Financial Review* every morning. Sometimes she'd be out the front waiting for it, standing there under that jacaranda. She loved that tree, was waiting for it to blossom — it's an old tree, but it would have been the first time for her, the blossoms like they are now." He was silent for a moment, then he went on, "I come across to see what might of kept her inside, she might have been sick or something, and I saw the front door open behind the security door. I come in and there she was —" He gestured at the floor. "Blood all over her front, none on the carpet. She was laying on her back, still dressed like she hadn't changed from the night before. Shoes, stockings, the lot. I told all that to the local blokes when I rang 'em and they come to take over. Are you blokes now on it, the case? From the city?"

"I'm with Crime Agency now, Nigger, a superintendent. Russ here is now the inspector in charge of Homicide. Yeah, we're on it."

"Then it's got big, eh? Superintendent, inspector, eh? Congratulations, I like to see me mates get on."

"Thanks," said Clements. "From your experience, Nigger, would you say this was a break-and-enter job that went wrong?"

"No way." Brown shook his head and a curl or two bounced. "I had a look at the front door. The stupid bastard had busted the lock from the inside. The security door was unlocked — Marilyn must of know-en him and let him in."

"You pointed all this out to the locals?"

Brown grinned. "You know better'n that. You never tell a cop his job, right?"

"Right," said Clements and grinned in reply. "Did Mrs Hyx have many visitors?"

"Hardly any. There was a bloke come to see her a coupla weeks ago. I seen him leaving, he had a Corolla, looked in need of a paint job. A while later Marilyn come across to have a chat with the wife, but she never mentioned him. But that was the night she told the wife she'd had a vision."

24

"A vision?" said Malone. "Like politicians have? The vision thing?"

"Nah. The real thing. She told the wife she'd seen the Virgin Mary. We knew she was pretty religious, but like I told the wife, that was going a bit too far. The Madonna of Rooty Hill — it don't have the right ring, you reckon?"

"If it did," said Malone, "you'd have all the Catholic politicians out here in no time, throwing holy water at the voters."

"He's a Catholic, sort of," Clements explained to Brown. "He doesn't believe in miracles."

"I think Marilyn did," said Brown. "Or she was praying for one. The last coupla weeks she was going to Mass every morning, not just Sundays. She was praying for *something*."

"For guidance, I think, Nigger. Marilyn had some problems at work. Did her boss ever come out here? Mrs Shipwood, woman with black hair?"

"Looks like Elizabeth Taylor," said Malone. "From a distance."

"I seen her, dunno I noticed the resemblance. She come a coupla times, in her big Bentley. What a job that'd be if it was ever in a smash! A bloke could retire on what he'd make outa it. I never spoke to her, neither did the wife. We only seen her at a distance. The wife would of said something, if she looked like Elizabeth Taylor. She knows every fillum star back to Clara Bow."

"An educated woman," said Malone, a professor of Late Late Movies.

"But you could see she had style, that's what the wife said. Wives notice that. You wanna see the rest of the house?"

Malone looked around. The house still had the smell, the look of newness; had Marilyn Hyx dreamed of this? It was two-storeyed and Malone guessed there would be at least three bedrooms upstairs; yet whom would she have dreamed of sharing it with? Who would now inherit it?

"I don't think we need to look any further," said Clements. "Everything been cleaned out? Papers, stuff like that?"

"The locals did all that. Once they'd closed down the crime scene, they gimme a key to keep an eye on the place."

"They know of your record? No offence."

Brown grinned again. "Who better to trust than someone you know's got a record?"

"You've become a philosopher," said Malone.

"You learn it in the tow-truck game. You win some, you lose some. It helps being part-Abo, me mum taught me that."

"Did Mrs Hyx ever mention any relative other than her husband? She had one, you know, divorced him years ago."

"Nah, she never mentioned him or anyone else. She was pretty lonely, I think. Nothing but work to occupy her. That, and this." He waved at the empty shell about them. "There's a Volvo in the garage. A nice inheritance, if there *is* someone."

Malone looked at Clements. "Was there a will in the strong-box?"

"None that I remember," said Clements, then handed Brown a card. "Call me if you think of something else. Or see anyone hanging around."

Brown looked at the brand-new card. "How does it feel?"

Malone had received his new card only that morning; just the one. More would be supplied "in due course", the public service euphemism for "when we get around to it".

"Same as sergeant or constable. You win some, you lose some. Give our regards to the budgie. Take care."

3

Driving back to the city Clements said, "What d'you reckon?"

"Someone in Orlando did her. How big is the business overall?"

He knew Clements would have the answer; the big man collected facts as for a scrapbook. The same way Malone had collected items for his murder-box, an old shoe-box, before computers had come in and taken over. Malone remembered the murder-box with some sentiment, when clues had been three-dimensional. Now everything, well, almost everything, came to you on a screen. Progress had to be acknowledged, though reluctantly.

Clements said, "It's in Victoria, Queensland and here in New South Wales — it stretches from Melbourne to Cairns. Its head office is in Sydney, in Sussex Street. It has pretty close to a thousand staff. Where d'you suggest we start looking?"

"Cairns would be a good place, a coupla thousand miles from Mr Sweden. How'd Orlando get into this mess?"

"Ambition, or something, must of gone to Mrs Shipwood's head. And the board of directors. I dunno whether they were thinking of turning themselves into a bank. But they've been buying small banks in the UK, the States, Canada. They started paddling and now they're outa their depth."

"How far out?"

"The talk is three billion, maybe more."

Malone, a tight one with a dollar, let alone a billion of them, was still bemused by how values had changed in the past twenty years. But then Clements, the moneyman who had started reading racing forms and now read the *Financial Review* and knew that Bloombergs was a financial service and not a delicatessen, had told him that the stock market was now the barometer of the nation. Real value had gone the way of beautiful unsliced bread and sixpenny meat pies and fly-zippers that zipped far enough down to acknowledge that your penis didn't grow out of your navel. It was a whole new world and Malone was only gradually coming to terms with it.

"Let's go and see Derek Sweden," he said.

Chapter Two

❧

1

Natalie Romal had been born with one eye open, suspicious of everyone congregated about her mother's wide-open legs. When she opened her other eye she was on her way to suspecting the rest of the world. She took no-one on trust at first sight. She had had a dozen lovers, all discarded like empty shopping bags, before she met Harry Shipwood. When she married him she had already skinned and gutted him, even though she loved him in a sort of way. It had taken him some time to realise it.

He had been a lecturer in economics at Macquarie University when she, at twenty-eight, had arrived there as a mature student. She had spent ten years as a typist and secretary in a stockbroker's office, taking notes on advice she was not supposed to hear and doing some trading at another stockbroker's. At twenty-eight she had a sizeable bank balance and decided she needed a degree if she was to go further. By the time she graduated, she and Harry, to his surprise, were married. He saw all her faults now, she knew; but against his better judgement, a not uncommon fault with economists, he loved her and she, though sometimes with difficulty, loved him. She needed someone to bounce ideas off, to tell her she was right, which she invariably was.

She had had enough money left to take out the franchise on a small branch office in an old-established building society that didn't recognise a whirlwind when it saw one. Lending money to society members to pass on to rapacious builders, she saw she was on the wrong side of the fence. She had sold the franchise and started Orlando Development. By luck that went to her head, though she didn't see it that way, she survived the Crash of '87. She wooed builders and investors, went public and the rest, she had hoped, would be history. Unwritten histories, unfortunately, are too often remaindered.

She had Brandon Jurgen when she was forty-one and Chloe a year later and, despite their late arrivals, neither child had any handicap other than an ambition to live on their mother's ambition. Harry, still a university lecturer, had by then given up on ambition, not that he had ever had much.

Now Natalie was standing on their jetty looking at her son in the well of their motor cruiser. "Brandy, the police have just been to see me."

He squinted at her from under the brim of his expensive straw hat. He was a good-looking young man, except for his eyes; one couldn't be sure whether they were lazy or shifty. He had a powerful body that showed the effect of hours in the gymnasium; women rubbed their faces against his abdominal muscles as they might against Vuitton handbags. Virtually all the women B.J. knew could afford Vuitton handbags.

"You better get used to it, Mum."

Last night, on Harry's insistence, she had told B.J. and Chloe about the disastrous state of Orlando's affairs. She had not told them what had caused the disaster and neither of them had enquired. They had just looked shocked that everything, *everything*, might be taken away from them.

Sometimes she wondered why she had bothered to have either of them, but it had been on Harry's insistent pleading and she had given in, twice, having two brainstorms that she was creating a dynasty. She knew that Harry was now disappointed in both of them, but he had come to accept them with that philosophical shrug that was almost a physical tic. She loved both her children, but sometimes it was an effort.

"In the next couple of days there's going to be some stuff in the newspapers and on talkback radio and TV. If you're asked to comment, you walk away, you know nothing."

He pushed back his hat. "That's exactly it, Mum. Chloe and I know nothing. You told us fuck-all last night —"

"Don't swear at me —"

"There's no other way to describe it. You think we're a coupla bloody idiots. Marilyn is murdered, then you tell us Orlando is in the shit ... Mum, for Crissake, what's going on?" He was standing up now, his body tense, as if he expected the boat to suddenly take off. She had never seen him so on edge, he who made a fetish of being relaxed, laid back. He looked past her: "Has she told you anything?"

Natalie turned; Chloe, in her dressing-gown, stood behind her. Chloe Shipwood was a brush-stroke or two short of beautiful; it was difficult to tell where the imperfection lay. She had better-than-average features, thick dark hair worn long and an eye-catching body that even the dressing-gown couldn't hide. Yet there was something missing, a lack of interest, even of intelligence.

"The police have been here," she told her brother.

"So Mum says."

They both looked at Natalie and, all of a sudden, she had the feeling she was being interrogated by strangers. They had changed since last night.

"Are you hinting I had something to do with Marilyn's murder?" It was an effort to get the words out.

Brother and sister looked at each other as if the thought had not occurred to them. Or as if it had, but they had not spoken about it.

"Oh, for Crissake, Mum!" B.J. took off his hat, looked as if he would swirl it away on the slight breeze. Then he looked at it, put it back on again and jumped down on to the jetty.

But Chloe, calm as a prosecutor, said, "Do the police know who killed her? They came and told you?"

"No, they didn't!" They were close together on the jetty, as on a stage. Natalie looked around, aware of an unseen audience. Windows of neighbouring houses stared back at her; a small cruiser floated by, seemingly with no-one aboard. But she *knew* they were being watched. Everyone in the neighbourhood watched her. "Let's go inside!"

She spun round and led the way back to the house. Even in her state she noticed the lawns needed mowing; she would have to tell Harry, who insisted on doing them himself. His insistence on independence, of being a dependant who earned his keep, angered her.

B.J. and Chloe looked at each other, then, with the shrug they had both inherited from their father, they followed their mother. They had also inherited his patience, but for a different reason. They knew where the money came from.

Harry, father and husband, but as remote as a

relative on the other side of the world, was standing in the French doors of the living room.

"Why have a family donnybrook right out there in centre stage?"

"Shut up, Dad," said B.J. "This is no time for your sense of humour. Why were the cops here?"

Harry looked at Natalie as she swept by him into the house. "Don't you think it's time, sweetheart, that we sat down and had a real heart-to-heart with our darling kids?"

"Jesus!" said Chloe and moved past her father and slumped down on a couch. "Will you for Crissake stop playing the university don!"

"I was never a don," said Harry, sitting down, making himself comfortable. "We don't have dons in our universities. I was just a plain old lecturer who could add two and two together and produce a prize student —" He gestured at Natalie, who took no notice of him. "I think it's about time you two heard a lecture. From your mother ... Bullshit time is over, sweetheart." He stared at Natalie challengingly. "Give 'em the facts of life. Our life."

Natalie had sat down. She was composed again; she was, as Malone had thought of her, lacquered from head to foot. She looked at her two children, side by side on the couch in front of her. She was not accustomed to complete honesty; she saw it as a weakness in others. But B.J. and Chloe were close to home, too close.

35

"We —" She stopped; taking blame was another weakness. "That is, Orlando. It's about to be investigated by the Securities Commission and there will be a lot of dirt flying around."

"She's being polite," said Harry. "She means shit."

Natalie ignored him. "Mistakes have been made by the board —"

"Mum —" B.J. had done a year of law before dropping out and deciding to be a professional footballer. He was one of the few footballers who didn't have an agent and he negotiated his own contracts. "You run the board, we know that. The board knows it, the financial writers know it —"

"And we know it," said his father. "If you want us to stand by you, sweetheart, you have to come clean."

"We're *family*, Mum," said Chloe, suddenly looking interested, intelligent. "Why do you keep trying to forget it?"

For a moment something hit Natalie, weakened her. It was not the first time: love, like malaria, recurs and recurs. She looked at them as if they were suspects: "You'll really help?"

Son and daughter nodded, but didn't rise to take her in their arms; there was still ground to be covered. Harry said, still in his chair, the most relaxed of the four of them, "Sweetheart, the truth, that's what they want to hear. Better from you than from the Securities Commission or the financial writers."

So she told them the truth; or almost. Truth never hurts the teller, said the poet; little did he know. There are limits to love and truth. She was sure another poet had said that, but she couldn't remember which one. Poets are so unreliable, like proverbs and philosophers, they contradict each other. Harry, the economist, had told her that.

"We — that is, *us* — we'll be okay. Everything we have is in a trust that can't be touched. But everything else is gone and we'll never get it back. We spread Orlando too widely."

"All over," said Harry. "The only place they didn't invest in was Patagonia."

"Do you want me to go on?" She turned a hot stare on him.

"Go for your life, sweetheart." He was, she realised, playing spectator, one who had come in on a free ticket, but had improved in the years since. Abruptly she hated him. Love, in that quarter, went out the window. Let the poets make what they wanted of that.

"Are you going to piss off overseas?" asked B.J. "Like those cowboys in the Eighties?" He had been at school then, a spoiled brat, a teacher's pet. Fortunately he had improved since then, if only marginally. "I can't see myself spending the rest of my life in Majorca."

"I can see myself there," said Harry. "An expensive villa, a swimming pool and thou beside me in the wilderness —" He looked at Natalie. "I think we had better start thinking of exits, sweetheart."

"No." She was emphatic; she was no coward. "I am not, as you describe it, going to piss off anywhere."

"Well said," said Harry.

B.J. and Chloe said nothing. She suddenly felt alone, something that had never worried her in the past. She must be getting *old*, at a frontier she had pushed back with facelifts, hair dyes and a mind as sharp as the day she had started Orlando.

2

It was lunchtime by the time Malone and Clements got back to the city, coming off the free-flowing freeway to the sludge of traffic on Parramatta Road.

"I could use the blue light," said Clements, "but I'd have to drive on the footpath."

"I'm having lunch with Lisa," said Malone. "Where does Sweden hang out these days? I'll meet you there."

"He's in the Orlando building, he has a suite of offices there."

"What does he *do*?"

Clements jerked his finger at a road-rager who wanted to cut in. "He's on the board of about a dozen companies. That's the way it is these days — boards of directors are like a club. They stick together like sheep, only they've got more power than sheep. Shareholders are the sheep."

"Stop bleating. What else does he do?"

"He's an investment adviser, though he doesn't have any title. He doesn't need one, those who want to use him, know him. He's still a mover and shaker."

"He still married to that same woman, one of those Roumanian sisters?"

"Still with her. She's one of his assets."

"How do you know so much about everything?"

"Everything? I don't know how women think."

"Who does?"

Secure in their blokey ignorance, Clements drove back to Strawberry Hills and Malone went to lunch with Lisa, his principal asset. She no longer worked as a public relations consultant for the city council, but did two days a week as a volunteer with the Red Cross. They met once a week for lunch in a café-restaurant on Macquarie Street, down from the bear pit of State parliament and across from the tranquillity of the Botanic Gardens. It was like a lovers' tryst, except that they slept together the rest of the week.

When he went down the steps into the restaurant Lisa was already at their table. With her was Tom, their son: bigger than his father, better looking but now worried-looking.

"What are you doing here?" At trysts you didn't expect your *kids* to be in attendance.

"We'll talk about it when we've ordered," said Lisa, cool and in command as usual. In middle age she still had most of the beauty she had had when young; slightly faded around the edges, perhaps, but still there like a challenge to the years. Malone, a slow learner in the climate of women, had come to recognise how women enter their middle and later years differently from men. Not all of them, of course; age and circumstances can be more ravaging on women than on men. But some, the fortunate ones, sailed almost imperceptibly into calm seas. Lisa was one of them.

A waitress took their orders, went away and Lisa said, "We have a problem. Tom has got a girl pregnant."

"*We* have a problem? What did we have to do with it?" He looked at Tom. "How'd it happen?"

"The usual way."

"Don't be a smartarse. What happened? Is it a girl we know?"

Tom had no regular girlfriend; he had more girls than a women's hockey team. He worked for an investment bank, made good money, was more than presentable and he parlayed those assets in a social life where they counted as capital. He might have made the Bachelor of the Year contest, except that he could not take anything seriously and would have been disqualified for laughing. He was not laughing now.

"Didn't you ever get into a situation like this?"

It was Lisa who kicked him under the table. "Ask another question like that and you can leave the table."

"Thanks," said Malone gratefully. There had been a couple of worrying times in his youth, but the girls had come good with reassuring news in time.

Tom nodded. "Sorry. I didn't mean that — it's just..." He rearranged the cutlery on the table in front of him. His mobile rang and he put his hand to his belt, but Malone shook his head.

"Don't answer it. You're talking to us. Is it a girl we know?"

Tom clicked off his phone, tried to settle himself in his chair. "No. I met her only the once. I'd seen her around, I knew who she was, but I hadn't taken her out. Then this night, down at The Sheaf in Double Bay, she was there. We had a drink, one thing led to another —"

"Her place or yours?" Tom had moved out of the Malone home in Randwick only three months ago, saying goodbye to his mother's cooking, fending off the jibes of his two sisters who had left home as soon as they were earning enough to be independent. He now shared a house with two other men in Paddington.

41

"Mine."

The restaurant had begun to fill and they had to lean forward to keep their talk private. At every second table a mobile had either rung or was being answered; the herd instinct was at work. The waitress came back with their orders and *her* mobile rang. She put down their plates and went away, phone to her ear. The whole world is connected, thought Malone.

Then he said, "Have you been seeing her since?"

"Dad, I went to bed with her *once* —"

"Unless sex has changed, that's all that's necessary. It doesn't need multiple injections —"

"Don't be crude," said Lisa, picking at her prawn salad. "Why didn't you use a condom?"

"Do you mind?" Malone was about to bite into his crab-avocado-and-mayonnaise sandwich. "Why couldn't we have waited till we were having coffee?"

"I have to get back to the blood bank. We're running out of blood."

Malone put down his sandwich. "Righto, do you think the baby is yours?"

"It can't be!" Tom wasn't letting his problem upset his appetite; he chewed on a hamburger with all the trimmings. "It was eight — no, ten weeks ago. Then last night she rings me and tells me she's missed her period —"

"Who is she?"

"She's a model, one of those you catch glimpses of in TV commercials. She's always there, too, in those miles of smiles in the Sunday gossip pages and you wonder who the hell she is, why they've bothered to take her picture. She's a party girl — a party animal, as they call 'em. Last week she was at some fashion wing-ding on Friday, something else on Saturday, another one on Sunday night — somehow she couldn't fit in the triathlon on Sunday afternoon."

"Being pregnant doesn't seem to have upset her too much."

"Forgive me for putting the woman's view," said Lisa, a prawn impaled on her fork, "but aren't we being a little hard on this girl?"

"Maybe," said Malone. "But he's got a cop for a father and I don't know how to act like a feminist counsellor."

"Don't get shirty with me," she said and gave him a wifely smile, which has a dozen meanings. "She didn't get him into bed with a gun at his head —"

"Look," said Tom, "can you leave this to me?"

"You came to us for advice," said Lisa, chewing on the prawn.

"Yeah, I know. But so far I haven't got any. I'll go and see her, work it out myself."

"Be careful," said Lisa.

"That's the woman's view?" said Malone. "Seems to me none of us is on the girl's side right now. But your mother's right — be careful, get a few facts from the girl. Now, can I finish my sandwich?"

Tom bit into his hamburger again, chewed a moment, then said, "How's the new job? You settled in okay?"

"So far. I'm back with Russ and Homicide at the moment. A woman from Orlando Development was murdered. I'm keeping watch because there are some names involved."

Tom cleared his mouth, raised an eyebrow. "That's interesting. There are rumours afloat about Orlando."

"Bubbles in still waters," said Malone, all at once cautious.

"What?" said Lisa, sipping her wine.

"Nothing." He rarely discussed his work with the family; that was one of Lisa's house laws, that he didn't bring murder home. Yet, being a wife, she rarely could resist asking questions. "What have you heard at the bank?"

Investment banks are hot springs where rumours are part of the working atmosphere. "Nothing definite down at my level. But there have been scraps on the e-mail, warnings to hold off —"

"You spread that sort of stuff on your e-mail?" said Lisa.

"Mum, you and Dad, in your day, you got little notes in cleft sticks. Now we get it on e-mail —"

Connections, connections, thought Malone.

"It's not supposed to be there, but it turns up on your computer and you note it. I'm not likely to be investing in a development company —"

"You might, if you become a father," said his father.

"Don't joke, Dad, this is serious."

"So are we," said Lisa. "If you have any trouble with your girl —"

"She's not my girl!"

"Keep your voice down. All right, she's not your girl. But if she proves troublesome, bring her to us."

The waitress was beside them. "Everything all right, Mrs Malone?"

"Everything's fine," said Lisa.

They went back to their lunch; then Lisa said, "That's a new suit, isn't it?"

Tom stroked the navy blue suit. "It's a Zegna. I got it for twelve hundred bucks. It was reduced."

Malone, in his off-the-rack Fletcher Jones three hundred dollars with free extra pants, went white. "No, you were reduced. Mentally."

"How did Mum ever marry a dag like you?"

"I was wearing a safari jacket, shorts, long socks and sandals when she proposed to me. Right, darl?"

"Thanks for mentioning my taste."

The three of them smiled at each other and nobody would have known they had a problem in the world. But then nobody was noticing them. Everybody was on his or her mobile: concerned with his or her own problem, with love, with gossip. Connected.

3

Derek Sweden was a sublime egotist: he recognised ego only in others. He was blind to his faults and deaf to criticism. He went through life wielding the white stick of arrogance, thrashing hecklers out of his way. He would have been his party's leader, State Premier or even Prime Minister, only no-one knew how to harness his ego. Flattery wasn't enough; he, unlike weaker egotists, didn't need it. He had left politics because he knew that, in this small country, there were wider worlds to conquer. Everyone was talking globalisation and he was sure there was a place for him in it. He had been the one on Orlando's board who had backed Natalie Shipwood all the way in her ventures abroad.

His office had been styled and furnished by his wife, his second wife, a sensible woman from Bucharest who believed that expense, like indulgence, should never be spared. The Orlando building was ultra-modern, but Rosalind Sweden had turned the clock back in Sweden's suite. The walls were wood-panelled, the carpet a soothing green, the furniture antique and leathered. There were a Monet and a Pissarro on the walls, plus a portrait of Rosalind herself by a flattering traditionalist. The insurance on the Impressionists she left to her husband, an old Roumanian tradition.

And now, sitting opposite Superintendent Malone and Inspector Clements, he was at the top of a long swift slide. He had expressed no surprise when they were shown into his office. Twenty years in the bear pit of State parliament had told him that showing surprise was a point for the other side.

"You're lucky to catch me. I was just about to leave for a meeting."

"Orlando?" asked Clements; Sweden's face showed nothing. "An Orlando board meeting?"

Sweden was a master of the long pause, an otherwise unAustralian oratorical skill; but his expression didn't change. He had a long bony face under a bald skull, a whiteboard with nothing written on it. He had put on a little weight since Malone had last met him, but he was still an elegant dresser, in the European style, his extra fat hidden by a tailor whose bias was expensive.

"What has Orlando to do with two detectives from Homicide? You're still with Homicide?" He hadn't forgotten his drill as Police Minister.

"You have a good memory," said Malone, another not to show surprise. Politicians, in the main, could remember a voter's birthday. "Yes, we're still with Homicide — or Inspector Clements is. I'm with Crime Agency now. We're investigating the murder of a woman named Marilyn Hyx. H-y-x. She worked for Orlando."

"Oh, yes, I read about her."

"Just read about her?" said Clements. "Mrs Shipwood didn't tell you about her? She was her private secretary."

No pause this time: "Yes, she told me about the murder. After I'd read about it."

Smart, thought Malone. As if still on the floor of the bear pit.

"Did you have a discussion on it?"

"Only in general terms. Mrs Shipwood was very upset and didn't want to talk about it. Why are you here questioning me?" There was no umbrage, just a polite question. Well, almost.

"We'll be questioning the rest of the Orlando board," said Clements. "And some of the senior managers."

Sweden took another long pause. "There's more to this than the murder, isn't there?"

"Funny you should say that," said Malone. "We were surprised, too." He took his own pause, let Sweden wait. Then: "Mrs Hyx left a strong-box full of Orlando papers."

This time the pause was too studied, like that of a bad actor. "I didn't know that."

Not bloody much, thought Malone. "It's all

been turned over to the Securities Commission. Maybe you were going to hear about that at today's meeting?"

Sweden was sitting perfectly still, but like a man recovering from dizziness in the inner ear. Clements said, "This is just a routine question. Where were you the night of September 12th between eight o'clock and, say, midnight?"

Sweden remained perfectly still. "Are you suspecting me of murdering Mrs Hyx?"

"As I said, it was a routine question. We ask them in all murder investigations. It helps elimination."

Sweden, surprisingly, smiled; or anyway, bared his teeth. "You should've gone into politics."

"He wouldn't have lasted ten minutes," said Malone. "But perhaps you'll answer the question. Where were you?"

"That night? I was at the ballet — no. No, I wasn't. I was at home with my wife. We both had colds and didn't want to throw the dancers off by coughing."

"You're over your cold now?"

Sweden bared his teeth again. "You're a terrier, Malone. Yes, I'm over it. Now is that all?"

"No," said Clements. "I saw what was in Mrs Hyx's strong-box before we sent it to Securities. Most of it was what I should imagine your board would have discussed. All pretty questionable. Round-robin cheques paying off loans, from company to company, some of them subsidiaries of Orlando, some of them privately owned. The sorta thing that went on back in the Eighties, a sorta merry-go-round of debt."

Malone was not surprised at what the big man knew. If Sweden was, he didn't show it.

"I don't know what you found," he said, "but what right did you have to go through her personal strong-box?"

It was Malone's turn to smile: "Mr Sweden, you were our Police Minister, you know we'd never get anywhere if we started checking our rights first."

"May I quote you on that?"

"I'll deny I ever said it. Did you hear me, Inspector?"

"Eh?" said Clements and put his hand to his ear.

Then Sweden genuinely laughed, a good strong sound that almost made a different man of him. "Okay, you win, you bastards. Yes, we discussed certain matters, the board, I mean. When we found out about them, which was only last week."

"When last week?" asked Clements.

"Monday."

"Did the board know Mrs Hyx had copies of all those transactions?"

"No, not then."

"Did Mrs Shipwood?"

"You'd have to ask her."

"We've done that. She was as evasive as you are."

Sweden looked at the two of them as if suddenly realising he needed more armour. "I remember you two. You were as shitty as this when you were investigating the murder of my son."

"Not shitty," said Malone. "Just persistent. And if you remember, we nailed your son's murderer ... Did the board know about those papers in the strong-box?"

"Basically —"

No-one in the nation over the age of five, whether illiterate or tertiary-educated, could make a statement without saying *basically*. It drove Malone up the wall. Basically, that is.

"We heard about them only yesterday. We had an emergency meeting and Mrs Shipwood told us the damage."

"You were shocked?"

"Naturally." He was unnaturally composed.

"Would any of the other board members have known? Beforehand?"

"You'll have to ask them. All I can tell you is *I* didn't know."

"You knew everything was going down the gurgler," said Clements. "Three billion, that wasn't an oversight. How were you gunna hide all that? It would of all come out, whether we found Mrs Hyx's strong-box or not."

"We didn't know." Sweden looked like a man ready to ward off blows from any angle.

"Yes, you did, Mr Sweden —"

Clements was now leaning forward. The bugger knows more than he told me, thought Malone.

"— I've read all Mrs Hyx's papers, every one of them. You and Mrs Shipwood went to America together to buy the first two banks, one in the US and the other in Canada, that started to get you into trouble. The ones that had big mortgage-lending subsidiaries, the ones on which you didn't do due diligence. You weren't with her when she went overseas again and bought the other three banks that have put Orlando in the shit —"

"You're talking through your hat," said Sweden.

"I haven't finished yet. You have a two-dollar company, StatCopy, that lent Mrs Shipwood eighteen million dollars just before the board was due to draw up the annual report for auditing. You lent it to her private company, Sylvan, she on-lent it to another of her companies that had a debt to Orlando and it paid the eighteen million on to Orlando. It went into Orlando's annual report, no questions were asked by the board, and everything looked okay — or would have looked okay at the end of the financial year. There was a bigger hole, a helluva bigger hole, but that eighteen million plugged the leak for a month or two. No money changed hands — the cheques were just bits of paper, your company StatCopy, couldn't have bought a plane ticket to Melbourne. Unfortunately for Orlando, Mrs Hyx was murdered before the house fell down. A house of cards," said Clements and sat back in his chair. "I'm surprised someone as shrewd as you ever bought into it."

Sweden said nothing, still in armour, the visor down. After a moment Clements looked at Malone. "You have any more questions, Superintendent?"

"No, I think you've asked enough," said Malone and stood up. "Take care, Mr Sweden."

Sweden still said nothing, his eyes cold as marbles.

Out in the corridor waiting for the lift, Clements said, "We only dented him. He won't fall down."

"It's a start."

Going down in the lift they said nothing more, silenced by the presence of the other passengers, two of whom already had their mobiles at the ready, waiting to get out into the open and be connected.

As the two detectives stepped out of the lift they were confronted by Natalie Shipwood and three men who looked as if they might be board members. She looked at Malone and Clements with surprise, then anger.

Malone got in first: "Order bandages, Mrs Shipwood. We think Mr Sweden is wounded."

He went out of the lobby, feeling better than he had felt all day. Malice is one of the least admirable of feelings, but there is no law against it. Basically, I'm not perfect, he told himself with satisfaction.

Chapter Three

❧

1

"Is Tom coming tonight?" asked Claire.

"He'll be late," said Lisa. "He has to see a girl."

"Which one?" asked Maureen. "He's got a coupla dozen."

"He's going to get into bother one of these days," said Claire. "Why can't he have a small harem, say three or four?"

"There's safety in numbers," said Maureen.

"You'd know. Who's your latest? Neddy or Freddy from the ABC?"

"I'm virginal at the moment. I've given up men for Lent."

"Lent's been over for months," said Lisa.

She always enjoyed the company of her two daughters. Claire looked like her, blonde, close enough to beautiful and with the same calm approach to life and its problems. Maureen had her father's dark hair, was good-looking but never still enough for one to decide whether she was beautiful; she met life head-on and so far had not been knocked down. Both listened to their mother, but she tried never to preach.

Malone came into the kitchen carrying Cornelius Malone Junior.

"You don't look comfortable," said Lisa.

"He's got no conversation," said Malone, handing the baby to Claire, its mother. "Why can't kids be born twelve or upwards? What wine do we have tonight?"

Tonight was the family dinner night, a ritual Lisa insisted on once a week. It held them together, a glue thicker than mere blood, even if argument was often the tone. Lisa was an only child who had known loneliness and she was determined that her children should never feel that way. Conversely, she was not overly possessive.

"How's the new job?" asked Maureen, helping Malone with the wine. She had just been promoted from researcher to reporter on ABC television and Malone had become cautious of her questions, no matter how innocent she made them sound. Reporters were always to be suspected, even those in the family.

"Easier. Much less blood."

"From what we hear, there's more blood *in* the Police Service now than out of it."

"Typical hack journalism. Why don't you report *good* news?"

"Who wants good news? Unless it's about sport." She sniffed the wine cork; she was the wine expert in the family. "Good … I'd love to be sent to Afghanistan, it's going to be interesting there."

He kept the alarm out of his voice: "Settle for what you've got. You're still learning."

Then Jason, Claire's husband, came to the kitchen door. He was very tall and came in under the lintel with only three or four inches to spare. "Tom's on the phone, Scobie. He wants to talk to you. He sounded a bit edgy."

"He's having a bit of girl trouble," Malone said as he went past Jason and down the hall to the phone. "Righto, what is it?"

"Dad —" Tom seemed to be having trouble with his breathing. Malone heard him take a deep breath: "Dad, she's dead. Lucinda."

"What do you mean — dead?" As soon as he said it, Malone thought, what a stupid bloody question.

"We've just found her. Idaho, her housemate, and me. I got to their house just as Idaho arrived home. We went inside, I looked in Lucinda's room and there she was. She looks as if she'd been strangled."

"Have you called anyone?"

"No, not yet. Only you."

"Get out of there —"

"Dad!"

Malone was instantly ashamed of his advice: a cop telling his son to leave the scene of a crime before the cops arrived. "Sorry ... Where are you? Where does she live?"

"Pyrmont. Juniper Street, Number 22."

"Righto, don't call Triple 0, call Bay Street direct — City Central, that's their area. Tell 'em you'll stay there, but don't give 'em your name. How's the housemate?"

Tom lowered his voice: "Pretty hysterical. The other one's just come home — she's off her head, too."

"Calm 'em down, don't let them call anyone till the fellers from Bay Street arrive. I'm on my way."

He hung up, stood a moment, feeling nerves trembling inside him. Then he took a deep breath and went out to the kitchen, looked past Claire and Maureen and Jason, spoke directly to Lisa: "There's trouble —" Then he turned to the others and, as shortly as he could, told them of Tom's problem and the murdered girl. "I'll be back with Tom as soon's I can get him away —"

"I'll come with you," said Lisa, untying her apron.

"No!" He couldn't help the sharpness of his voice.

"No, Mum," said Maureen. "You stay here, I'll go with Dad —"

"No, Mo, I don't want you there. Keep this under your hat —"

"Dad, for Crissake, what do you think I am?"

"Sorry —" He kissed her cheek. "I'm just trying to protect Tom."

"Don't you think I am?" She was angry and hurt.

"Yes," he said. "But this is a police matter. Not mine, but City Central's. The less family are there, the better."

He went down the hall to the main bedroom, found a jacket and pulled it on. When he turned round Lisa was in the doorway.

"Simmer down before you get there. You're going to be no help to Tom, the way you are."

He nodded, kissed her. "I'll try and get him out of there before the press hacks get on to it. But later —"

"Later?"

"You know the drill. There'll be an inquest … The post-mortem will tell 'em she was pregnant, Tom will be questioned —" He kissed her again. "Better say some prayers. And call Russ, ask him if he can get there —" He gave her the address. "Don't elaborate, just tell him I want him there."

He drove into the city under a cloudless sky, a full moon smiling sardonically at him through the mesh of the Anzac Bridge as he crossed it and swung down into the narrow streets of Pyrmont. The past came up like shadows. Con Malone, his father, had worked on the wharves here and Malone remembered being brought down as a boy to watch the ships being unloaded. Con had hoped he would come to work on the wharves, not doing the donkey-work but as a tally clerk; he had almost died of shame when Scobie had told him he wanted to be a cop. Those days were long gone, for him and the area. Gentrification had crept in, a cloak thrown over old scabby sights.

Pyrmont was once a maze of factories, a brewery, a distillery and a sugar refining complex; one could get drunk just on the air. There had been wharves and marshalling yards; one's head could split from the noise. Hidden in the maze were terraces of narrow houses, now exposed and gentrified, looked down upon by hotels and expensive apartments. Progress had once again given the back of the hand to history.

Malone found Juniper Street, parked his car behind the two police cars double-parked outside Number 22. He sat a moment getting himself together, then stepped out to be greeted by a young uniformed officer.

"You can't park there, sir. Please move it —"

Malone showed his badge. "I'm Superintendent Malone, from Crime Agency."

"Sorry, sir. I didn't know you had been called in so soon —"

Malone didn't enlighten him, ducked under the crime scene tapes and went in through the open front door of the house. The first person he saw was Clements.

"I was coming out the door when Lisa rang —"
The Clements lived at Drummoyne, only ten
minutes' drive from here. "Romy was with me.
She's in there —" He nodded at a doorway into a
bedroom. "She's doing the medical."

Jesus, thought Malone, the cover-up had
already begun! His best mate here as the
Homicide chief, his best mate's wife here as the
medical examiner. Romy Clements was deputy-
director of forensic medicine at the City Morgue
and normally would never turn out for a routine
murder case. Her work was done at the morgue,
where the secrets lay. Like the pregnancy of a
murdered girl ... His mind was getting away.

"Where's Tom?"

"In the living room. Rupe Steeple, from Bay
Street, is interviewing him. How well did he know
the girl?"

Was going to bed with a girl a barometer of
how well you knew her? "Just casually, I think.
I'll talk to you later."

He went past Clements, who looked at him
curiously but said nothing. He went down a
narrow hallway into a room that had been
widened, with a wall knocked down, and
lengthened. It looked out on to a small patio, once
called a backyard, where two Physical Evidence
men were examining the back wall that seemed to
lean in against the stares of all the windows in the
tall block of apartments behind it.

Tom sat opposite two girls; Steeple, the local senior detective, sat across from them. He looked up as Malone came into the room. "Who are you? Don't barge in here — oh, it's you, Scobie!" Then he seemed to remember that Malone had gone up in the world since they had last met. He stood up. "Sir."

"G'day, Rupe. Everything going okay?"

"Yeah, so far. Lucinda's friends here, Idaho and Frenchy —"

Lucinda, Idaho and Frenchy (Frenchy?). Whatever had happened to Dot, Shirl and Beryl?

"— they've been filling me in on some of Lucinda's boyfriends —"

Malone kept his eyes from looking at Tom, who sat with hands clasped between his knees, his face watchful.

"— your son was evidently not the only one."

"I was never her boyfriend!" Tom looked ready to leap out of his seat, but restrained himself. "I met her casually a few times at a pub in Double Bay —"

"He brought her home only once —" Frenchy was a small, dark-haired girl who looked as if she had spent too much time watching French movies of the *nouvelle vague* period or even earlier. She was a *gamine*: or wanted to be thought of as one. "Tom was not a regular, not like some of the others —"

"How many others?" asked Malone, looking for camouflage for Tom.

"Yeah, how many others?" said Steeple, as if annoyed that Malone had taken the questioning away from him.

"Three or four —"

Idaho was a big blonde who somehow suggested a double image of herself, now and in middle age: a galleon of a woman, sailing big-breasted into luncheons, charity meetings, Liberal Party galas. Despite her tear-swollen eyes she was good-looking, in a magnified way as if she should be projected on to the walls of a glass skyscraper. She had a soft pleasant voice that warmed one to her:

"I shouldn't say it, but Lucinda was never careful, she liked a good time too much —"

"Does — did she have family?" asked Steeple.

"Not here, no. She was from New Zealand, she came here a couple of years ago. That's her mum and dad there, that photo on the mantelpiece."

There was an old-fashioned fireplace in one wall, a timber mantle above it. Invitation cards jostled each other on the mantle, like votes for popularity; a tall lean man and a stout blonde woman, arms wrapped round each other, smiled at their expatriate daughter who now would never come home.

Steeple took the photo, turned it over to check what was on the back of it; then suddenly changed tack and said to Tom, "Why were you here tonight?"

Malone felt an instant, unreasonable resentment: he should be asking Tom the questions. Or maybe not asking: just getting him out of here as quickly as possible.

Then Romy Clements, pulling off plastic gloves, came into the room. Each time Malone saw her he was struck by her composure. It was a different composure from Lisa's, like a uniform she had donned when she had first gone to work in the morgue and which now fitted her like a second skin. She looked at him now, her broad good-looking face showing nothing, then she looked at Steeple.

"She was strangled — whoever it was must be very strong —" Frenchy made a retching noise; Romy looked at her, then went on, "There had been intercourse —" She still had a faint German accent and she tended, like Lisa sometimes, to speak in precise terms: "A condom was used, there is no semen in the vagina —"

Frenchy retched again and Idaho put a comforting hand on her arm. Steeple said, "How long's she been dead?"

"A couple of hours, I should say, no more. Have you ordered an ambulance to take her to the morgue? Good. I shall do the autopsy tomorrow. Are you girls all right?"

She really is formal tonight, thought Malone. Keeping a wall between herself and Tom. Between her and himself.

"Don't stay here," she went on, talking to the girls, still ignoring Malone and Tom. "Find someone to stay with. Do you want a sedative?"

"No, we'll be okay," said Idaho; you knew she had been the mother in this house. "We have somewhere to go and stay the night."

"Can we see Lucinda?" Frenchy had trouble finding her voice. "To, you know, say goodbye?"

"No, I don't think you should," said Romy. "Remember her as she was."

Frenchy thought about it, then nodded. Then Idaho said, "Who's going to tell her parents?"

"We'll do that," said Steeple, who had done it more times than he cared to remember. "You can find her parents' address or phone number?"

The mechanics of bad news, thought Malone and looked at Romy, who said, "I'll be out in the car. Come out when Russ does."

Malone jerked his head at Tom and the latter rose. But Steeple said, "I'd like to finish talking to your son, Superintendent."

Here we go, thought Malone. The police knew more about the territorial imperative than David Attenborough's birds and animals ever would. "Of course. I'll wait outside, Tom."

For a moment Tom looked as if he were being abandoned; then he nodded. "Sure, Dad. I won't be long."

"I'll be in touch, Rupe," said Malone. "Take care, girls."

He followed Romy out of the house. Clements, coming out of the bedroom, joined them. The three of them stood beside the Clements' Volvo.

"All right," said Romy in her official voice, "what's the story? Why is Tom in there?"

"Lisa didn't tell you?"

"No," said Clements. "She said Tom was here and could I get down here soon's I could. I'm here and so's Romy and we'd like a bit of background."

Malone didn't hesitate, but at the same time felt a certain unease. He was, without asking them, pulling them into the defence of Tom. "He came to see her, Lucinda, because she told him she was pregnant."

"He'd been to bed with her?" said Romy.

"Once, a one-night stand about three months ago. Or nearly that. Lisa and I think she took her time telling him —"

"Some girls can be two months pregnant before they know, depending on their periods. I'll check when I do the p.m. tomorrow. Tom might not have been the only one."

"Her flatmate said she played around. You said there was someone in her tonight — had she been raped?"

Romy shook her head. "No, no sign of that at all. If it was the same guy, he killed her after they'd had sex. If she was pregnant, why was a condom used? Unless it was someone she hadn't been with before and she'd got late ideas about safe sex?" She opened the door of their car. "I don't think Tom has to worry."

"Romy —" She waited while Malone hesitated; then he went on, "I'm doing my best to keep Tom out of this —"

"So will we," said Clements.

"I feel pretty bloody about this —"

Romy was almost clinical: "Darling, we'll be doing no DNA on the foetus if she was pregnant."

Then she got into the car, closed the door but did not open the window. Clements pressed Malone's arm. "Tom's safe, believe me."

"Rupe Steeple is questioning him —"

"Okay, so he's being questioned. He didn't kill the girl and if she was pregnant, chances are it was some other guy. Take Tom home with you for the night. I'll talk to Rupe Steeple tomorrow."

He went round his car, nodded sympathetically to Malone, got in and drove away. As Malone turned to go back into the house the ambulance arrived. He went in ahead of the medics, straight through to the living room at the back. He jerked his head at Steeple, led him out into the patio yard. Up above them watchers were congregated on balconies like birds waiting for carrion. The flashing blue-and-red lights of the police cars and now the arrival of the ambulance had been like the smell of death.

"Rupe, have you finished with my son?"

"Scobie —" No rank: just birds of a feather at odds over territory. "Are you taking over this case?"

"No, Rupe, I'm not. Have you got kids?"

"Yeah, two girls."

"Rupe, all I'm trying to do is see my son doesn't get hit with any of the shit from this. He didn't kill the girl —"

"I know that, Scobie. But a murder case isn't just the victim and the killer — you know that. If it were, there wouldn't be any need for us. The DPP could just step in right away and prosecute. Unfortunately, they ask for something called evidence —"

"Righto, Rupe, don't lay on the sarcasm … Sorry." He had seen Steeple's face stiffen. He tried, as Lisa and Clements often advised him, to simmer down. He was all fingers, thumbs and bumble feet on this one. "No, you're right. Has he had anything worthwhile to tell you?"

"No, not much. The two girls say they've only seen him around here the once — he's in the clear," said Steeple. "For the moment."

Malone knew what he meant: *the investigation ain't over yet*. "Good. And thanks, Rupe. I won't be interfering. If he tells me any more than he's told you, I'll let you know."

"No, you won't, Scobie," said Steeple. "Neither would I if my girls were in trouble."

2

Mick Kelray was planning murder when the police knocked on his door later that night to tell him about the murder of the girl down the street.

The young officer said, "Sorry to disturb you, sir —"

"No worries, mate. I seen youse down there. What's the problem?"

"There's been a homicide, one of the girls in Number 22. Did you know 'em, the girls?"

"I didn't *know* 'em. I've seen 'em around, I'd nod to 'em, but that was all. Which one got it?"

Then Phoebe called from upstairs, voice as weak as a small child's. "Who is it, love?"

"It's the Salvation Army," he called; then lowered his voice as he turned back to the young policeman: "The wife's an invalid, arteriosclerosis." He didn't stumble over the word; he had been using it for four years now. "She gets upset easy ... which girl was done in?"

"Lucinda Rossiter, she was a model, they say. Tall, blonde. You didn't hear anything? Screams, for instance?"

"Mate, I'm four, no, five doors up from them. These terrace houses are old, the walls are thick, none of your cardboard stuff they build these days. And I don't keep the front door open, not now. We did in the old days, but not any more."

"So you didn't see any stranger's car out here?"

"Mate, I'm not a car man. I got that old bomb out there —" He nodded out towards a grey Toyota Corolla. "That was the last time I took any interest in cars. Ten years ago when I bought it. I'm sorry, mate, I can't help you. It's crook, a pretty girl being murdered."

"Yeah," said the young officer. "Well, thanks, Mr —?"

"Kelray. Mick Kelray." He grinned to himself, dredging up some humour out of the cellars of himself. Here he was planning murder and he was giving his name in advance. "Everyone used to know me one time, I'm what I think they call the Oldest Inhabitant. Not any more. I been here in this house forty-two years and I'm the stranger."

"Yeah, well —" said the young officer, lost for words, and left.

Mick Kelray closed the front door and climbed the stairs to their bedroom. He was a big man with a big friendly face under thinning iron-grey hair. He had once been muscular, but the muscle had turned to limp cord under flesh turning to fat. Each night he took Phoebe out of her wheelchair and carried her upstairs and each morning he carried her down again. Light though she was, just skin and bone, the task each morning and night was becoming harder. But he would never let her know.

"Who was it, you said?" She was propped up in bed, a once-pretty woman now lost in a mask of pain.

"The Salvos, collecting. I give 'em a dollar."
Pretty soon, unless he and Phoebe were dead by
then, he'd be calling on the Salvos for help.
"What's on TV?"

"Another cookery show, *The Naked Chef* or
something —"

"He's running around in the nuddy? Does he
chop his dong instead of a carrot?"

Because she spent so much time in bed they had
a second television set in their bedroom. The world
for her was soap operas and he couldn't blame her.
Though there were times when he watched with
her and he thought, but never told her, that the soap
characters went through more bloody misery than
Bangladesh peasants in a flood.

"Mick, sit down —" She moved painfully in the
bed, patted a place for him to sit. "What's the
matter? What's on your mind?"

"Nothing. Why?"

"Love, I've been reading you for years.
Something's worrying you."

I'm gunna murder a woman, love. A Mrs
Natalie Shipwood, who's taken all our money and
lost it, every bloody skerrick of it.

"Nothing, love. I'm just getting old, I think. I
ain't what I used to be." He could feel the rust, the
crumbling inside him.

She was silent a while, looking at him almost
wistfully, then she said, "Mick, are you sorry we
never had kids? They'd be looking after us now."

He took her hand, a shrunken claw. "Love, that water went under the bridge a long time ago." She had been a passionate lover, but had been unable to have children. He had got over his disappointment, but he knew, watching her watching other people's children, that she still felt as if she had let him and herself down. "We dunno we'd of had kids who wanted to look after us like we are now. Kids today are different from what we were. What if we'd of had a coupla druggies, bastards who thought only of 'emselves?"

She grimaced: it was a smile, one that had once lit up her face. "You're trying to make me feel better. Forget it, love. We've been happy."

"Yeah." He leaned forward and kissed her shrunken lips. "Yeah, we've been that."

He hadn't told her what her sister Marilyn had told him last week.

3

The board meeting of Orlando directors earlier that afternoon had been a bomb-throwing exercise. Derek Sweden, a cynical man, had likened it to a board meeting of Afghan warlords. The bomb-throwers, with the exception of himself, had been the other directors and the target had been Natalie Shipwood. She had sat there hating them. Orlando was *her* company and these men, all outsiders, had their positions only at her invitation. Sweden had sat at the far end of the table saying nothing, holding his silence as if it were something of value. Which, of course, it was.

"Natalie —" Curtis Leshner, a solicitor from the Central Coast, was an overweight man who, when angry, always looked one breath short of apoplexy. He was new to the board and she had made a mistake in inviting him. His practice was in a small town, he had aspirations towards Big Business, but he had left it too late. "What the hell were you doing? These North American banks, how much did you look into them? Into their mortgaging — basically, their system is so different from ours —"

"Everything I knew about them, I told you. I laid it all out here on this table and you endorsed it, agreed to our buying them, all six of them —"

"Natalie, you rode roughshod over us —" Garry Faulks was the oldest member of the board, a builder with his own company. He was short, blunt-faced and energetic. He had begun as a hod-carrier, but now, with success, carried only chips on his shoulder. "Come to think of it, that's the way you've always been. We're down the toilet, basically, but I tell you — we're not staying in the shit with you!"

"Steady on, Garry —" Another of the directors remonstrated with him, but only because he could think of nothing else to say.

"At the end of the day —" said another director and said nothing more, as if all clocks, including his own, had stopped.

The bombing had gone on, but Natalie Shipwood had sat there, hurling none of the bombs back at them. At last she looked down the table at Derek Sweden.

"You have nothing to say, Derek?"

"Basically, I think we should tread water —" He did not believe what he was saying; but he had been a politician and was practised.

"How the fuck do we do that?" Faulks was back on a building site, speaking the language he knew best. "For Crissake, Derek, there's no water to tread!"

"Basically," said Leshner.

"There's so much else going on," said Sweden, who had wide vision. The world, and companies, were falling apart. Disaster can hide disaster. "Till the media gets wind of this —"

"You've just told us the Securities' jokers are on to what's happened. You think they're not going to leak this?" Leshner looked ready to burst, an exploding tomato. "There are no secrets any more —"

"A pity," said another director and looked wistful, as if remembering old love affairs.

Sweden said, "We deny everything till we've got the full picture. Basically —" But, basically, they would never get the full picture. Natalie had seen to that.

The meeting broke up ten minutes later; no more bombs thrown, but no truce declared. Natalie Shipwood and Sweden remained, still separated by the length of the long table. She sat waiting for him to move down to join her, but he didn't budge and said nothing. At last she stood up and walked stiff-legged down to join him, aware as she went down the table that she was surrendering, that at last they were equals.

She sat down round the corner of the table from him. "I hope we're not going to fight?"

"Not yet," he said discouragingly. "I had two cops to see me this afternoon, a Superintendent Malone and an Inspector Clements. Two dogged bastards who never give up. I saw them at work, solving my son's murder. They asked me what I knew about Marilyn Hyx's murder."

"You know nothing!" She hadn't meant to be so forceful.

"That's what I told 'em and I think they believed me. Up to a point."

"What point is that?" She was cautious now.

"They think I might know who did kill her." He had had plenty of experience with women, he knew how to test them.

She had had experience of men. "Don't be bloody ridiculous! You're suspecting me? She was my *friend*."

"Natalie —" He was patient, in the way that some men can be, so annoyingly. "I'm not

74

suspecting you. But that's not to say that, basically, you won't fall under suspicion. She worked for you, she was your private secretary — too private, some of the board members think. If she was going to blackmail you —"

"She would never do that! She was too honest, too religious —"

"Natalie —" His patience was insulting. "No-one's too honest, too religious, when the stakes are high. Thirty pieces of silver has been the going rate —"

"You'd know." She knew his background, in politics and business. She had done due diligence before she had invited him to join the board. "Don't lecture me, Derek. I'm getting enough of that from Harry and the kids."

"Do they know how much you still have of what's missing?"

She gathered up her briefcase, stood up. "I shouldn't talk like that if I were you, Derek."

"Ah, but I'm not you, Natalie." He, too, stood up. "If I'm sued for liability as a director, you'll find I'm very much not you and not on your side."

4

Tom sat silent in the car, leaning against the door as if putting distance between himself and his father. He was dressed in his new suit and wore a tie, as if he had come straight from the bank to Lucinda's house. His dark hair was rumpled and he ran his fingers through it now. Malone had never seen him so deflated.

They drove in silence through the night for five minutes before Malone spoke: "Did you visit Lucinda more than once?"

Tom looked at him cautiously. "Do you think I've been lying about how well I knew her?"

"You knew her well enough to go to bed with her."

"Oh, for Crissakes, Dad!" Tom looked out the car window; then turned back. "Don't start playing the old-fashioned father. My generation didn't invent one-night stands. Yeah, I knew her — but except for that once, it was just to drink with her and half a dozen others down at The Sheaf. She hadn't given me a second look up till that one night and she never gave me a second look afterwards. Not till she called me and said she was pregnant."

"She sounds a tramp."

"Dad, don't start judging her. You never knew her."

Malone looked at him with sudden new respect. "No, you're right. You judge everyone like that?"

"Till I know them better, yes."

You'll never make a cop; but he didn't say that. Tom had never shown the slightest interest in following him into the Service.

Claire and Maureen greeted Tom as if he were still only five years old. They hugged him and kissed him; he was their favourite brother, he was their *only* brother.

"God!" cried Maureen, "why aren't you more careful?"

"Listen to her," Claire said, "the promiscuous virgin."

"Have I missed dinner?" Now he was safely home Tom was relaxed, almost insouciant. The bugger should never have left home, thought Malone.

"Humble pie for you," said Lisa and kissed her son. Tom looked over her shoulder at Malone and the latter saw the sudden pain in the dark blue eyes.

"We've waited dinner for you," said Lisa, "and there'll be no discussion of the case. Understand, everyone?"

"Who said the Dutch weren't autocratic?" asked Jason and blew his mother-in-law a kiss.

It was at dessert, old-fashioned sherry-flavoured trifle, that Maureen said, "Dad, are you on that case of the developer's secretary who was murdered?"

Malone was abruptly wary. "Only at a distance. Why?"

"*Four Corners* is doing a piece on companies that have gone belly-up. We won't be running it for several weeks, not till we find out what's going to happen with the Americans and the Taliban. If *that* gets big, really big, then nobody will be interested in companies belly-up or arse-up."

"Every other inch a lady," said Lisa. "The Brigidine nuns must be proud of you. Are you on the story?"

"I may be, they're still making up their minds whether women or men are more probing."

"Oh, women, easily," said Jason and leaned away from Claire's sideswipe.

Stay out of it, Mo. Malone looked around the table, at the happiness here, the bond, even with Jason, the outsider. But wondered at the accidents of chance.

Chapter Four

❧

1

Clements settled himself into the chair opposite Malone.

"Two visits in two days," said Malone. "Is your bum comfortable in that chair or shall I get you another one?"

"I'm working on it. I'll be coming over pretty regular, mate — I need you on this case. One of my contacts —" He had more contacts than an electricity power station. "She tells me our mate Mr Sweden is already working on *his* mates, in Macquarie Street and down in Canberra."

"What does he think he's going to achieve? With things the way they are everywhere, why would anyone in government be interested in bailing out Orlando? That's what you're talking about?"

"Don't ask me how people at that level think. The thing is, he's trying to stop the fan whirring." He shifted in the chair, as if it was too new to make him comfortable. "All I'm interested in, forget the ramifications, all I'm interested in is the actual murder of Mrs Hyx ... I've been talking to the locals out there. They've found out Mrs Hyx had a second male visitor — another one beside the guy in the Corolla that Nigger Brown saw. This was a night or two before, a guy in a Honda Civic."

"Any identification?"

"Vague. Both guys were middle-aged or older, they said. But —"

"Another but?"

"She also had a visit from a girl. Tall, dark-haired girl in a yellow Saab convertible with black upholstery."

"I'll bet it was a young bloke made that identification. Now I remember something —"

"So do I. In the Shipwood garage, a four-car job, there was a yellow convertible that might have been a Saab." He stood up. "I thought I'd let you know. I'm on my way out to talk to Miss Shipwood."

Malone hesitated, then he, too, stood up. As he did so, Greg Random came to the door of his office. "The Shipwood case? I've just had a call from Charlie Hassett —" Assistant Commissioner in charge of Crime Agency. "He's had a call from the Commissioner, who's had a call from —"

Malone held up a hand. "That's far enough. What's the word?"

"I'm within six months of retirement —" Random already looked retired, he was so relaxed. "I've reached an age and a stage where I couldn't care a stuff about strings being pulled —"

Malone looked at Clements. "I think he's giving us free rein."

"Sure," said Clements. "but who gets the kick in the bum if we stuff things up?"

"Good luck," said Random, grinned and departed.

A chain of command develops rust if no-one moves. Malone looked at Clements, saw something there that he had recognised twenty-five years ago. The big man had fibre in his character that might bend but would not break. His reaction to prodding was to become more stubborn. He, Clements, was now the boss of Homicide and Malone owed him.

"Are you enjoying the job?"

"Being boss?" Clements thought a moment, then shook his head. "No. I think I might be a good example of the Peter Principle. Promoted above my worth."

"Balls. It just takes a bit of getting used to." But he wondered if the years of service had taken a greater toll on Clements than he had thought. Life in the Police Service over the past four or five years had not been easy. There had been reorganisation that the Old Guard had resented and done its best to wreck. There had been corruption and back-stabbing and there was no longer the feeling of certainty there had once been in the Service. The Good Old Days had been also the Bad Old Days, but one had been younger then and more resilient. Clements looked *worn*.

As they drove out along the freeway to the south, just a long swift river of traffic, Clements abruptly said, "Do you think there'll be war?"

In the bustle of traffic, everyone going about everyday business, not a ruin or a bomb crater in sight, it took an effort of imagination to put an image to the question. "I don't know. How do you go to war against shadows?"

"Yeah, I was reading that. There are these terrorist cells in some sixty or seventy countries. If war breaks out, do you think we'll still be chasing homicides?"

"You know we will," said Malone and changed the subject. For the first time he saw the possibility of Tom going off to war. He was afflicted with the long view, something he valued in most circumstances but, abruptly, not now. "Let's concentrate on Miss Chloe for the time being."

When they pulled into Sylvania Waters and drew up outside the Shipwood mansion, the yellow convertible was backing out of the garage. Clements pulled their car across the driveway and the two detectives got out. There was an angry blast from the Saab's horn and an arm waved at them to get out of the way.

"Watch out for road rage," said Malone as he and Clements approached Chloe Shipwood, who had now got out of her car and looked ready to declare war on motorists who parked across her driveway.

"Will you move that —"

"When we're leaving, Miss Shipwood," said Clements and showed his badge. "Remember us? Detective Inspector Clements and Superintendent Malone. Can we go inside or would you like to talk to us out here in front of the neighbours?"

Pull your head in, Russ. But Malone could see that Clements was in no mood for argument. And, he had to remind himself, this was Clements' case, not his. He gave Chloe what was meant to be a friendly smile, but she was unfriendly.

"What's it about?" She was dressed in a lemon shirt and black slacks and had a cardigan that matched the shirt thrown over her shoulders. Her eyes were hidden behind dark glasses, the mask that can hide idiocy as well as intelligence. "I'm busy —"

"So are we," said Clements, "so this shouldn't take long. Inside?"

For a moment it looked as if she would refuse, then she abruptly turned and led them towards Gog and Magog. As they went past the still-open doors of the garage Malone saw that the Bentley was missing, but a Range Rover occupied one of the spaces.

"Anyone else home?" he asked.

"My father. He's down on our boat, housekeeping."

Car washer, boat housekeeper: Harry Shipwood seemed at the bottom of the totem pole in this household.

She led them into the house, into the living room where they had been before. She didn't invite them to sit down, but turned and demanded, "What's this all about?"

"May we sit down?" said Clements. "Superintendent Malone and I are both getting on —"

Malone wanted to laugh; instead, he took a seat, uninvited. "Let's be friendly, Miss Shipwood. Sit down."

It was an order; it took her a moment to realise it. Then she sank into the chair that her mother had occupied yesterday. "Like I said — what's this about?"

"That car, the Saab," said Clements. "Does anyone else but you drive it? No? Then —" He looked at his notebook. "On September the 10th, you went out to Rooty Hill to visit Marilyn Hyx, right? Why?"

She was no longer angry; more uneasy, even afraid. Nothing showed beneath the dark glasses, but Malone could see the tension in her body and long legs. "Why?"

"Yes," said Malone, taking over the bowling from the other end of the pitch, the change bowler. "Why?"

She licked her very full lips that looked slightly unnatural. Malone wondered if they had been collagen-injected. Women's mouths, for those who could afford it, were starting to look as if they all came out of the same mould. Mona Lisa might smile at the fashion.

"Take off your glasses," said Malone.

"What?"

"Take off your glasses. We don't like talking to a mask."

She hesitated, then took off the glasses. Malone looked at her eyes and wondered if they would tell him any more than the glasses had.

"Marilyn rang me," she said, "asked me to go out there. She said not to tell my mother —" She licked her lips again. "My mother doesn't know I went."

"Does your father or brother know?" asked Clements.

"My brother does —"

"But not your dear old dad," said Harry Shipwood from the doorway. He was in a T-shirt, shorts and sandshoes again, the family handyman. "Why wasn't I told?"

Malone held up a hand. "A moment, Mr Shipwood. Inspector Clements is asking the questions. Sit down and join us."

It was another order and Shipwood recognised it at once. He sat down, looking out of place in the room of which, supposedly, he was the master. But he was not ill at ease, not like his daughter. "Go ahead, Chloe."

She looked at him and for a moment the eyes came alive with a shine, which might have been tears; she looked at him as if she saw him for the first time. Then she blinked and looked back at the two detectives.

"Marilyn said she had something to tell me, something that sounded as if it was upsetting her very much. She was almost crying over the phone. But when I got out there, she had changed her mind, said she was not going to tell me anything. I — I tried to get her to tell me, but no go. I guess I got a bit angry — I mean, going all the way out there, the back of beyond —"

Out in Rooty Hill, the back of beyond, Malone could hear the fringe-dwellers stirring.

"I just left, got out. I'm sorry now — I mean, in view of what happened. We'd been friends — she used to pet me, comfort me when I was a kid —"

"She was a good woman," said Harry Shipwood; but didn't move to comfort his daughter.

"Did you ever visit her at Rooty Hill, Mr Shipwood?" asked Clements.

"No. She'd only been out there — I dunno. What? Two, three months, that was all. She never invited my wife and me to dinner, anything like that. I only saw her here, when she'd bring work for my wife. And we'd invite her sometimes to business receptions here — she'd organise them. She was a great organiser."

"We've learned," said Malone, taking over the bowling again, "she had visits from two men, each on a separate occasion. Your wife said she had a husband. Did you ever meet him?"

"Never." Shipwood looked at his daughter. "Did she ever mention him to you?"

"Just once." Chloe was herself again. "She'd had a couple too many drinks — I drove her home." All the way to Rooty Hill, the back of beyond. She isn't entirely without heart, Malone thought. "She said never to trust men with big ideas and little minds."

"Good advice," said her father. "The country's full of them."

"Care to name them?" said Malone.

Shipwood smiled, but didn't take up the offer.

"Did she have any family?" asked Clements. "Brothers, sisters, nephews, nieces?"

"I think she had a sister," said Chloe. "But where or who, she never said."

"She was a very lonely woman," said Harry Shipwood.

"It seems so," said Clements and looked at Chloe. "What about your brother? How did he get on with Marilyn?"

The switching of the bowling seemed to be unsettling the Shipwoods. Harry said rather sharply, "We're spreading the suspicion a little widely here, aren't we?"

"Just elimination," Malone told him. "As we explained to your wife yesterday."

"Marilyn doted on him," said Chloe. "After that hullabaloo when he turned down the Bachelor of the Year invitation — you know about that?"

"Vaguely," said Malone. "Inspector Clements and I were non-vintage bachelors."

He saw Shipwood smile, but the latter said nothing.

"After that," said Chloe, "Marilyn sent him a big box of chocolates. She told me once she'd have liked a son like him."

"She had no children?"

"She couldn't. She told me that night she'd had too much to drink, she was glad she hadn't had any. Not with the father they'd have had."

Malone began to feel sorry for Marilyn Hyx and not solely because she had been murdered. She was beginning to sound a lonely, unhappy woman. But what had driven her to make copies of so many incriminating documents, to salt them away in her strong-box? Whom had she turned on and why?

"She had no men friends?" said Clements.

"None that we knew of," said Shipwood, but with the uncertainty of a man who mistrusted his knowledge of women. "But that's not to say she didn't have some secret lover. Marilyn, though we knew her for fifteen years and thought the world of her, had her secrets. Who doesn't?"

"Sure, that's one of the things we cops learn," said Malone, another man careful in the climate of women. He looked at Clements: "Any more questions, Inspector?"

Clements closed his notebook, in which he had made notes. He had a library of notebooks, not all of them transferred to the computer. Cops, too, like their secrets. "I think we have enough. For the time being."

"For the time being?" Shipwood must have been an alert lecturer in class, ear tuned to the student evading a question.

"It's the way we sign off," said Malone.

"Always leave 'em dangling?"

"Who?" said Malone, innocent as a first-day cop.

But Shipwood merely smiled; he had faced too many innocent students. He rose and began to lead them towards the door. Then he stopped and looked back at his daughter: "You still going out?"

"No," she said, staying in her chair. "I've changed my mind."

Her father studied her for a long moment, saying nothing; then he turned and led the two detectives out into the hallway. He opened the front door, stood with Gog (or Magog?) looking over his shoulder.

"You'll be coming again?"

"There's always the possibility," said Malone. "Is Mrs Shipwood home?"

"No, she's at a board meeting. The second in two days. As you have gathered, things are crook in Tallarook."

It was a saying Malone hadn't heard in years, replaced by Americanisms. "She never asked for your advice? You being an economics lecturer."

Shipwood laughed, sounded genuinely amused. "Superintendent, how many students ever come back to ask advice of their old teachers? No, my wife, I'm afraid, is like most of today's entrepreneurs. They all forget that the shortest memory is the financial memory. Every generation makes the same mistakes. You go back to the Dutch tulip fiasco in the seventeenth century, the South Sea Bubble — Christ knows, there may have been entrepreneurs amongst the money-lenders in the Temple. No, my wife never asked my advice."

"What would you have told her if she had asked?"

"I'll never know," said Shipwood and closed the door on them.

The two men walked down the driveway, past the yellow convertible, to their car. On the grass verge of the dead-end street, a few metres from the unmarked police car, was a white wooden bench. On it were two very elderly men who looked at Malone and Clements with frank interest.

"Is it up for sale?" He was a tall bald-headed man with a face that looked as if it had been carved out of soft putty. But the blue eyes were shrewd and bright. "You putting a price on it?"

"We're not estate agents," said Clements. "You know the Shipwoods?"

The old man looked at his companion, who was shorter, had a shock of white hair and a face that was a mass of wrinkles under his gold-rimmed glasses. "Do we know the Shipwoods?"

"I forget," said the second man.

The first old man gestured at the second. "This is my friend, Dan Ovenden. Eighty-four and still has all his own teeth."

Mr Ovenden cackled and supplied the punch line: "In a jar." He laughed again, showing teeth as false as a political promise. "We're getting past it, too bloody old. I've forgotten something Ralph Waldo Emerson once said."

"Who?" said the first old man.

"Henry Wadsworth Longfellow ... Who brought him up? What did you just forget?"

"I dunno, I can't remember."

Malone got into the car beside Clements before the two old gagsters got too far into their act. Were they old-time comedians or just two old men taking the mickey out of two younger men?

"You ever notice? The old laugh at being old, but the young never laugh at being young."

"What about middle age?"

"No man's land, son. I dunno whether to joke or cry."

Then, looking sideways at Clements as the latter swung the car back up the street, he wondered if, down the track, he and Clements would be like that, fending off senility with jokes. He looked back, saw the second old man laughing heartily, his face wrinkled, contoured with mirth, his glasses small pools of sunshine as he looked up at the sky.

Let me go like that, thought Malone. Die laughing.

2

Clements turned the car out on to the main highway back to the city. They went up over the arc of the Captain Cook Bridge and Malone looked to the south-west. Clouds of smoke smudged the sky; two helicopters crawled across the grey-yellow swirls. A decorated Holden zoomed past the unmarked police car, two youths lolling back in the front seat, the car's radio booming out defiant rock. For a moment Clements' foot pressed down on the accelerator, then he eased it off.

"I'd have the time of my life on the Highway Patrol."

"You'd grow tired of it. Where do we go now? The Orlando board meeting?"

"I don't think so," said Clements. "John Kagal and Gail Lee —" He said the names as if Malone had already forgotten who had once worked for him. "They've interviewed all the board members. Preliminary stuff, but enough for the time being. No, I'm going to lunch with Jack Aldwych, Senior and Junior."

"Was I asked?"

"No, but I'm sure Old Jack would be glad to see you. I didn't mention it, because I'm still not sure how far or how close you wanna be to this case. The murder and the Orlando business."

"Russ, for Crissake, I'm just around the corner from you, on the same floor —" Then he stopped and nodded. "No, I see your point. Is it always going to be like this, not wanting to get me involved, taking a chance on someone else in Crime Agency?"

"If you were a football or a cricket coach and you were picking a team, who would you pick? Guys you know or some scrubbers from elsewhere?"

Malone grinned. "There are some superintendents and some chief superintendents in the Agency who'd strip you down to probationary constable for that. Yes, I'll come to lunch with you. Call Jack and ask him if its okay."

"I'll have to call his daughter-in-law, she's putting on the lunch, her and Jack Junior. Out at Point Piper." Then he changed the subject. "How's Tom?"

"I thought you'd never ask. No, he's okay — I called him this morning. He's still upset at what happened to that girl, but he knows he's not under suspicion."

"I talked to Rupe Steeple, he thought he could keep the case under wraps. No go," he said with some asperity. "The girl was one of those social nobodies you see every Sunday —"

"Don't tell me." *We're as old as those two old buggers we just left. Still believing you got your photo in the papers for being Somebody.* "The *paparazzi* want photos of the suspects?"

"That's what they'd like. The only thing that might keep Tom out of the papers is that the girl's two housemates are keeping their mouths shut, Rupe says. I think I might have a word with them, thank them."

"I'll do it —"

"No, you won't. You and Tom stay well away. Understand?"

Malone understood and was grateful.

Clements rang Juliet Aldwych and she said she would be delighted to have Superintendent Malone to lunch. So, after checking in at Strawberry Hills, where some of the staff were just getting out their plastic-wrapped sandwiches, Malone and Clements drove out to Point Piper where plastic-wrapped sandwiches were thought of as what one sent starving refugees.

Point Piper was named after a lecherous entrepreneur of the nineteenth century who laid schemes and women with equal skill. Since then generations of entrepreneurs, not all lecherous, have nested there on the narrow finger of land. Old money, too, has nested there, but old money no longer has the cachet it once had. Money in Sydney brings its own benediction, irrespective of whether it is old or new or, lately, honestly acquired.

The Aldwych apartment had cost Jack Junior and his then new bride three million dollars eight years ago; now it was worth eight million. Harbourside prices are not related to the rest of the city or, indeed, to commonsense. Malone, a man with no sense of real estate values, always felt light-headed in these surroundings.

"You don't beat terrorism with bombs and planes —" Jack Aldwych had been appalled by the attack on the World Trade Center in New York; he had used terror in his attacks on banks, but that had just been a sales technique. "It'll be a long clean-up campaign —"

"Darling —" said his daughter-in-law, "let's talk of brighter things. Like swindling the poor investor."

Aldwych smiled at her, then at Malone and Clements. "The Roumanians know how to put things into perspective. I'm glad you married into the family, Juliet."

She accepted the compliment with the amused grace she had used to accept compliments all her life. She was a beautiful woman and would be into her old age. She was also clever: at being intelligent, puzzled or dumb. Men would always be two steps behind her, never certain that what they thought they saw was really her. She was the perfect wife for Jack Junior, who was only half a step behind her.

He, a younger version of his father except for scruples, sipped the semillon that came from his own boutique vineyard in the Hunter Valley. Both father and son were big and handsome and both had an air of authority. Jack Senior had developed his through the use of gun, iron bar and razor, but Jack Junior's was that of a very successful businessman.

"You're on the Orlando case," he said to their two guests, "the murder and the business schemozzle."

"Half right," said Malone. "Russ is on the murder enquiry and I'm — well, I'm like your dad is with you."

"*Eminence grise*," said Aldwych Senior, who had taken to trying to educate himself in his old age. "Whatever the hell that means."

They were having lunch on the wide terrace of the apartment, shielded from the sun by a loggia on which bougainvillea burned with rich redness and purple. Out on the harbour the sails of yachts sliced into the wind like giant knives; in the distance a Manly ferry ploughed magnificently into the swell coming through the harbour heads.

Somewhere, way out of sight, the poor were doing whatever it was the poor did. Jack Senior knew, he had once been poor, but Jack Junior and Juliet had not a clue.

"Why are we here?" asked Clements, a fork of barramundi raised to his mouth.

The Aldwychs' cook had just brought fresh warm rolls to the table; Jack Junior waited till she had gone. "We'd like to know how much you know that we don't. Who killed Natalie Shipwood's secretary?"

"Why would you want to know about that?" asked Malone.

"We've done a million two with Orlando going down the hole," said Aldwych Senior. "Juliet's brother-in-law, Mr Sweden — you've talked to him?"

"You know we have, Jack," said Malone. "Otherwise we wouldn't be here."

Aldwych gave him an approving smile. He had never hated cops, only the bent ones, and he had real affection for Malone. "Derek was the one who conned us into putting money into Orlando."

Malone waited for Clements to take up the bowling, but the latter was chewing on his fish; he never neglected the inner man. While he sought his own answer, Malone raised his fork to Juliet: "Nice fish."

"I'll tell Magda, she does all our buying and cooking." Juliet had once boiled water successfully and thought it a culinary achievement. "Is Derek under suspicion?"

"For what?" Clements had cleared his mouth of fish.

Aldwych laughed. "You blokes are tighter than a fish's arsehole."

"I couldn't have put it better myself," said Juliet, smile as sweet as a choirgirl's. "Only it sounds better in Roumanian."

"Jack," said Malone, "and you too, Jack Junior. You know something you haven't told us."

The two Aldwyches looked at each other, then Jack Junior said, "There's a guy on the Orlando board, Curtis Leshner. He came to see me a couple of months ago, said he wasn't happy with the way things were going. He knew nothing about the losses then — at least I don't think so. But he said Mrs Shipwood was very uptight, telling the board nothing. And there were payouts that were rushed through, for her and Derek Sweden and the managing director. Bonuses that the board rubber-stamped. Boards do that these days," he added with obvious knowledge.

"Why did he come to you, this — Leshner?"

"Because we pay him," said Jack Senior. "Russ, you blokes have your pigeons, gigs, moles, whatever you wanna call 'em. It's no different in business. Not any business I'm in," he added with a smile that had no humour in it.

"Did he mention Mrs Hyx?" asked Malone.

"No," said Jack Junior. "We had just started to look into Orlando when Mrs Hyx was murdered. Then we bailed up Derek and he told us that things were pretty drastic. It's only since then we've found out how drastic."

"What do you intend to do?" said Clements.

"We want Mrs Shipwood nailed to the wall," said Aldwych and looked at his son, who nodded. Juliet sat quietly, only her eyes moving. She had the most beautiful poker face Malone had ever seen.

"Jack —" said Malone, taking his time. "You too, Jack Junior. You know we can't do anything. We're limited to the murder of Mrs Hyx —"

"That's it," said Aldwych. "Natalie Shipwood could have done it or paid someone to do it. I dunno the woman, but Jack tells me she's capable of it."

Malone looked at Jack Junior. "How do you know her so well?"

The younger Aldwych looked at his wife, who said, "She's on a charity committee with me. She hates us all, the ones who live out here in the eastern suburbs. As if we're different," she said and succeeded in looking surprised: a nice acting job, thought Malone. "It's ridiculous, but it's true. She's a woman who can really hate. I've seen her cut up some of us on the committee when we've come up with an idea —"

"Not you, Juliet," said Malone. "She'd never cut you up."

She looked at her husband, smiled. "Is he complimenting me?"

"I think he is," said Jack Junior. "Go on."

"There's no need," said his father. "She's the one, Scobie. That Mrs Shipwood."

The barramundi turned sour in Malone's mouth: the taste of unexpected disappointment. The old man had been a hardened criminal, ruthless and sometimes vicious; but he had never been petty. He was worth — what? Three, four hundred million? More? And he was pointing the finger at a woman for a mere fraction of one per cent of his fortune. Since the old crim's retirement and their occasional meetings, Malone had developed a liking, almost an affection, for the old man. But now greed, the recurring disease, had bitten Aldwych, turned him into a cheapskate.

"That's enough, Jack." He put his knife and fork together on his plate, a deliberate action. Then he stood up. "We're leaving, Russ."

Clements didn't look surprised; he had learned never to show it. He, too, stood up, and said, "We'll let you know if we find Mrs Hyx's murderer. Thanks for lunch."

"I'll show you out —" Jack Junior rose.

"There's no need," said Malone. "The three of you sit here and think about what you were asking us. You can call me or Russ when you want to apologise."

He and Clements went in from the terrace,

leaving a silence behind them broken only by a ferry's piping siren out on the harbour, like the echo of a jeer.

When they got outside he looked across the roof of their car at Clements. "You think I'm a stuffed shirt?"

"No-o. But I always thought you and Jack Aldwych were mates."

"I guess we'd become mates. But never bosom buddies." They got into their car; then he said, "You think he might have something? I mean about Mrs Shipwood?"

"It's a possibility."

3

Mick Kelray had been out in the street cleaning the interior of the Corolla when he saw the young bloke come out of Number 22. He had come out in a rush, stopped and looked up and down the street like a man who was not sure where he was or how he had got there. Kelray was inside the Corolla and perhaps that prevented the young man from seeing him at first. He came up towards the Corolla, stopped when he saw the older man, then turned and hurried down the street, almost at a half-run, and disappeared round a corner.

Kelray paused in his wiping down of the top of the dashboard. He took the Disabled Person parking label from inside the windscreen and put it in his shirt pocket; then paused and stared down towards the corner round which the young man had disappeared. Kelray had had time to observe him, though he would not have looked at him twice except that he seemed so agitated. Kelray minded his own business in the street since it had been taken over by yuppies; he still thought of them as that, though he had read somewhere that the term had gone out of fashion. This young bloke, though, was asking to be looked at. Something had obviously upset him. He was well-dressed, but without a tie and his shirt was undone down the front, as if he had put it on in a hurry. He was young, in his early twenties, and he had the sort of good-looking face that men like Mick Kelray never noticed; except now, because the face was showing fear and bewilderment. He had very blond hair, done in the style that Mick Kelray thought showed they couldn't afford a comb, cut short and standing up as if some hairdresser (Mick Kelray never went to a hairdresser, he went only to a barber) had teased each individual hair to stand up as if its owner had been frightened out of his life. The young bloke had certainly looked like that. Shit-scared, Mick Kelray thought.

He had told none of this to the young cop who had knocked on his door last night. When you were planning a murder of your own, you didn't want to be involved in anyone else's.

He had learned in his years of working on the wharves that you minded your own business and didn't get involved in anyone else's. He had been in trouble, but never seriously, and he was not going to start looking for trouble now. Except, of course, to kill that bitch Shipwood ...

It would not be a drive-by shooting, the way kids were doing it these days. He wanted to face her, tell her why he was going to kill her, tell her that she had ruined his and Phoebe's life. Tell her that he thought she had done in Marilyn, murdered her herself or paid someone to do it for her. He would tell her all that, trying to keep his temper, then he would top her. As Marilyn had been topped, with a knife.

The events of the past three weeks had kept Marilyn's murder to no more than three lines in an inside column. He had let it remain there, telling Phoebe nothing. But then a TV news broadcast had given the game away; Phoebe followed the news on TV as avidly as she did the soap operas, often telling him that some of the items *were* soap operas. Then, there on the screen, was Marilyn's new house and her shrouded body being carried out to an ambulance and Phoebe had looked at him and he had nearly cried at the pain and shock in her face. She and Marilyn had never been close, had not spoken to each other in almost twenty years. And then, there in her face, was a sense of the loss of those twenty years.

Six weeks ago Marilyn had looked him up in the phonebook and called him, told him not to say anything to Phoebe. He had gone out to her house at Rooty Hill, been impressed by it but had not said anything, and there she had told him what had happened to their money.

"How did you know we had money in Orlando?" he had asked.

"I saw you come into head office one day, oh, it must have been two or three years ago."

"If you saw me, why didn't you stop me, talk to me?"

"Mick —" She had looked at him — sadly? He hadn't been sure. "Mick, would you have wanted to talk to me? Phoebe and I never got on ... How is she?"

"Not too good. She's in a wheelchair all the time now ... So how much have we lost?"

"The lot, Mick. I looked up what you'd invested — an awful lot? Your superannuation?"

"That and a bit we'd saved. It was returning enough to live on. It was enough — we own our house, we get concessions as senior citizens — but now you tell me it's gunna be bugger-all. There's no hope of getting it back?"

She had shaken her head. She was a good-looking woman, not as pretty as Phoebe had been, but now she looked older than her — he wasn't sure — fifty years? "It's all gone, Mick. It and millions more. Natalie, my boss, got greedy."

"What about her? Is she broke, too?"

"No way. She's lost none of her own money — well, not much of it. She will cry poor mouth, but she's got a lot stashed away overseas, Switzerland and a bank in the Caribbean. She had the board pay her and a couple of the others bonuses — I just don't know how the board fell for it, but that's what a lot of them are like these days. I don't think her own family know how much she has stashed away. *I* know because I was the one who transferred it for her. She trusted me," she said and looked embarrassed. Or ashamed.

"Have you lost any?"

"No. What I had I took out to buy this." She waved at the house around them. He looked around, then back at her and had the feeling she didn't yet belong to the house. "I have some shares, but nothing in Orlando."

He looked around him again, compared it with the terrace house in Pyrmont. He once might have promised something like this to Phoebe, but if he had he had never been able to deliver. "You live here on your own?"

She nodded and he noticed for the first time the loneliness in her.

"You ever see your husband? Clem, that his name?"

"Klement, with a K — he was a Czech, from Prague. He came to see me a couple of weeks ago.

Just to stickybeak, I think, see how well I was doing. He wanted to borrow some money."

"How much?"

She looked at him in surprise. "Somehow I never thought you'd ask a question like that, Mick."

He grinned. "I'm surprised, meself. Okay, forget I asked."

"No, I'll tell you. Thirty thousand. I told him no. He's living with some floozy, the third or fourth since I kicked him out. He got pretty nasty and only left when I threatened to call the police." She looked at him again, said without any coquetry, "Why couldn't I have picked someone like you? Does Phoebe know her luck?"

"I think so. I know mine." Then he had said, "What do I do about our money in Orlando?"

"It's gone, Mick."

When he had left she had kissed him, on the cheek. Her lips had hovered for a moment before his, then moved to his cheek. He had gone out to his car feeling uneasy, as if somehow he had almost betrayed Phoebe.

Marilyn was murdered the night after the terrorist bombing of the World Trade Center in New York. Phoebe had sat in her wheelchair and watched TV and cried for those dying in the flames and smoke and dust and falling masonry. Then she had seen the item on Marilyn's death and had bent her head and wept almost uncontrollably. The tears closer to home this time: he had held her to him and felt the years of lost family shuddering within her.

"We should never have stayed apart," she had said at last. "We were both stupid. They know who killed her?"

"I dunno. You want me to find out?"

"No, let it lay. We can't do anything, not now." She dried her eyes, blew her nose. "I wonder if she'd been happy?"

"I dunno," he said and told her nothing of his visit to Marilyn.

And now he was planning to murder Natalie Shipwood.

4

Malone sat in the living room and channel-surfed on the TV.

One station was replaying a recent football final: "And now he's taking the penalty in close proximity to the uprights."

He switched to another channel, where two ex-footballers were discussing an overseas soccer star: "Basically, mate, he's absolutely fantastic!"

"Yeah, mate, fantastic!"

He switched to the ABC where a politician was commenting on the coming Federal election: "Basically, at this point in time and at the end of the day —"

He switched off. Illiteracy would never be dead while television was alive.

Then he heard a key in the front door and a moment later Tom appeared in the living room doorway, filling it. "I want to talk to you, Dad. Where's Mum?"

"Out in the kitchen."

Tom went out to the kitchen, then came back after a moment or two. Lisa followed him, but he looked over his shoulder at her.

"Mum, this is police business —"

"If you're involved, it's *my* business." She sat down on the couch beside Malone. "Go on. What's the police business?"

Tom sat down opposite them and looked at them as if sizing them up. And Malone, to his own surprise, found himself sizing up his son. He guessed this happened in many families; at least in those families that tried to understand each other. It was as if Tom had passed through an invisible door and a new character, or a new side to him, had emerged. There was still the familiar image: the trainee at the investment bank who was doing well; the cricketer following his father into the State squad as a fast bowler; the rugby fullback who was tipped for representative honours. But now there was someone else, someone for whom the world had suddenly changed ...

"Everything's gone arse-up, hasn't it?" said Tom.

"I guess so," said Malone, not sure what in

particular had gone arse-up in a world that had been splintered like a glass ball.

"Get to the point," said Lisa with Dutch directness. The Zuyder Zee, she would tell them, hadn't been held back by vacillation.

Tom looked at them again, then he spoke to his father. "Dad, one of the guys down at The Sheaf, he'd been seeing Lucinda."

"From what Lucinda's housemates, Idaho and Frenchy —"

"Who?" said Lisa. "You're kidding."

"Are you accusing this bloke of killing Lucinda?" said Malone and even in his own ears sounded like an interrogating officer.

Tom flapped a helpless hand. "Well, no, not exactly —"

"Is he one of your mates?" asked Lisa.

"No, not exactly —"

Malone, trying for patience, said, "You're giving us a lot of *not exactly*. Exactly what are you trying to tell me?"

"Well —" Tom chewed his lip. "Well, he's not a mate, no. He's a guy in the crowd I have the occasional drink with, there are eight or ten of us, not all together at the same time. But one of *his* mates asked him what he thought of Lucinda's murder, seeing as he'd been seeing her, and the guy wouldn't answer. He just put down his glass, said he had to go and left. He was almost running out the door."

"That's not much to go on."

"I know that. That's why I came to you first —"

"You shouldn't have. It's Russ' case." But then, because he was a cop and couldn't help it, he said, "What did he say? His mate?"

Tom took his time, as if he now realised he should not have brought home his suspicions. "He said how much Barry had been boasting how well he was doing with Lucinda."

"Nice man," said Lisa. "I hope you don't boast like that."

"Mum —"

Malone said, "Barry is the bloke you suspect?"

"Yeah, Barry Mackaw." Tom spelled it out. "Like the parrot, only with a *k*. Look, maybe I better keep my mouth shut —"

"You've opened it," said Malone. "Russ will have to look into it."

"His mouth?" said Lisa, then shook her head. "Sorry, that's crass. I didn't mean it." She was obviously upset, more so than Malone could remember her being earlier. She reached for Tom's hand and he gave it to her, like a small boy. "You're in the clear, darling, but you may still finish up in court giving evidence."

"It's not going to look good, Dad being on the case."

"I'm not on it!" Malone couldn't stop the sharpness in his voice. "It's got nothing to do with me. I keep telling you, it's Russ' case. Or rather, it's Rupe Steeple's. But it's not mine."

"Nonetheless, I'll be identified as your son." There was resignation in Tom's voice. "Thomas Malone, son of Superintendent Scobie Malone. They'll make something out of it, hanging out with a possible murderer. The drug scene —"

"You're not into drugs?" It was Lisa's voice this time that was sharp.

"Of course I'm not! Nor are the other guys — at least they never talk about it. The media are always looking for an angle —"

"What does this feller do, Barry Mackaw?" asked Malone.

"He's an accountant. He's with Foxglove, Berenger —" Tom named one of the city's big accountancy firms. "What's the matter?"

"I'm not sure, but I think they're the auditors on the Orlando mess."

"He'd be too junior to be on something as big as that. He's like me, still working his way up from the bottom of the heap."

"What did this — Lucinda? — see in either of you?" said Lisa.

"Mum, did you tell Dad, when you first met him, what you saw in him? I dunno what she saw in me, even if only for one night ... I just wish she hadn't."

Malone said, "I think you should go and see Sergeant Steeple."

"Does he have to?" said Lisa.

"Darl —" He was tempted: let the police on the case find their own suspects. "No, if he thinks this bloke Mackaw —"

"Dad, don't put the onus on me —"

"Well, why'd you come to me? For Crissakes, Tom, I'm a cop! Would you have come to me if I'd been a fireman or a bus driver? You'd have kept what you thought to yourself. Now you have told me, because I'm a cop I have to see you carry it through. Or do you want me to go to Rupe Steeple?"

"You could," said Lisa.

"No, I couldn't. It would look as if I were asking for special treatment for Tom, to keep him out of the case —" He looked at his son. "Was that what you wanted?"

Tom hesitated, then shook his head. "No, I'm in it, if only on the outer. Okay, I'll go to Sergeant Steeple tomorrow morning. I'm dobbing in Barry Mackaw and that doesn't make me feel good. But, Jesus, this is murder!"

"That's the point," said Malone. "A girl is dead."

Lisa was still holding Tom's hand; she was mothering him as she hadn't in a long time. "Do you want to stay here tonight?"

"No, I'll be okay." He stood up, big enough to take care of himself; and yet, Malone thought, still vulnerable. "Thanks, both of you. I'll let you know how I get on with Sergeant Steeple."

When he had gone Lisa said, "I think you're right, telling him to go and see Sergeant What'shisname. But I wish it didn't have to be."

"How would you feel if he was in the army right now? There are kids facing worse prospects than his, the way things are going."

"Don't —"

He kissed her. "I'm not trying to find a bright side. At the moment he thinks he's in a helluva situation. And he is, from his perspective. But in another six months a — year —" He shrugged, not wanting to draw the picture; then changed the conversation, trying to lighten the mood: "What did you mean, what did Lucinda see in him? She saw a stud bull, that's what she saw."

"That's my son? A stud bull?"

"Better get used to it. Let's go to bed."

"With a stud bull?"

"I wasn't thinking of *that*. I'm dog-tired. I think I'm getting old."

She pushed his head back, kissed him fiercely. She was suddenly afraid of the future, a fear she had never contemplated.

Chapter Five

❧

1

His sister-in-law had told him of Natalie Shipwood's driving habits. "Mick, she has a chauffeur drive her around town on appointments, but she likes to drive herself to and from the office. What other career woman in Sydney drives her own half-a-million-dollar Bentley. She sits up there like Boadicea —"

"Marilyn, when did she start getting up your nose? You've been with her a long time."

"Mick, I wouldn't know. It was just gradual. Maybe it was the first time I saw her behind the wheel of the Bentley. She just looked as if she was ready to run right over everyone."

So he had spent a couple of nights watching Natalie Shipwood, leaving Phoebe alone on the excuse that he had to get into town to see about their seniors' cards. He often left her alone for an hour or two and she never minded, content to be left undisturbed with Bert Newton, Oprah Winfrey or the beleaguered characters on the battlefield of *The Bold and the Beautiful*. He had never left her alone at 6.30 in the evening and he had had to invent an elaborate excuse.

"Hon, I've got an appointment with a solicitor about our wills —"

"Our wills? At tea-time?" But she wasn't suspicious, never had been. She was too trusting, he had often thought, for the shit of a world they lived in.

"He's free, one of those volunteer blokes they have in Legal Aid. For people like us, pensioners, people on super."

"Are we that hard up, Mick, we have to have free legal advice?"

"Love, we're not hard up —" *Not bloody much*. "But these days, if you can save a dollar, you try to save a dollar. Everything's going up, love."

"All right, but don't be long. What time'll you be back?"

"Seven-thirty at the latest. I'll bring something back with me for tea. Pizza or something."

"I thought you were saving money?" But she smiled and kissed him and he had left the house feeling an absolute bastard. He was burdened with love, they both were, and it was a heavier load than he had ever had to carry down on the wharves.

He drove into the city in the Corolla, found a parking space in a street a block from the Orlando building. He was about to get out of the car when he noticed that the Disabled Person parking ticket was missing from the windscreen. Bugger! It was still in the pocket of his shirt where he had put it and the shirt was back at the house in the laundry basket. It was not meant for his use, but he used it anyway, parking the car and getting out and limping away as if he were minus hip-bones. He got out of the car and went to the parking meter. Holy Shit! A dollar for every fifteen minutes. And the smallest cash he had was a five-dollar note.

He looked around, saw a coffee bar across the street and headed for it to change the note. The young bloke behind the counter was unobliging.

"This ain't a bank, dad."

"I know that —" *Smartarse*: but he restrained himself. "Banks don't change money any more. They just take it."

"Have a cuppa coffee and I'll change a hundred dollars for you."

Jesus, where do they breed these kids? "I'll come back and have a cuppa. But right now I need cash for the meter."

The young man changed the note and Kelray went back across the street and put four dollars in the meter, cursing at inflation and the greed of councils. He had an hour to top the bitch or he'd be booked and maybe traced to knowing Marilyn and then ... His mind was running away from him. He should have caught a bus to murder.

He went in through the front entrance of the Orlando building, into the lobby of terracotta and timber and the water dribbling down one wall like a public urinal. The security desk was vacant, as he knew it would be at this hour, and he went to the emergency door at the rear of the lobby and went down the stairs to the garage.

The Bentley was in its usual double parking space; no risk was taken of its rich doors being dented by careless lesser makes. Two vans that he knew did not go out overnight were parked opposite the big car. He stepped in behind them, crouched down and waited.

He had been waiting ten minutes, getting impatient, before Natalie Shipwood appeared. Three men and a woman, separately, had come down to the garage, got into their cars and driven out. The garage was almost deserted, occupied only by two cars and the two vans besides the Bentley, when the bitch stepped out of the lift.

He took the ski-mask from his pocket and slipped it over his head. He felt bloody ridiculous, but the mask must be effective; everyone was wearing them these days in hold-ups, like a criminal fashion item. He took the butcher's knife out of the paper-bag in which he had carried it and stepped out from behind the vans.

Natalie Shipwood was at the driver's door of the Bentley when she turned round and saw him coming at her. Then he heard the shout from behind him. A bald-headed bugger had appeared from nowhere, was rushing at him with a laptop raised to belt him over the head. Jesus, where had the bugger come from?

He swung round, his back to the bitch, and slashed at the man. He felt the knife go into the man's arm, heard him scream and drop the laptop, then he was running away down the length of the garage towards the exit, pulling off the ski-mask as he ran. He was surprised to find himself crying with frustration.

2

In the morning, not telling Lisa or Russ, going against the grain of being a good cop, he went down to Pyrmont to see if Idaho and Frenchy had returned to their house.

Idaho was standing at the front gate with a big grey-haired man. "Oh, hello, Mr Malone. This is Mr Kelray."

The man put out a hand that could have cupped a football; the calluses on the palm could have sandpapered a table. "I live just up the street. I stopped to tell Miss Breslin how sorry we are about what happened the other night, see if she was okay. You're Con Malone's son, I remember you down the wharves some years ago."

"You knew my dad?"

"Well, not exactly knew him —" Mick Kelray had a gravelly voice, as if there were calluses in his throat. "I knew *of* him. Everybody did. Every demo, every strike, he was up there at the front, waving the Red Flag — he still a commo?"

"Only in his memory. He's mellowed, like they all do."

Kelray nodded. "Me, too … He had the spirit — we all had it in them days. Not any more. We had the soul-case kicked outa us — enterprise bargaining. Give him my regards."

"I'll tell him. He might get the Red Flag out of the cupboard."

"Salt of the earth, they don't make 'em like him any more. Well, I gotta be going. Nice talking to you. You want any help, Miss Breslin, knock on my door."

He went up the street and turned into his own front door. Idaho said, "He's nice, what I guess good neighbours used to be. I hardly know him, but he's always pleasant. Did you want to see me, Mr Malone? I'm on my way to a job."

"Is your friend — Frenchy?" The name was like a bubble of mirth on his lips. "Is she home?"

"No, not here, she's gone home to her parents, up at Pennant Hills. I don't know if she'll be coming back. Look, I've got to go —"

"Where do you work? You got a car? No? I can drive you."

"Would you? Trying to find a taxi ... I'm going to Chippendale, a recording studio. I do voice-overs — you know, commercials. I have to tape three this morning. One for cat food and I hate cats." She shivered.

He put her into the family's Fairlane, walked round and got in beside her. "Do you do much of this work? You have a good voice."

"Thank you. I'm surprised you noticed — most men never notice a woman's voice."

"I do," he said.

"I get enough work to pay the bills. But some of the crap I have to say, I don't think anyone notices my voice. At least I don't have to shout — I turn down those jobs." She turned in her seat and looked at him. "Why did you want to see me?"

The small talk was over. "I wanted to see both of you. Frenchy — is that her real name?"

"No, it's Nancy Delarus. Her grandfather was French or Belgian, something like that." She was still facing him. "You didn't come out here to Pyrmont to talk to me about my voice."

He started up the car, drove carefully. He always drove carefully, especially when holding a conversation. He glanced sideways at her as he turned the car out of Juniper Street. The puffiness of tears had gone and she looked younger this morning; middle age had receded into the future, where it belonged. "How many boyfriends did Lucinda have?"

"Oh —" For a moment he thought she was going to tell him to mind his own business. But then, as if she realised it *was* his business: "Like I said, she played the field, she was pretty reckless at times. But one or two were regular, you know, she might see the same guy once or twice a week."

"But not my son?"

She gave him a shrewd glance. "That's why you came this morning?"

"Partly. I believed him when he said he'd brought Lucinda home only once."

"That's true. Frenchy — Nancy and I saw him only that once. He's nice. But you're worried?"

"Not about him, no." He wasn't going to tell her too much about Tom; certainly not about Lucinda accusing him of being responsible for her pregnancy. "Do you and Nancy have boyfriends?"

"Yes. Not regulars, though."

"What did your boyfriends think of Lucinda?"

She took her time: "That's not a nice question."

"I know. But what we're talking about, murder, isn't a nice question, either."

Reluctantly she said, "She was our friend, we all got on well together. But —" She glanced at him again. "The boys thought she was a slut."

"You said there were one or two fellers who were a bit more regular than others —"

"There was one she seemed to like more than the others. A guy named Barry Something."

"Did you mention him to Sergeant Steeple?"

"No-o. No, I don't think so, unless Nancy did. The other night I was pretty, I dunno, shell-shocked. Is that the word? I'm not used to murder."

Not like me. "Idaho — is that your given name?"

She smiled, relaxed, looked very attractive. "No, I was christened Ida Hope. I put them together, did away with *p-e*. Idaho. I wanted to be — I still hope to act. But whoever heard of an actress named Ida?"

"Ida Lupino?"

"Who?"

"You don't watch the Late Late Movies on TV? Or Bill Collins' Movie Classics?"

"Only if they've got Cary Grant in them. Is your favourite actress that old? Late Late Movies?"

"Even older. Theda Bara."

She smiled, looking even younger. "You're kidding."

He drove a while in silence, then said, "Do me a favour, Ida. If Sergeant Steeple comes to see you again, don't mention you've seen me."

"Of course not. You're trying to keep Tom out of this, aren't you? I don't blame you. I just wish Nancy and I could be kept out of it."

"I'll talk to Inspector Clements, he's on the case." *Jesus, I'm pulling strings as I've never done before.*

When he drew up outside the recording studio in Chippendale she pressed his arm before she got out of the car. "Tom's safe, Mr Malone. And thanks for the lift. I hope I didn't take you out of your way."

"No, my office is just up the road, in Strawberry Hills. Take care, Ida. Good luck — as an actress. Watch the Late Late Movies."

3

When he got to his office the first thing he did was phone Romy at the morgue: "Have you done the p.m. on Lucinda Rossiter?"

"Yes. It would seem that Tom's in the clear." Romy sounded calm, matter-of-fact; he could imagine her taking off medical gloves as she spoke to him. "The girl was six weeks pregnant, no more. I can't give you any clues on her killer."

"I'm just a bystander on this one."

"The hell you are," said Romy. "But I love you, Scobie."

He put down the phone as Clements came into his office. "Your wife has just told me she loves me."

"I've heard her say that to a corpse." Clements sat down, looking comfortable in the chair. Malone wondered how many times he would come here to sit in the chair. And didn't mind. "I've just had a call from Bay Street, from Rupe Steeple. Someone tried to get at Mrs Shipwood last night."

Malone waited.

"Our girl Natalie was saved by our friend Derek," Clements went on. "She was gunna give him a lift home to his apartment, he still lives at The Wharf, and he'd stopped on the ground floor to speak to someone. He came down the emergency stairs just as the guy did the rush on Natalie and tried to carve her."

"How's Sweden?" asked Malone.

"Four stitches in his arm. He tried to whack the guy with his laptop."

"Did Compaq or Apple design them with that in mind? It's another selling point."

"I'm thinking of getting one."

"Balls. You'll never give up your notebook." Then Malone said seriously, "You think Jack Aldwych might have arranged this job?"

"It'd be a laugh if he had. His son's brother-in-law getting the knife instead of Natalie. But we'll look into it. Where've you been? I came around here half an hour ago."

Malone took his time. "Tom came to see us last night, me and Lisa. He thinks one of the fellers he drinks with, not a mate but one of a group, he thinks the bloke might've had something to do with the murder of that girl, Lucinda. I went over to Pyrmont this morning to have a word with her housemate, Idaho."

Clements looked at him. "You're poking your nose in."

"I know. I was just checking. Tom was going over this morning to see Rupe Steeple, tell him about this other bloke."

"He's been. Rupe called me, told me about Tom after he'd told me about the attack on Natalie."

"What did he have to say?"

"They've already talked to this other guy —" He took out his notebook, flipped over the pages. He would be taking notes at his own funeral, checking on who turned up. "Barry Mackaw. He has an alibi for the night of the murder."

"Well, then, Tom was wrong."

"Yeah." Clements put away the notebook. "You mind if I give you an order."

Malone checked himself from bristling. "Can you do that?"

"You mean the rank? No, I guess not. But as one mate to another, yes, I guess I can. You and Tom stay out of this case. Rupe Steeple is taking care of it and he's letting me know how things go. You are out of the circle."

Before Malone could answer, Greg Random was standing in the doorway. "Who should I be more afraid of? Osama bin Laden or Derek bin Sweden?"

"Oh, bin Sweden," said Clements.

Random came into the room, sat down on the other chair opposite Malone. "He's already been on to the Commissioner. Why haven't you buggers got all this sorted out?"

Clements looked at Malone before he said, "You don't mean that."

Random sighed. "I'm only repeating what the Commissioner said."

Clements looked at Malone again, then said, "Jack Aldwych is pissed off with Mrs Shipwood."

Random said nothing, waited: at which he was an expert.

Clements went on, "He's done a million, two hundred thousand in Orlando."

"Why does my head no longer swim when I hear those sums? What gets me is how did this swindle, or whatever it is, how did it happen? Did management keep something from the board? Or vice versa?"

"The mushroom syndrome," said Clements.

"The what?"

"Mushroom syndrome. Feed 'em bullshit and keep 'em in the dark. One does it to the other. Or vice versa."

Random looked at Malone. "He's a mine of information."

"It's all in his little notebooks."

Random changed tack: "Jack Aldwych is an old mate of yours. Would he have paid for this bungled hit?"

"I don't think so. Jack would have used a pro and pros don't use knives, it can be messy. But we'll look into it."

"Good," said Random and it was difficult to

note whether he approved or not. Then he said to Clements, "What else have you got on your plate?"

"Things are quiet. Everyone must be at home watching TV, looking for bin Laden. There aren't even any domestics."

"I saw on the reports there was a girl murdered over in Pyrmont. You're not on that?"

"No, Rupe Steeple, from City Centre, is handling it." Clements hadn't glanced at Malone; the latter might not have been in his own office. "I'll let you know how we get on with Jack Aldwych."

"Do that," said Random and stood up. "There's something you buggers are not telling me. But I don't want to know, not till it's all tied up in a neat bundle on my desk."

He left them, going out as quietly as he had come in, and Malone looked at Clements. "Thanks, but eventually he'll know about Tom and that girl."

Before Clements had time to reply Gail Lee had appeared in the doorway. "Sorry to interrupt, boss —"

She had spoken directly to Malone. She called me *boss*, he thought, even though I'm no longer her boss. And was pleased. She was half-Chinese and one of the best detectives in Homicide; he had always liked working with her. I still haven't left there, he thought; and said, "Something the matter, Gail?"

127

"Yes, sir." But now she was speaking to Clements, her boss: "There's panic stations at Orlando, someone's sent a letter with white powder in it to Mrs Shipwood."

"Shit!" said Clements. "Anthrax?"

"They don't know yet, but the Fire Brigade decontamination squad is there, hosing down everyone."

"Anyone infected? Mrs Shipwood?"

"I don't know. I think we should get over there —"

Malone was on his feet before Clements; but then the big man had always been a slow mover. "Let's go —"

Clements, out of his chair, looked at him, was about to say something, then changed his mind. Without a word he pushed Gail Lee out ahead of him and, without a backward glance at Malone, followed her. Malone hesitated, then he, too, went out of his office. He had to keep reminding himself, because it had not yet become habit, that Homicide was under Crime Agency command and he was still Clements' boss.

Gail Lee drove the unmarked car, using the siren and the blue light to demand passage; she drove with calm skill, while Malone sat in the back with his feet trying to bore holes in the floor. When they reached Sussex Street they found the Orlando block had been cordoned off and a crowd had gathered. As they got out of the car they heard cheering and whistling.

"What's going on?" Clements looked angry.

They pushed their way through the crowd, showed their badges to the uniformed officer who tried to stop them; then they slowed up as they saw the scene ahead of them. Some effort had been made to form a screen with fire trucks and police cars, but the show was still visible. Eight women and four men, stripped to their underwear, were being hosed down, one at a time in a portable shower-stall. Under the hose at the moment was Natalie Shipwood, in brassiere and panties, hair hanging down about her face, her arms held tight across her bosom as she shivered and gasped under the strong stream of water directed at her.

Clements spoke to the fire brigade officer in a yellow decontamination suit: "What happened? Were they sprayed by the powder?"

"No ... Listen to those clots!" The fireman looked back at the crowd with disgust as they whistled and hooted; Natalie Shipwood had been replaced in the shower-stall by a young blonde in very brief panties and no brassiere. "No, we do this as a precaution."

"Is the building quarantined?"

"No, just the two top floors."

"Why are you showering them out here?" As more hoots and whistles came from the crowd.

"You trying to tell us how to do our job?"

Malone jerked his head at Clements and the two men and Gail Lee crossed to the lobby of the Orlando building. Natalie Shipwood, wrapped in a blanket, escorted by two women, went in ahead of them. She glanced at the detectives, but didn't appear to recognise them.

"Hullo, Scobie, what are you doing here?"

Malone turned as he went through the revolving door. A tall lean man with a grey moustache and a weary air had stopped on his way out.

"Paul, are we on your territory?"

Paul Ascott was the inspector in charge of the detectives at City Central; his and Malone's paths had crossed for twenty years, always without getting in a tangle. "If it ain't one thing it's another . . ." He looked at Clements. "When did I call in you and Crime Agency?"

"Paul —" Malone took Ascott by the arm, led him aside. The lobby was full of people: firemen, police officers, office staff; this was no place for an argument about territory. "We've been on this for the past two days —"

He explained the connection with Orlando, rising out of the Hyx murder. Ascott listened patiently, then nodded, almost with relief. "Okay, it's all yours. But Jesus —" He stared out at the last of those being sprayed in the street, a middle-aged man with a belly and underpants that hung on him like a surrendered flag. "If this is anthrax —"

"How soon will they know?"

"I dunno. The letter has gone to the lab. It was posted at the GPO, addressed to the boss lady in block letters. It was opened by her secretary —" He glanced at Malone. "The new one, the one that replaced that Mrs Hyx. She's hysterical — and I don't blame her. I don't think it's got anything to do with terrorists — I hope to Christ not! But the bastards have given some moron fucking ideas!" For the moment he was no longer weary; his lean face flushed with anger and his teeth were bared under the moustache. "If we catch 'em, we'll throw the book at 'em!"

"I'll see Russ keeps you up to scratch on what we learn. Let me know soon's you get a report on what was in the letter. Take care, Paul."

"We'll need to," said Ascott and Malone knew he was talking about the world in general.

Clements and Gail Lee were waiting by the lifts for Malone. "What's the word?" asked Clements.

"They don't know yet what was in the letter. You tell Mrs Shipwood we want a word with her?"

"She's gone back up to her office with Sweden —"

"He's here?"

"Arm in a sling, looking like a war hero. And bloody angry. Or frightened."

"Not our man Sweden. He'd stare down the entire Taliban mob."

They got into the lift with three young women and a man, all wrapped in blankets, all soaked and bedraggled. One of the young women, shivering still, tried for some humour: "Did you see those TV cameras? My mother will die when she sees me having a shower in the street!" The others tried to laugh, but they were too cold or too afraid and they managed no more than weak smiles. Tides were creeping out from New York, fear was a new virus.

The lift stopped at the twentieth floor and when the doors opened a young police officer in a jumpsuit and weapons cap motioned for all of them to get out. "End of the line, folks. Everything above here is quarantined."

Malone showed his badge. "Where is Mrs Shipwood? She on this floor?"

"In the big room at the end of the corridor, sir. She's with one of the directors, a Mr Finland."

"Sweden."

"Pardon, sir?"

But Malone let him off the hook, just smiled and led Clements and Gail Lee along the corridor. Sweden had been Police Minister before this young man's time; politicians came and went like clouds, often making no more impression. Sweden's influence was at a higher level than the young cop's.

He tried to swing that influence as soon as the three detectives came into the big room: "Jesus, do you have to come barging in *now*? Mrs Shipwood —"

"We appreciate what's happened —" Malone let Clements do the talking. "But do you want us to stand back and do nothing? I'm sorry, Mrs Shipwood —"

She was dressed in a blue canteen coat, a nameplate stuck on her left breast: Tiffany-Amber. The elegant coiffure was now just flat black dough on her head; all her make-up was gone and she suddenly looked ten years older than when Malone and Clements had seen her last. There was no resemblance to Elizabeth Taylor, not even at a hundred metres.

The room was evidently the office of four senior executives; their desks faced each other across the floor like the steeds of four combatants. Two large windows looked out across the roofs of the buildings on the opposite side of the street; beyond was a glimpse of water, like a promise of better views when the executives rose higher up the ladder. On the walls were framed awards, memorabilia from Orlando's better days.

Gail Lee, on a nod from Clements, sat down opposite Natalie Shipwood. "Are you up to talking to us?"

Natalie Shipwood looked at the three detectives as if wondering whether to trust them. "Why would anyone do such an awful thing?"

Gail said, "Last evening someone tried to kill you with a knife —" She glanced at Sweden, who raised his slung arm as if to say, *Don't forget me*.

"This morning, with the anthrax — if it *is* anthrax, we don't know yet — it seems someone holds a very deep grudge against you and Orlando. They started off by murdering Marilyn Hyx —"

Hold it, thought Malone, there's no connection … But then he saw the way Gail was going:

"You are the target, Mrs Shipwood, and you are endangering everyone else at Orlando."

Natalie Shipwood saw the anomaly. She stared at Gail Lee, then she turned to Malone and Clements. "Aren't you two the senior officers? How dare you let her talk to me like that!"

Malone had to strangle a laugh. Indignation demands the proper face; under her black cap of dough Mrs Shipwood just looked like a cartoon character. He managed to say with his own face perfectly straight, "We agree with what Detective Lee has just said." He looked at Clements, who nodded, then at Sweden: "Wouldn't you agree, too?"

Sweden looked for a moment as if he was going to *dis*agree; but he was no fool. Defender of the faith, knight in shining armour: that was for losers. "They're right, Natalie —"

"So what am I supposed to do?" she snapped. If she had been frightened by what had occurred, she was now recovered. "I can't just *disappear* —"

"It would be best if you stayed in your own home," said Clements. "We can give you police protection —"

Nice work, thought Malone. The teamwork, without practice or intent, had nailed her down.

"Perhaps she could go abroad till all this has settled down?" suggested Sweden.

Like other absconding entrepreneurs? It was obviously something the two of them had discussed; Sweden was just too casual in his suggestion.

"I don't think the Securities Commission would allow that," said Clements, never one to ignore unused nails. "I understand they are putting a restraining order on everything to do with Orlando. That, I think, would include you personally, Mrs Shipwood."

If it was a shot in the dark it was a good one. Natalie Shipwood frowned at Sweden as if he had sold her bad advice. "Can they do that, Derek?"

Sweden sighed, raised his wounded arm, winced and dropped it. "They can do anything these days, Nat. Bloody regulations!" Then he glared at Malone. "What are you grinning at?"

"Come on —" Malone was now totally relaxed; they had won the small battle. "You were a politician, you spent — what? ten? fifteen years? — drafting regulations. Every time something went wrong, you drafted new regulations, playing catch-up. One thing about the insurance game, it's never behind what might happen. I'll bet they've got Orlando covered, protecting themselves. ASIC are slow out of the traps sometimes, but after —"

He named a major company that had collapsed. "They're on the ball now. And I'll bet Orlando's insurance company has got a gun at your head. And then, of course, there are police regulations."

"You should have been a politician," said Sweden without rancour.

"Never in your class," said Malone and they smiled at each other like hyenas.

"I am not going to have my home overrun by police," said Natalie Shipwood.

Ignoring that, Gail Lee asked, "Have you been swabbed and tested?"

Shades of the Olympics. But Malone bit his tongue before it became facetious. Distance took the threat out of terrorism, but that was not to say that it was not getting closer. Today's scare had nothing to do with terrorism, he was sure, but the example had been set. Australia Post could now deliver death, unregistered.

"Yes." For a moment Natalie Shipwood did look frightened. "How soon will we know?"

None of the detectives knew; this was all new ground for them. Malone said, "I'm sure they won't keep you waiting. Are you ready to go now?"

"*Now?*"

Malone was patient. "Mrs Shipwood, killers don't run to timetables. You have been threatened — *twice*. The sooner we get you into protection, the safer you'll be."

"You'd better take their advice, Nat," said Sweden. "What about the rest of the board, Superintendent? Are we threatened?"

"I'd take precautions," said Malone and wondered at the taste of malice in his mouth. "Where is the woman who opened the mail?"

"They've taken her to hospital," said Natalie Shipwood. "I should go and see her —"

"We'll do that," said Gail Lee. "On our way back from your home."

The older woman stood up. She looked down at the tunic she wore, twisted her head to read the label on her breast. "Tiffany-Amber?" Then she suddenly lifted her hands: "Where's my jewellery?"

"It's being fumigated or whatever they do to it —" Sweden was beginning to sound impatient. "Go home, Natalie. You've got more than jewellery to worry about."

Her glare was as hard as a diamond. "Don't lecture me, Derek —" For a moment there were only the two of them; the three police officers could have been out in the corridor. "I'm a long way from finished."

Chapter Six

❧

1

Phoebe Kelray liked to joke, a little bitterly, that when she was light-headed with pain, she was having "a fit of the vapours". When Mick Kelray opened his front door in response to the knock and saw the two young people there, a man and a woman, the man holding up a police badge, he, too, had a fit of the vapours.

"I'm Detective Sergeant Kagal," said the young man. "This is Detective Constable Dallen."

"What's it about?" He wanted to shut the door in their faces. Anything to stop Phoebe hearing what they had to say.

"We believe your wife is the sister of a woman named Marilyn Hyx —"

"Yeah," he said cautiously.

"May we come inside, Mr Kelray? We'd like to talk to your wife, too, if she's here."

Kelray hesitated, then he stepped out on to the narrow porch. "Look, this isn't gunna upset the wife too much, is it? She knows about Marilyn being done in, but we don't talk about it … I don't want her upset — she's an invalid —"

Kagal looked at Sheryl Dallen, then back at Kelray. "That's a problem, Mr Kelray —" He was handsome and well-dressed, an advertisement for the Service; he knew it but managed not to be obnoxious about it. He was also not insensitive: "But we do want to talk to her —"

"I dunno —" Kelray shrugged hopelessly; or helplessly. He was still not sure why they were here, but he felt a little safer. Except for Phoebe: "She's an invalid, like I said — arteriosclerosis —" Again the word slid effortlessly off his tongue; he was fluent in maladies. "Can I help?"

"How much do you know about your sister-in-law?" Sheryl Dallen spent six hours a week in a gymnasium; health, shining out of her, made her almost good-looking. "Did you see her frequently?"

Kelray shook his head. The blonde girl down the street, Idaho, went by and he nodded to her. Then he looked back at the two officers. "Nah. Her and the wife, they hadn't spoken in years. They —"

Then Phoebe called faintly from inside the house. "Who is it, Mick?"

"Coming, love." Then he turned back to the two detectives, sure now that they were not here for him. "Can you forget how Marilyn was done in? I mean, don't lay it on —"

"We never do, Mr Kelray," said Kagal.

Kelray led the way along the short, narrow hallway into the small living room. Phoebe was in her wheelchair in front of the downstairs television set. Oprah Winfrey was interviewing another of the 799 experts on terrorism: "Of course, we can't be certain," said the expert with certainty. "But —"

Phoebe switched off the TV with the remote control, looked at the two young people with interest and some welcome. She and Mick rarely had visitors and certainly not any young ones.

"They're police, love. They want to talk to us about Marilyn."

"Marilyn?" She frowned and for a moment he thought she was going to cry.

Kagal said, "May we sit down?" Kelray pushed forward the other two chairs in the room; he remained standing. Kagal sat down, automatically arranged the creases in his trousers and went on, "We've been trying to trace her family. You're the only ones, you and her husband. He's the one we want to find."

"Clem?" said Kelray, anxious to keep Phoebe from being too upset. And wanting to keep Marilyn out of the frame as much as possible, not wanting Phoebe to know he had visited her sister. "He's still around. Last we heard he was living up around Collaroy, Dee Why, somewhere there on them beaches."

"You haven't kept in touch with him?"

"Why should we?" said Kelray and looked at Phoebe, who nodded. "He was a first-class bastard. Him and Marilyn divorced, I dunno, ten or fifteen years ago. Maybe more, maybe less. He was history."

"No children?" asked Sheryl Dallen.

"No," said Phoebe. "That was the only thing we had in common, my sister and me."

She didn't look at Kelray and he was glad.

"We've tried to trace Mr Hyx," said Kagal. "It's an unusual name. H-y-x."

"He changed it," said Kelray, glad to get away from Marilyn, even if she was still in the room with them. "He was a Czech. I think H-y-x was only part of his name. He changed it to Hicks — H-i-c-k-s — after him and Marilyn were divorced. He changed the spelling of his first name, too. It was Klement with a K. He changed it to a C. We knew him as Clem."

"Did you know him well?"

"Nup." Kelray looked at Phoebe. "We never wanted to, did we?"

"No," said Phoebe. "We never got on, my sister and me, but she never deserved someone like him. Like my hubby says, he was a first-class bastard. But he'd come around here occasionally, never with my sister. We never knew why."

"He was a salesman," said Kelray. "Always looking to sell something. Or himself. I was on the wharves in them days and I think he thought I could work some sorta finagle, getting things through Customs."

"You don't know whether he kept in touch with her after the divorce?" asked Sheryl.

"We wouldn't know," said Kelray, feeling the questions running down and beginning to feel safe.

"So, to clear things up," said Kagal, "you're the only surviving relative, Mrs Kelray?"

"For what it amounts to," said Phoebe. "Have you found out who murdered her? Or got a clue?"

Bugger, thought Kelray. She's spent too much time in front of the TV. She knows all the police procedure. She's walked the beat with *NYPD Blue*, with *Law and Order*, *The Bill* and *Blue Heelers*.

There was a moment before Sheryl Dallen said, "Not yet, Mrs Kelray. She was the private secretary of a woman we're interested in."

"Natalie Shipwood? What's she been up to?"
Jesus, Phoebe, let 'em go!

"That's what we have to determine," said Kagal and stood up. He looked around him. "You look very comfortable here. These old houses are — well, *solid*."

"We moved in when we married," said Kelray, eager for them to be gone. "Forty-one years ago. A different neighbourhood in them days. You could leave the front door open —"

"And watch the world go by," said Phoebe, who had not been in a wheelchair then, who had been young and pretty, as Mick Kelray still remembered her. Then she tapped the arms of the wheelchair: "I wasn't in this thing then."

It was a remark to shut the door on them now. *Good on you, love*. Kelray led the way back along the hall, opened the front door, said quietly, "Thanks. We weren't much help —"

"Oh yes, you were, Mr Kelray," said Kagal. "Hicks, H-i-c-k-s. Now we know where to find him. Look after yourself."

He went out off the narrow porch. Sheryl Dallen was about to follow him, but turned and put out her hand. She said nothing, just squeezed Mick Kelray's hand and was gone. Suddenly he couldn't see the other side of the street nor the world going by.

2

"It wasn't anthrax," said Clements. "It was powdered ecstasy tablets."

"Some sick bastard having fun?" asked Malone. "Or someone adding pressure?"

Clements shrugged. "We're still treating it as someone pressuring her, but it could be some sick lamebrain. They come out of the woodwork when someone else sets an example. You seen this morning's papers? Bloody firebugs starting bushfires again and summer hasn't really started.

We oughta declare a *jihad* on them if we could find them."

He had come around once again to Malone's office, almost as if he had to report in each morning. Malone had begun to wonder if Clements had not wanted the promotion to head Homicide, if he had felt much safer as second-in-command. Ambition is not always a ready sale.

"They've picked up Mr Hicks, got him through his driver's licence and car registration. They're holding him down at Dee Why. You wanna come down with me?"

Malone considered. His desk was still comparatively empty; Crime Agency had not yet got him on target for bumf. Soon, though, someone would notice the empty desk and the blank computer and then the dam gates would be opened. There are no bigger sins against bureaucracy.

"I'll come," he said and stood up.

Then Greg Random was lounging in the doorway, "Gallivanting again?"

"The Orlando business. You told us to leave no stone unturned."

"Where are you unturning stones this time?"

"Dee Why," said Clements, chipping in. "They've picked up Mrs Hyx's ex. He's on our list of suspects."

"That business yesterday, the anthrax scare —"

"It wasn't anthrax, we got the lab report this morning. It was powdered ecstasy tablets."

Random's smiles were always slow-motion creases; Malone and Clements had rarely seen him actually laugh. "I could do with a little ecstasy. Mr Sweden is pulling strings again. I'm told all he has is a six-inch gash in his arm. Pity. Don't quote me."

"I'll say this for him, he saved Mrs Shipwood's life," said Clements.

"That may disturb my dreams." said Random. "I'll let you know."

"Just don't quote any Welsh poets at us," said Malone.

"The Welsh don't have a monopoly on the melancholy. You Irish had the voices for it. Synge and O'Casey weren't Happy Little Vegemites. I never hear you quoting the poets, Russ."

"Wish in one pocket and piss in the other, see which one fills up first," said Clements. "It doesn't rhyme, but it covers most of today's business. Especially Orlando."

"Good luck," said Random and went as he came, always without fuss.

Malone and Clements went downstairs to Clements' car, and headed for the northern beaches. As they drove Malone said, almost too casually, "Heard any more from Rupe Steeple on that girl's murder?"

"He's no further on it than we are on this one. Tom talking about it?"

"We haven't seen him since he talked to Rupe. I hope he's out of it now, finished with it."

The day was fine, but the sky at the edges was a dirty beige. The bushfires had started, or been started, early and smoke was drifting in from the south-west. The natives' natural lethargy had shredded over the past month, there was an edginess now as if they were waiting for disaster. True, next week would be Melbourne Cup Week and the nation would come to a standstill and bugger the war, bugger terrorists, bugger the bushfires. Perspective had to be kept.

Then at the end of the week there would be the Federal election, one of the nastiest Malone could remember, and two generations of voters would go to the polls with more on their minds than they had had to face so far. The smoke from the bushfires, for those with imagination, was a reminder of the smoke of war. And Afghanistan would come back out of the history books they had read at school ...

"How do you think the Yanks are going against the Taliban?"

Clements took his time. He was a good driver, but had little patience with road-hogs; he would have notched up record hauls if he had been on Highway Patrol. He cursed as a grey-haired daredevil cut in front of him, but held off the horn.

"I think they're a bit like that old dill up front there. Hasty."

"You used to be like that when you were young."

"Like the old guy? Or the Yanks? Have you seen the terrain they've gone into? Maybe I'd of made a poor soldier, I'm too cautious —"

"You could have fooled me. But yeah, you're right, about the terrain. We're lucky."

"How's that?"

"We know the terrain. It's only the crims who change."

Dee Why is a beachside suburb some ten kilometres north of the harbour. There are several guesses at how it got its name. Some say it is a garbled version of an Aboriginal name for a bird that nested in the local lagoons. Others claim it is the initials of the *Donna Ysabel*, a Spanish galleon wrecked off nearby rocks centuries ago, but they are romantics; *caballero* are in short supply locally. There are a dozen beaches north of the harbour and they have their own culture, bound to the surf. There was, and still is, a drug culture and several police were under current arrest for their dealing in it. But the atmosphere, generally, is laid back and the locals feel under no threat. The only terror is the occasional shark cruising beyond the surf.

The police station at Dee Why was next to a church. A funeral was in progress as Malone and Clements drew up. Someone from the Pacific Islands was being buried; burly brown men in wrap-round skirts were carrying the coffin out of the church. Malone took off his pork-pie hat as a mark of respect and one of the men nodded in thanks.

Someone's troubles are over, thought Malone, no more rough terrain. He followed Clements into the station and met Sergeant Alex Lorre, the senior detective.

"We've got him in an interview room —" Lorre was a big, overweight man, his baldness disguised (he hoped) by the current fashion for shaving the skull. He had bright blue eyes and a big nose that suggested he liked a drink or two. "He's not happy —"

If Clem Hicks wasn't happy Malone didn't want to meet him when things were going well. He was the glad-hander of all time: politician, salesman and public relations man. "Oh, what a pleasure to see you! The inspector told me you were coming —"

"Sergeant," said Lorre.

Hicks didn't hear him. There was just a trace of accent in his speech. He was as big as Malone, but (Malone would hate to admit it) fitter. He had a thin handsome face, a trim grey moustache, dark wavy hair with grey sideburns, and eyes that (Malone was sure) could see all sides of a box at once. He was dressed in a London Irish rugby shirt and cargo pants with pockets on the shins, knees, thighs, hips and backside. Malone had a momentary vision of his being weighed down in the pockets with wishes and piss.

He shook hands with both Malone and Clements; his handshake was that of a long-lost relative, one glad to be home. "This is about my wife Marilyn? I couldn't believe it when I read of it —"

"Let's sit down, Mr Hicks —"

Malone gently cut him off. He and Clements sat down, motioned to Hicks to sit on the other side of the table from them. Lorre sat on a chair under the eye of the video recorder. Hicks looked up at it, then sat down.

"We just want to ask a few questions about you and your ex-wife." Malone put just faint emphasis on *ex*; but Hicks caught it. "Had you seen her just before she was murdered?'

The *murdered* was brutal, but Malone had decided they would get nowhere glad-handing Mr Hicks. The latter's blue eyes froze for just a moment, then he shook his head. "I hadn't seen her in months — I've been busy —"

"What do you do?" asked Clements.

"Do?"

"Whom do you work for?" said Malone.

"Whom?" A big smile, another glad-hand on the way: "What a pleasure to hear an Australian with respect for the English language! Usually it is only educated foreigners who respect it —"

"Mr Hicks," said Clements, an uneducated native, "who do you work for? What do you do?"

Hicks gave up the glad-handing; there was no sale. "Do? At the moment I'm weighing up several offers —"

He's out of work, thought Malone: like those sacked executives who were always going to pursue other interests. "Whom *did* you work for?"

"You think I might have worked for Orlando? No, I was with —" He named an IT firm, one of the many that had gone bust over the past year. "I was a marketing consultant —"

"A salesman?"

An offended look. "Ye-es."

"We have evidence that you visited your wife — your ex-wife — at her home about a week before she was murdered." Again the slight emphasis on *murdered*. "You drive a Honda Civic, right?"

Hicks all at once changed character. The smile was gone, the glad-hands were wrapped in each other on the table in front of him. Then a mobile phone rang.

Lorre reached into his pocket, took out a mobile: no, it wasn't his. Malone and Clements checked theirs: both dead. Then Hicks was searching in his ten pockets; his hands scrambled over his cargo pants like frantic crabs. Then he found the mobile, took it out:

"Yes? No, my love, I'm at the police station … No, I don't know how long I'm going to be —" He looked at the three detectives. "It is my lady friend. She wants to know how long you are going to keep me."

"Three years," said Lorre sourly, "if you don't put that bloody thing away."

"I have to go, my love," said Hicks into his phone; then clicked it off and put it away in one of his many pockets. "She is never separated from her toy, carries it everywhere with her, like a weapon of some sort."

"Speaking of weapons," said Malone, "do you carry one?"

"Only my smile," said Hicks and threatened them with it.

"Jesus!" said Lorre.

"Inspector —"

"Sergeant."

Hicks gave up, he was selling nothing in this small room.

"Mr Hicks —" said Clements, "we are trying to establish things relating to your ex-wife's death. Were you in touch with her again after that visit to her house at Rooty Hill?"

The smile was gone now, put away for a more favourable occasion. He took his time, then glanced up at the video recorder. "Is that on?"

"No," said Lorre. "Unless you want it on?"

"No," said Hicks, as if he had been offered an unfavourable deal. Then he turned back to Clements: "No, I did not visit her again. That is the truth, so help me, God."

He sounded truthful; but he was a salesman. Clements, a born cynic, said, "What prompted you to visit her in the first place? Had you kept in touch with her?"

"I would send her a Christmas card — I'm a romantic —"

"I send Christmas cards to my grandparents," said Clements. "I'm not a romantic. Were you hoping for a reconciliation?"

"We have it on good authority," said Malone, taking up the bowling again, "that you asked her to lend you thirty thousand dollars for some project you had in mind."

If Hicks was surprised by what they knew, he didn't show it. He gave another smile, not a salesman's one, but man-to-man: "Camouflage. I was there for another reason."

"To blackmail her?" said Clements.

Hicks was horrified. "Blackmail her? My God, no! I have principles —"

"Then why were you there?" asked Malone. "Behind the camouflage?"

Hicks looked at his clasped hands again, then spread them on the table. They were elegant hands, the nails looked as if they had been manicured. Appearance with him would be important, part of his camouflage.

"I was asked to get some information from her. An acquaintance knew I had been married to her —"

"Who was the acquaintance?"

"Well, basically, I don't think I can divulge that —"

His English is good, thought Malone: basically, that is. Now all he has to say is *fantastic* and he'll be all-Australian.

"Mr Hicks, I think you'd better send for a lawyer to give you some legal advice. Then we'll turn that on —" He nodded up at the video recorder. "Things will start to get serious. Give Sergeant Lorre the name of your lawyer and we'll send for him right away."

Hicks hesitated, looked less assured. "No. No, I don't need a lawyer. Not yet."

"You will pretty soon, if you keep mucking us about," said Clements. "Who was your acquaintance?"

Hicks took a deep breath. "A Mr Leshner, he's on the board of directors of Orlando. He is a solicitor from somewhere up on the Central Coast, Gosford or Terrigal, I think. He's not with one of the big legal firms."

Malone and Clements looked at each other; then Malone said, "How did you know him?"

"He was on the board of —" Again he named the IT company that had folded. "I congratulated him when he was appointed to the board of Orlando and told him my ex-wife worked there."

"And that was the extent of your acquaintanceship?"

"Well, no-o —"

All at once Malone could see Hicks' life laid out like a map. The glad-hand would be extended in every direction, connections made, the chance of a sale never neglected.

"Get a move on," said Lorre impatiently.

"I was the sales manager at our company. Mr Leshner was the sort of director who wanted to know everything that went on. He would come to me and ask for weekly figures — he didn't trust our accountants and auditors —"

"Throwing a little light on the mushrooms," said Malone.

"Pardon?"

"Nothing. Go on."

Hicks glanced at him quizzically, then went on, "He came to me and asked me if I still saw my ex-wife. I said yes —"

Malone didn't ask why he had said yes. Hicks would have seen a glow-worm in a mushroom tunnel.

"He said things weren't what they seemed at Orlando and he wondered if Marilyn — if my ex-wife might know a thing or two. He said there would be something in it for me if I could find out —"

"Was there?" asked Clements.

Hicks shook his head at the false promises in business these days. "I found out nothing. That was what Mr Leshner paid me. Nothing."

"So Marilyn gave you no hint of anything wrong? She didn't seem upset when you put the question to her?"

"She was more upset when I asked her for the thirty thousand," said Hicks and looked at the three detectives as if they should understand how obdurate wives, or ex-wives, could be.

"You met no-one but Mr Leshner?" said Clements. "I mean, on this question of what was going on at Orlando?"

"No, no-one. Is there someone else involved?"

"Not as far as we know," said Malone like a practised liar. "Did you hate your wife, Mr Hicks? Marilyn?"

Hicks looked as if he had been asked if he had raped his mother. "Oh, my God, no! I loved her, Superintendent — I was wrecked when she told me our marriage was over. It took me years to get over her — I never did, not really —"

"Have you married again?"

"No — I always thought of myself as still married to Marilyn —" He was selling himself again. "There have been other women, of course — one has to be comforted —"

His mobile rang again, but before he could reach for a pocket Malone said, "Don't answer it." He stood up. "That'll be all, Mr Hicks. You may go. You have no further questions, Inspector?"

"None," said Clements.

Malone looked at Lorre, who said, "He's your pigeon, sir."

Hicks stood up, the mobile still ringing in his pocket. He was awkward for a moment, as if all his cartilages had become displaced and his bones were rubbing against each other. But the smile was not displaced nor misplaced: it was always at the ready: "It's been a pleasure, Superintendent. You too, gentlemen. If I can be of any more help —"

"We'll be in touch," said Malone. "Take care."

Hicks left, mobile now to his ear, heading for the comfort of women.

3

"There's too much coincidence," said Clements when the three cops were alone.

"Coincidence makes the world go round," said Malone. "Did you ever see a movie called *Six Degrees of Separation*?"

"I did," said Lorre. "Couldn't make head nor tail of it. Seemed to be full of trusting idiots. The wife dragged me along. I dunno she got the drift of it, either. How many degrees of separation are there at Orlando?"

"Not separation," said Malone. "Connection ... That movie put the proposition that we're all just separated from each other by that much —" He held up thumb and forefinger an inch or two apart.

"The converse works. At certain levels we're all connected. Us in the Service, politicians, people in religion — right at the top, all the rulers and ex-rulers of Europe. And nowhere are connections as close as they are in business. Right, Russ?"

Clements nodded, ready to admit he might be wrong. "Company boards, yes. There was —" He named a retired politician. "At one time he was on twenty boards — he was in a revolving door, he used to meet himself coming and going. Over in the West in the Eighties, the cowboys used to sit in each others' laps on company boards."

"What an innocent world I live in," said Lorre and shook his head.

"Righto, Russ, use *your* connections." Then Malone turned to Lorre and explained: "Russ has more connections than the Pope or the Queen. He can connect you to MPs, bookies, brothel owners or some girl who's been buried in the cellars of Telstra for the past twenty years and knows everyone's number, including silent ones. Watch him. He will now get us Mr Leshner's phone number without you and I having to wade through Central Coast phone books."

Clements spent two minutes on his mobile with the girl from the cellars of Telstra, hinted he still loved her and clicked off his phone. "Mr Leshner has offices in Gosford." He gave the number. "You wanna call him or will we just surprise him?"

"We're not going to drive all the way up there on the off-chance of finding him at work." Malone took out his own mobile, rang the number. "Is Mr Leshner in his office today? I'd like to see him, just for five minutes."

"Yes, he's here. Who's calling?"

"Seamus Cleary."

"Shamus? S-h-a-m-u-s? You're a private investigator?"

A reader of Chandler and Leonard ... "No, S-e-a-m-u-s, it's Irish. I'll be there in a couple of hours." He clicked off the phone. "We'd better get started."

"There's no need to go back up to Wahroonga and on to the F3," said Lorre. He looked at his watch. "A ferry leaves Palm Beach for Gosford in thirty minutes. That's the quickest."

"How long to Palm Beach?"

"Twenty, twenty-five minutes. Fifteen if you use the light and the siren."

"He's a revhead," Clements told Malone.

"Ain't we all?" said Lorre, leading the way out of the station.

"Not Superintendent Malone," said Clements. "He thinks the Highway Patrol should have Shetland ponies and dogcarts."

The funeral cortege had gone from the church outside. A man was sweeping the steps, cleaning up for whoever and whatever was to come next. He looked across at the three detectives as they came out of the station, raised his broom and waved it at Lorre.

"A nice — what's the word? Juxtaposition? Police station and church next door to each other. We lock 'em up or send 'em next door for enlightenment."

Malone and Clements didn't have to use the siren, but Clements put the blue light out on the roof when a Toyota Landcruiser, complete with bullbars against feral pedestrians, tried to overtake them on a narrow winding stretch of road between Newport and Avalon, two more beach suburbs. They reached the jetty on the Pittwater side of Palm Beach just as the ferry was about to leave. They galloped along the jetty, two lumbering big men on a picnic gambol, and scrambled aboard. They sat up front, getting their breath, as the ferry ploughed out across the swell coming in through the heads of Broken Bay. There are few coastlines in the world that have as many good inlets as New South Wales. Malone, not a waterman, always enjoyed the few occasions when he did venture to put a foot on a boat.

Breath back, relaxed, Malone gulped in a couple of lungfuls of the freshest air he had tasted in weeks. Far to the west the sky was tinged dirty yellow, but there was no smell of smoke out here.

"I wonder what the poor are doing today?"

"Battling to make a living," said Clements, a realist in every fibre. "Up here, where we're going, all these retirees, I'll bet there are some who did all their dough in Orlando."

The ferry eased into the calm stretch of Brisbane Water, then nudged into the wharf at Gosford. The town, a small city, was half-asleep for many years; then it was rejuvenated by superannuation. Retirees began moving in, lured by the cheaper prices; light industry began to invest heavily, and the young stayed at home to work instead of being deceived by promises from the Big Smoke. The Central Coast is now one of the fastest growing areas in the State. Developers can't believe their luck.

Leshner and Partners had offices in a three-storeyed building in the main shopping centre. The woman on the front desk looked old enough to be a retiree, to have read Hammett and Chandler in the original editions, a shamus fan. "Mr Cleary?"

"No," said Malone and showed his badge. "Superintendent Malone. And this is Inspector Clements. Will you tell Mr Leshner we're here, please?"

"I'm afraid he's not free at the moment —"

"Tell him we're from Orlando, that'll free him up." *Jeez, I'm talking like a shamus. Move over, Marlowe.*

She was a stout, grey-haired woman; and shrewd. "But you did phone and say your name was Cleary?"

Malone nodded, "But now I'm Superintendent Malone and we'd like to see Mr Leshner. *Now.*"

She got up and went into an inner office, taking her time because she was long past alacrity. Clements said, "Have you ever met anyone who called himself a shamus?"

"Only in books. What's your bet Mr Hicks has already called him?"

"I'll bet Mr Leshner has also called Jack Aldwych."

The woman came back, still unhurried. "Mr Leshner will see you." She held the door open for them; she was not antagonistic, just intrigued. Obviously Leshner and Partners was not an office that had visits from senior detectives from Sydney. "Would you like coffee?"

"Two with milk, neither with sugar. Ah, Mr Leshner —" Malone didn't put out his hand because Leshner hadn't put out his. The lawyer, Malone decided, was not a glad-hander. He decided to open with a back-hander: "Superintendent Malone, from Crime Agency. And Inspector Clements, from Homicide."

"Homicide: Crime Agency?" Leshner's face was too big and round to frown easily; indeed, it showed almost no surprise or puzzlement. "One of my clients?"

"In a way. Orlando. And Mrs Marilyn Hyx. H-y-x."

Leshner remained motionless for a moment, then he gestured for the two detectives to sit down in the chairs fronting his desk. The desk itself looked like an asbestos heap and Malone wondered how many wills and deeds were lost amongst it.

The woman came in with two cups of coffee. "It's instant," she said, not apologetically but as if to tell Malone and Clements she was on the ball. "Do you want me to take notes, Mr Leshner?"

"No, Myrtle, I don't think that will be necessary." She went out reluctantly and he nodded after her. "A treasure. She worked for my father when he started our business. They don't make 'em like her any more."

No, the Myrtles of the world, like Agatha and Clarice, were gone forever.

"Mr Leshner," said Clements, taking out his brass tacks, "why did you ask Mr Hicks, Clem Hicks, to go and visit his ex-wife?"

"He told you that?"

Clements nodded. "And we believed him."

Leshner put his elbows on the arms of his chair, put his hands together and steepled his fingers. He rested two chins on them. "I think that is Orlando's business that I'm not at liberty to discuss."

"Would you like to call a lawyer?" said Malone, then smiled. "Come on, Mr Leshner. We know you're Jack Aldwych's mole in Orlando and we know you suspected Natalie Shipwood was not telling the truth about what was happening at the company. We also know that —"

Leshner unsteepled his fingers, a church crumbling. "Okay, okay. How do you know about Mr Aldwych?"

"We're old mates. We presume Mr Hicks has already called you about us interviewing him and you've called Jack? What did he say?"

"He warned me you would probably come up here to see me. He has great respect for your ability."

"He was pretty good, too. Only he was on the wrong side of the law."

"Before I knew him," said Leshner, lawyer-like. "How much do you know about Orlando?"

"Pretty near everything," said Clements. "It's a big black hole. When did you become aware of it?"

Leshner steepled the fingers again. "I should like to point out to you that the Securities Commission is investigating all this —"

"Mr Leshner, I don't give a stuff about ASIC, they're not in our territory. We're Homicide, we are investigating a *murder* and I'll take any route I can to find out who murdered Mrs Hyx. Do we understand each other?"

Leshner looked at Malone. "You approve this approach?"

"All the way," said Malone. "A few sensible answers from you and we'll be saved the trouble of taking you back to Sydney with us. You don't want that, I'm sure?"

The fingers were still steepled, Leshner looking past them like a cleric who had just been told the difference between moral sins and legal sins. But he was also a lawyer who knew the value of lost time.

"Well, we don't want that, do we?" He separated his hands, put them on the desk, palms down, a man making a decision: "I got an anonymous note — I think I was the only one who did. It said Mrs Shipwood and another director were unloading shares, something the rest of us on the board knew nothing about."

"The other director being Mr Sweden?" said Clements.

For the first time Leshner registered surprise; or at least an eyebrow went up. "Yes."

"You had no idea who had sent you the note?" asked Malone.

"None at all. It was typed, not hand-written. I thought it could be Mrs Hyx, but I wasn't sure. I didn't want to approach her direct — she was at all the board meetings, taking notes. So I got in touch with her ex-husband." He pursed his thick lips. "That was a mistake. I should have approached her myself."

"Why didn't you?"

"Because I wasn't sure how loyal she was to Mrs Shipwood. I have a loyal secretary out there —" He nodded at the closed door, at the invisible Myrtle. "I thought Marilyn Hyx might be the same."

"So what was Hicks supposed to tell Marilyn?"

"He was supposed to have heard rumours from outside, that he was a shareholder and worried. You must understand that Mrs Shipwood is a lady with a very vengeful streak in her, a mile wide. If Mrs Hyx had gone back to her —"

He threw his hands up like a drowning man, though Malone was sure he would have floated in any depth of water or circumstance.

"Did you approach Mr Sweden?" asked Clements.

"No-o. I left that to Mr Aldwych. I understand they are related by marriage."

"An embarrassment to both of them," said Malone. "Would anyone else on Orlando's board have checked with Mrs Hyx?"

Leshner shook his head; chins also shook. "Garry Faulks is the only one with balls enough to stand up to Mrs Shipwood, but I don't think he ever went near her. Every inch of him is male chauvinist, he thinks women should never have been allowed out of the kitchen. It must have strangled him when she invited him on to the board."

"Then why did he accept?" said Clements.

"Because Orlando had steered such a lot of work his way as a developer and builder. Business is full of unhappy bedmates. Money is the Viagra."

Malone grinned at Clements. "Look at what we miss not being on the boards of directors." Then he looked back at Leshner and threw a beanball: "Who do you think sent the anthrax to Mrs Shipwood?"

"Was it anthrax?" No attempt to duck the beanball.

"No, it was crushed ecstasy tablets. Someone had a crooked sense of humour. You any idea who might have that sense of humour?"

"Nobody on the board. Mrs Shipwood herself has no sense of humour at all, not even crooked. It scared us, the anthrax. Or the powder, whatever it was. But I have no idea who sent it."

Malone nodded, then stood up. "When you call Jack Aldwych to report, tell him we're looking forward to our next meeting with him."

"When will that be?" Leshner remained seated, looked relieved.

"Soon."

On their way out through the outer office Malone passed by Myrtle's desk. "Do you read crime novels, Myrtle?"

She had been too long at the front of a lawyer's office to be offended or caught off guard. "Of course. I read 'em all the time, the old stuff. I even have a first edition of W.R. Burnett, *Little Caesar*. Mr Leshner gave it to me."

"Was there a shamus in it?"

"Not one spelled S-e-a-m-u-s."

Malone grinned, said goodbye. Sometimes the best talent was in the outer office. It might have been that way at Orlando.

Chapter Seven

❦

1

"Derek," said Jack Aldwych, "you're on the board of Orlando and you're also on the Business Ethics Council. Don't you blokes know a conflict of interest when it bites you?"

"Jack —" Sweden's conscience was as pliable as a breast implant. "Conflict of interest is a medical term for cross-eyed. Accountants recognised that a long time ago. That's why they practise consulting and auditing for any corporation that asks them."

"Whatever happened to ethics?" asked Jack Junior, newly pious.

"Ethics are a moveable feast. They come and go, like Easter."

Aldwych, who had learned to spell *ethics* only in the last few years when he had heard there were such things, grinned his old crim's smile. "Don't let's tell the women. Let 'em keep their innocence or whatever they call it."

167

Jack Junior and Derek Sweden smiled in reply in that way men do when women's morals are discussed: it hides their uncertainty about such things. All three men looked in from the balcony at the three women in the apartment's big living room. The men, drinks in hand, were on the balcony of the Sweden apartment, overlooking Circular Quay. This small area, on the east side of the Quay, had over the last few years become a magnet for money. The hoi polloi, whatever they were, moved along the colonnade below, the evening light softening their vulgarity, whatever it was. They occasionally looked up at the cliffs where the wealthier birds, some of them vultures, lived. Sweden was a lammergeier vulture who swallowed whole the bones of fools who believed in ethics.

The Bruna sisters had lost their innocence when their mother, a Bucharest beauty, had had a servant remove their diapers for the last time. Ophelia, the eldest, was the widow of Cormac Casement, a man with a name and a fortune almost as old as the nation's; she lived in the penthouse here in The Wharf, as the building was modestly titled. Rosalind, who sometimes troubled her husband, her sisters and herself with snatches of conscience, was married to Sweden. Juliet, the youngest, was Jack Aldwych's daughter-in-law by marriage and osmosis: that is, she had to look up the dictionary to learn the meaning of *ethics*. All three sisters had married at least twice, but each had been generous in her offering: beauty, sex, intelligence and a talent for extravagance. They fitted perfectly into the upper echelons of what passed for Sydney society these days.

"I want our money back," said Aldwych, adding a little chill to the evening air.

"Jack," said Sweden and ran his hand over his bald head, as if looking for what had once been there; he marvelled at young men who wore no hair at all as a fashion choice. His gesture now could have been a sign of nerves, but it was hard to tell. "There's no money in the kitty. It's skint, empty."

"Derek —" Names were being exchanged like handshakes, hands that did not trust each other. "We're not expecting anything from Orlando's kitty. We want it out of Mrs Shipwood's account. Or yours."

"Are you threatening me, Jack?"

Aldwych looked at his son. "Am I?"

"Sounds like it, Dad," said Jack Junior and his voice had the same cold tone as his father's.

"We know, Derek, that you unloaded a truckful of shares just before the roof fell in. Likewise Mrs Shipwood. Now we can scare the shit outa her, but we'd rather —"

"Someone did that," said Sweden. "Scared the shit out of her. When they sent that anthrax through the post to her —"

"Was it anthrax?" asked Jack Junior.

"Well, no-o ... But it had the same effect. You didn't send it, did you?"

Jack Junior looked at his father, who said, "It's not my style."

Lifetime criminals have difficulty looking innocent; the eyes, the mirrors of the soul, are mottled. Sweden, who had been reading faces since he had lost his own innocence, at age seven, knew at once who had sent the fake anthrax. And was surprised at his own sudden fear.

"Let's go inside," he said and almost sprang out of his chair.

Aldwych rose leisurely, looked down at the hoi polloi, though his own term for them was "the mugs". He had never had a conscience, let alone a social one. "I wonder how many Orlando shareholders are down there? I wonder how many of 'em know you live up here?"

Sweden could see hordes of demonstrators at the doors of The Wharf. "You are really leaning on me, Jack. It won't work."

"I'm patient, Derek. I'm old, but I'm not dead yet. I always took my time — I had a motto, never worry, never hurry. But you look worried, son."

"Just tired, Jack. That's all, just tired."

He led the way inside and the two Aldwych men, after a glance at each other, followed him at their own pace. After the glance Jack Junior, like Sweden, had been surprised at what his father had done.

The three women looked up as the men came in. The room was expensively furnished and the women complemented it: they would have looked out of place amongst Ikea and Freedom. Rosalind, the hostess, rose and went across to an eighteenth century writing desk that had been converted to a liquor cabinet; with e-mail, billet-doux had given way to liquor. She looked at her husband:

"You look as if you need another drink, darling. Has Old Jack been giving you bad news?" She was brown-haired and still beautiful; she had come through the menopause as if that was what it was, no more than a pause. Like her sisters she was afraid of no man, least of all her husband. She held up a decanter: "You too, Jack?"

"No, I'm fine," said Aldwych and sat down beside Ophelia. In his youth he had never worried about beauty; in bed, with the light out, women had no looks, only sex. Then he had met a beauty, fallen in love, something he had never dreamed of, and married her. She was dead now but he was still in love with her. She had opened his eyes to the beauty in other women. "You're looking healthy, 'Phelia."

The sisters' mother had been taken to bed in Bucharest by a leading man from the Old Vic which had sent a troupe to Bucharest to educate them in the finer points of Shakespeare. Since the Roumanians had been indulging in Shakespearean intrigue for centuries, they were only mildly impressed by the plays and wondered why Hamlet was in such a quandary. But the Old Vic lover, each time he went to bed with Ileana, called her by the names of Shakespearean heroines and she had loved the sound of the names, even as he gasped them; she had always had an acute ear, even when it throbbed with blood. The Old Vic lover departed, worn out, to be replaced by a dozen locals, none of them classically inclined. Then she had married Adam Bruna, had three daughters and accordingly named them.

"One takes care of oneself," said Ophelia. She was sixty, but one would have had to see her birth certificate to know it. There wasn't a single grey hair on her blonde head; her hairdresser knew better than to allow that; there are diplomats in salons in Double Bay, an otherwise undiplomatic area. The jawline, that giveaway, was still firm, the lips still sensual, the eyes still clear and knowing. Even the hands looked young; or youngish. "There's a pleasure in looking in a mirror, if what one sees is still beautiful."

Aldwych grinned, lifted his glass to her. "You're on your own, girlie. You should of run my brothels. One was a takeaway. No overheads."

"I could never have brought myself to charge for sex," she said and sounded almost like a Mother Superior.

Juliet, the brunette of the Brunas, moved from her chair to the couch where Sweden sat, stiff, almost upright, like a commuter waiting impatiently for a bus. She had never seen him like this, but made no comment on it. "So you're not going to New York?"

"Who said we were going anywhere?"

"Ros. She said you were, then going on for a week in the Bahamas. Lovely — I've always wanted to go there." Out of the corner of her eye she saw her father-in-law had stiffened, as if he were waiting for the same bus. "You're not going because of the terrorist scare?"

"In my years in the bear pit —" the State parliament house "— I learned never to go looking for trouble, it'll come to you if it's looking for you. That's one of the first rules of politics. No, we're not going overseas, not at the moment. Things will settle down, there'll be time for other trips."

"The Bahamas, eh?" said Aldwych, like an explorer who had just been handed a new map. "Lots of palm trees. And banks."

"So I'm told," said Sweden; his bank was in the Turks and Caicos Islands, almost five hundred miles to the south-east of the Bahamas, just an hour's flight. "You must have used them at some time or other."

"Never. When I was in business, we had our own way of laundering money. Sometimes we'd put it back into the banks we'd robbed and they were glad to have it. Banks were no different then than they are now, just less blatant." He smiled at his daughter-in-law, who might have been a bank robber if she hadn't found an easier and quicker way to make a fortune. "You should of given me grandkids, Julie, so's I could tell 'em bedtime stories. You're good at bedtime stories, right, Derek? All them years as a politician."

"We're not going to talk politics, are we?" said Rosalind, coming back with a fresh drink for her husband. "Or terrorism? We've had enough of that, close to home. When Derek told me about the anthrax scare, I thought I'll never open a letter again. One thing about e-mail, it's poison-proof."

"Not with gossip," said Ophelia. "You have friends in the police force, Jack. That Inspector Malone —"

"He's a superintendent now," said Jack Junior.

"Well, he'd know more than an inspector. What does he tell you about the anthrax business? What a way to kill someone!"

"I'm surprised you Roumanians never thought of it," said Sweden, still stiff and sour.

"I haven't seen Scobie in months," said Aldwych, who never admitted to connections. He certainly was not going to admit any to Sweden: "Has he been to see you?"

"Just routine —" Sweden had gulped down half his drink. "About this —" He held up his arm, now out of a sling. "The police are concerned for

Natalie Shipwood. Two attempts on her life, it's not easy for her."

"You sound sympathetic for her," said Aldwych, sounding unsympathetic.

"Women in business, it's always harder for them," said Ophelia. "I'm glad I never had to go into it."

Aldwych smiled at her. "'Phelia, you've been in business since you left kindergarten."

"Of course. I just never had to answer to a board of directors," she said, unoffended, and smiled at Sweden.

Then the Swedens' maid came in to say dinner was ready. As they all moved towards the dining room, Aldwych touched Sweden's arm. The latter winced, "Careful!"

"Sorry," said Aldwych, who had deliberately chosen the arm to touch. "We want our money back, Derek. Don't forget. We're not finished pressuring you, not yet."

2

Malone was dreaming:

He was young again, but in the present, running up to bowl against an English batsman in a Test. Then his mobile rang. He pulled up, took it out of the pocket labelled Telstra; he was spattered with seven other labels, a human billboard. The caller was the team's coach, telling him he had taken only eighteen paces for his run-up instead of the recommended twenty-two ...

The umpire, who wore bifocals with Armani frames, label attached, stepped aside, took out his mobile and called his bookie, to say the next leg-before-appeal would be denied ...

The English batsman, taking advantage of the break, took his mobile out of the special pocket in his pads and called his wife back home in England. She, in bed with his county captain, a slow bowler but a quick lover, did not appreciate this *coitus interruptus* ...

"Darling! Scobie! Wake up!" Lisa was shaking him.

He struggled awake. "Wassamatter?"

"You were laughing hysterically — I thought you were having a fit —"

He blinked himself awake. "I was dreaming —" But he didn't tell her about it. He reached for his watch on the bedside table. "Seven o'clock."

Lisa was sitting on the side of the bed, and turned back to look at him. There are certain poses when all women, even plain ones, look attractive; looking over the shoulder, even without being provocative, is one of them. "You're getting jumpy or something. I thought in this new job —"

"You're a good sort, you know that? Take off your nightgown."

"Get up and have a cold shower." He was

176

surprised how concerned she looked. "Darling, what's the matter?"

He pulled her pillow across, put it on his own and lay propped against them. "I dunno. Is it that obvious, I mean do I look as if I'm walking around in circles? Something like that?"

"I don't know. You look sort of — *lost*. Uninterested." She was a stickler for proper English; she knew the difference between *uninterested* and *disinterested*. She would never be disinterested, impartial, in anything concerning him. "It's the new job, isn't it?"

He thought for a moment, then nodded. "You've put your finger on it. I was talking with Russ, he's not happy, either. Said he thought it might be the Peter Principle, he'd been promoted above his ability. He's wrong. But there might be another version of it. I think I've been promoted above my level of interest."

She considered that: "Could be. Maybe you were too long in Homicide."

Consideration on his part: "You could be right. But is that what I'm going to be missing from now on? Murder, blood on the walls, shit like that?"

She reached for his cheek, ran her hand down the stubble of it. "No, I'd never let it get you down like that."

He reached up, turned her hand over and kissed her palm. "I'll never lose interest in you. Come back to bed."

"I'll see you tonight." She headed for the bathroom. "I'm due at the blood bank at eight."

An hour later Malone was driving to his office. At some traffic lights a youth in singlet and shorts approached him with a squeegee and cloth, offering to wash his windscreen. Malone hesitated, his pocket instantly clamping shut, then he nodded. He wound down his window when the youth had finished, gave him two dollars; he felt charitable, but not reckless. "You a student or unemployed?"

The youth had a big-toothed grin. "I'm an entrepreneur, dad. Have a good day."

"Don't go broke."

"You're not helping, dad," said the entrepreneur and held up the small coin.

Malone drove on, heartened that there was still some ambition in the world. This morning's paper had been full of pessimism: terrorism, bushfires, companies collapsing. He had turned to the cartoon page, to Hagar the Horrible, a Viking always on the horns of his helmet. Anything for a laugh.

At Strawberry Hills he parked his car in the special section for senior officers, went up to his office, stood for almost five minutes staring out its window, then went round to Homicide. Slowly, like a long-term prisoner returning to a home that he could not be sure had not changed. Gail Lee and Sheryl Dallen were at their desks; so was Phil

Truach. All three looked up at him and smiled as if they had been expecting him. Things hadn't changed.

"Russ in?"

"Here." Clements came out of the file room, the morgue for cases not yet dead. "Come into my office, ladies."

"Ladies?" Gail Lee looked enquiringly at Sheryl Dallen.

"I think he means us."

They rose and followed Malone into Clements' office. Clements sat down behind the desk and Malone, smiling to himself, dropped into the couch under the window, into the indentation that for years had accommodated Clements' backside. The women took the two chairs opposite Clements.

"Gail and Sheryl have been at work —" Clements addressed Malone. "They looked at Mrs Hyx's phone account, from her home. The day before she was murdered, she made two calls to the Shipwood house out at Sylvania Waters —"

"The day before or the night before?" asked Malone.

"The day before," said Gail Lee. She was cool and at ease in a dark blue skirt and a white shirt; come to think of it, Malone had never seen her anything but cool and at ease. He wondered who had bequeathed her that quality, her Chinese father or her Australian mother. Immigration was turning out a new native. "We've checked — Mrs Shipwood was at a board meeting all day at Orlando, so the calls weren't for her."

"The first call," said Sheryl Dallen, "Was at 10.32 — it lasted just over three minutes. The second was at 10.54 — it lasted twelve minutes."

"Why was Mrs Hyx at home? A working day."

"We've checked on that — she called in, said she wasn't well. But she turned up at Orlando after lunch, around two o'clock. She was there the rest of the day." Sheryl, too, looked cool; but not at ease. She had a repressed vibrancy to her, as if somewhere in her mind treadmills were running, weights were waiting to be lifted. "Who took those calls out at Sylvania Waters? Mr Shipwood, Chloe or B.J.?"

"That's what we have to find out," said Clements. "We've talked to Shipwood and Chloe, but not to B.J."

"I called their home," said Gail. "His sister answered. He's at the gym and pool at the football stadium out at Moore Park."

"Did you say we wanted to talk to him?"

"No, I didn't want to scare him. I said I was from the *Rugby League News* and I wanted to interview him, take some pictures. All sportsmen love the camera, so Sheryl tells me."

"Our girls are learning to lie," Clements told Malone.

"They should go into politics," said Malone.

"I'm going out to the stadium now," said Gail. "Sheryl can't come — she's up to her neck in that Pyrmont case. The one —" She looked at Malone.

He turned to Sheryl Dallen. "How's it going?"

"Dead ends, mostly. I'm going down to see Sergeant Steeple at City Central this morning. His plate's full and I think he's gunna ask us to carry the can for a while. I hope you don't mind?" She sounded tentative.

"Sheryl —" He sounded tentative to his own ears. "Tom's in the clear, Rupe Steeple's told me that. Don't hold back because Tom knew the girl."

"I wasn't going to," she said defensively. "But it's awkward —"

"I know that. But forget who Tom's father is —"

Sheryl suddenly smiled, looked at Gail Lee. "He's kidding?"

"Okay, now we've got that straightened out," said Clements, "would you care, Superintendent, to go out to the SFS with Detective Lee and talk to Brandon Jurgen Shipwood?"

"Brandon Jurgen?" said Sheryl.

"Don't ask me," said Clements. "Ask his mum or his dad."

Malone tried to remember when he had asked Greg Random to stand in for him on an investigation; but couldn't. But he also understood that Clements had recognised he was at a loose end, out of one chair and not yet settled in another. He stood up:

"Let's go, Gail. You drive. Carefully." He waited till the two women had gone out of the office, then he turned back to Clements. "Thanks. But what's keeping you indoors?"

Clements gestured at the paperwork on his desk, much more than when the desk had been Malone's. "Keep your report short, mate. Don't add to this."

"Didn't you know? Superintendents don't write reports, we're like cardinals. Call Greg Random and tell him you sent me on this job."

"*Sent* you?" Clements smiled and nodded. "Enjoy yourself."

Gail Lee drove carefully all the way out to the Sydney Football Stadium, a ten minutes' careful drive from Strawberry Hills. The big complex had a certain heavy beauty to it, though Tom, who occasionally played there, had once remarked that, like many stadia, it looked like a huge toilet when viewed from the air. The big pool in the grounds beside the stadium was stirred by a mixture of swimmers: children, women in bikinis, young men in briefs and self-admiration, old men and old women in faded muscles and fading memories. Malone, like most men of his age who had to work, still wondered at the number of people these days who, apparently, didn't have to.

Malone and Gail Lee had trouble finding B.J. Shipwood. Then someone directed them out into the stadium itself; they found him sitting a dozen rows back from the sideline. He was in a blue T-shirt, stretched tight across the pectorals, and tight shorts that displayed, as the girl reporter from the football magazine would be expected to say, his magnificent thighs.

"I thought this would be a good place for an interview," he said, then looked at Malone. "You the photographer?"

"No," said Malone and displayed his badge, "Superintendent Malone. And this is Detective Lee from Homicide. Sorry, we didn't bring a camera."

Brandon Jurgen had been posing. Without moving it was no longer a pose; the muscles changed position in the magnificent thighs. "What's this about? I was told someone from *Rugby League News* wanted to see me."

"Someone must have dropped the ball," said Malone. "We're here to talk about Mrs Hyx, Marilyn Hyx."

B.J. said nothing. His silence was magnified by that of the stadium, 42,000 mute empty seats. At the far end of the field, behind the goal posts, a workman, a wordless puppet, was noiselessly stamping down loose turf.

"Mrs Hyx," said Malone, "you knew her?"

B.J. looked at them both without moving his head; then he abruptly relaxed. "Yeah, I knew her."

"On September 11, during the morning, did she call you?"

He had no hesitation in remembering the date: "The day before she was — murdered? Yeah, she did."

"Why?"

There was a little hesitation this time: "I took her out a few times."

It was the detectives' turn to be silent, at least for a moment or two. Then Gail Lee said, "She was more than just your mother's private secretary?"

He nodded. "If you want to put it that way —"

"How often —" asked Malone. "How long were you — *friends*?"

He smiled, not unfriendly. "Superintendent, I'm not gunna make out Marilyn was a middle-aged sexpot. She wasn't. She took a liking to me, I liked her, one thing led to another —"

He's the darling of older women, his father had said. But his father had never mentioned that Marilyn Hyx was one of them.

"How serious was it for her?"

"We never talked in those terms."

"Did your father and mother know about the relationship? Your sister?"

"It was not a relationship, it was — I dunno. An affair, if you like. It lasted a year, I guess, no more. Half a dozen times I took her out, we'd have dinner and then go back to her place."

"To her house at Rooty Hill?"

He laughed; he had wonderful teeth and knew it. "We used to joke about that name. I only went there once, the last time. Before that she lived in a flat in Burwood. She used to joke she was a born suburban girl. In case you think I was a bastard —" He looked directly at Malone, man to man. "I really liked her. We just didn't love each other, that was all."

"She told you she didn't love you?" asked Gail.

"It was never mentioned." He gave her his full attention. "You're young, you know what it's like. It's not like it used to be —"

"In my day?" said Malone. "Mrs Hyx would have been around my age."

"You haven't answered the question —" said Gail. "Did your mother or father know about the — the affair? Or your sister?"

"I think my sister guessed, but I never mentioned it to her. Marilyn said she would castrate me if ever I told them, especially my mother."

"I think I'm on Marilyn's side," said Gail and sounded as if she would have lent the knife for the operation. "You're lucky you still have your balls."

He looked at Malone again, man to man again. "It's always us to blame, isn't it?"

"How often did you go out to the house at Rooty Hill?"

"I told you, just the once. About a week after she moved in there."

"Your car or hers?"

"Mine."

"What do you have?"

"A Porsche."

Malone wondered how Nigger Brown and his wife had missed the visiting Porsche. And wondered if they had missed other cars.

Then Gail Lee said bluntly, "Where were you on the night of September 11, Mr Shipwood?"

He frowned, "I don't know —"

"B.J., everyone remembers September 11, we're still talking about it. But it was September 12 on our calendar, we're a day ahead of the Americans. Marilyn was murdered the day after the attack on the World Trade Center, our time. Where were you?"

"I'm trying —" He looked hard at her; she was one woman who wasn't going to fall for the pectorals and the thigh muscles and the brilliant teeth. "If I gave you an answer right off the tip of my tongue, what would you think? He's too smart, he's got it all worked out —"

"Have you?" said Malone, bowling from the other end. He was finding Gail a good partner, it was almost like the good old days with Clements. "Where were you, B.J.?"

He sighed; even the magnificent thighs seemed to go loose. "I was up at Terrigal with a friend."

"Who will verify that?" said Gail. "Your friend?"

"No, I don't think she will. It was — what's the word? — clandestine. She's a married woman."

"Did you stay at a hotel or a motel? So's we can check."

"No-o. It was at her holiday house. Look —"

"No, *you* look, B.J.," said Malone. "You're buggering us about. We're investigating Marilyn Hyx's murder, one of your lady friends, and you apparently don't want to help us find who killed her. So you'd better come back to Homicide with us and we'll see whose patience runs out first."

B.J. looked out at the empty stadium, at the big screens at either end, as if some message might be written there for him. But they were blank. He turned back to the two detectives.

"Her name is Dorothy Faulks, she's the wife of one of Orlando's directors, Garry Faulks. She's younger than him, he's a bit short on bedroom energy ... He'd kill her and me if he found out. He's a guy with a pretty short temper."

Malone sat back in his seat, took his own glance around the stadium. He came here to see Tom play in early games to Super 12 fixtures. Mayhem happened out there on the turf, but it was all good clean fun, not murder.

"You get yourself into some spots, don't you, B.J.? You ever thought of trying celibacy for a while?"

Gail Lee smiled, but said nothing. Then the smile faded and he wondered if she was thinking of Tom. Then he tried to remember how celibate he had been himself when he was B.J.'s and Tom's age. Not very, though he had stayed away from married women.

"We'd like to talk to Mrs Faulks, if only to get you off the hook —"

"Christ Almighty, you don't think I killed Marilyn!"

"We never take anyone's uncorroborated word, not in a murder investigation. It's our suspicious nature. Mrs Faulks —?"

B.J. hesitated, then he said, "She's down at the pool. We were there when I got your message —"

"Let's go, then. We can clear it all up now." Malone stood up, looked around the stadium again. "You've played here?"

"Two seasons." B.J. stood up. He was as tall as Malone and the latter, looking at him in the skin-tight shirt and shorts, could see why women fell over for him. "You ever play sport?"

There you go, Gloria, *sic transit* . . .

"He played State cricket," said Gail Lee, sounding for the moment like a cheer-leader. "How long ago, Superintendent?"

"Last century. Way back in the last millennium." He grinned at B.J., forgiving the kid his ignorance. "I was a fast bowler. Long in the leg and thick in the head."

B.J. had the grace to look apologetic. "Sorry. I understand now why my father said sporting fame is ephemeral."

"Written on the wind," said Malone.

"Let's go and talk to Dorothy. Can we keep it low-key?"

"People will just think we're Seventh Day Adventists."

B.J. led the way down the steps. Malone looked at Gail Lee, who rolled her eyes. Then they followed B.J. Shipwood, his buns hard as small curling stones under his tight shorts, out through a couple of tunnels into the open space beside the pool.

There B.J. pulled up short. The space and the pool were not crowded, but there were too many witnesses; eyes would follow like tiny searchlights as B.J. Shipwood and the man and the woman, both fully dressed, moved towards Mrs Faulks.

"Shit!"

"What's the matter?" said Malone.

"Garry's with her, her husband. That's him in the yellow trunks."

Malone saw the blonde woman in a bikini sitting at a table under an umbrella; beside her, towelling himself, was a beefy man with a belly in yellow trunks. They were not arguing, but even at a distance one could see they were at odds with each other. A man who has been married for twenty-five years doesn't have to be a detective to recognise marital chill when he sees it.

"We'll give you a day, B.J. You and Mrs Faulks come to Homicide tomorrow morning. Give him your card, Gail. Ask for Detective Lee or Inspector

Clements. Tomorrow morning, son, ten o'clock. Without fail. Otherwise we'll be visiting Mrs Faulks at her home, when Mr Faulks might be there."

On that, he and Gail Lee left. As they walked back to their car he said, "What do you think?"

"I don't think he killed Mrs Hyx," said Gail.

"What do you think of him, generally?"

"He must have trouble passing a mirror. But he's got lovely buns."

"You women," said Malone and eased his spongy buns into the car.

3

Tom Malone got out of the cab, having sat up front with the driver, being a true-blue Aussie. He tipped the driver twenty per cent. He was not tight with money, as his father was. Scobie tipped cab drivers only for acts of social service, such as putting out a bushfire or performing major emergency surgery on an injured passenger. The driver, a Turk from Anatolia, not a region noted for profligacy, flashed Tom a big smile of thanks and wondered if the kid, despite his accent and the *keep the change, sport*, could really be an Australian. Probably foreign-born with a heritage of generous forbears.

The cab drove away and another pulled into the kerb. Sheryl Dallen got out, paid the driver, gave him a woman's tip, which wouldn't weigh down his pocket. Then she stopped and looked at Tom. "Tom Malone?" She had met him once or twice when he had come to police functions with his parents. "What are you doing here?"

"I'm on my lunch hour. I thought I'd come across and see how Lucinda's housemate is making out, Idaho. You're Shirley Dallen, right?"

"Sheryl. What's your interest in the housemate?" Tom frowned. "Am I still under suspicion or something?"

"No." Sheryl looked a little embarrassed. "But you're a policeman's son, you know we ask questions all the time."

"Look, I hardly know Idaho. But she's here on her own, in a house where her friend was murdered —"

"Sorry, Tom," Sheryl apologised. "You're right. It was a nice thought. Let's see how she is."

Tom knocked on the door of Number 22. A moment, then the door was opened by Idaho. "Hello, Tom. When you called —" Then she looked at Sheryl Dallen. "Oh, I wasn't expecting you —"

"Constable Dallen," said Sheryl and showed her badge. "I was here for a few moments the other night, with a colleague. We'd been up the street to see your neighbour, Mr Kelray."

"Oh, sure. I just wasn't expecting … Come in. Would you like some coffee, both of you?"

They followed her back through the house into the kitchen. Tom, who had a neat mother, looked around: Idaho kept a neat house. The kitchen opened out on to the small patio at the back; sun shone on a border of pink flowers along one wall. Peace reigned here, if jelly-like.

Tom and Sheryl sat down at the kitchen table and Idaho got cups and saucers out of a neat dresser.

"Where's Dad?" Tom asked Sheryl.

"Out at the SFS talking to B.J. Shipwood. You ever played football against him? B.J.?"

"He plays league, I play union. And never the codes shall meet. Or that was the way it used to be. Now union's professional, we steal each other's players. You follow football?" He looked at both girls.

"Only off the field," said Idaho, bringing the cups to the table. "I wouldn't want to get into a scrum with any of you."

It was small talk, the cement that sometimes builds a base to work on. Sheryl evidently felt enough base had been built: "Idaho, did Lucinda have a mobile phone?"

"Did she!" Idaho poured the coffee, which had been simmering on a hot-plate, and sat down at the table. "She was never off it. Frenchy and I have got them, but hers grew out of her head. Why?"

"There was no mention of it in the Crime Scene report. Have you got it?"

Idaho shook her head. "No. I just assumed the police had taken it away with them."

"We've got her phone records from Telstra. A call was made on her phone an hour after she was reckoned to have been murdered."

Idaho's hand shook, she spilled coffee. She put her cup down, reached across for a dishcloth on the nearby sink and mopped up the coffee. But her hand was shaking and Tom took the cloth from her and finished wiping up the small mess.

"Something I said upset you?" said Sheryl.

"Of course it bloody did!" Then Idaho got her nerves back under control. "Jesus, that's — that's macabre! Creepy!"

"Neither," said Sheryl. She took a sip from her own coffee, as if this were no more than a café chat. "It looks as if the guy who murdered her took the mobile and made a call on it."

"Who did he call?" asked Tom. "You'd know the number."

"He called here," said Sheryl and nodded at the handset on the kitchen bench. "On that phone."

There was silence for a long moment; then Tom slapped the table. "I remember now! You took it, Idaho —"

She frowned, trying to remember an evening she had been trying desperately hard to forget. "Yeah. It was some guy, he said, who's that? I said, Idaho, and he just hung up."

"When was that?" asked Sheryl. "Before the police arrived?"

"Yes," said Tom. "We'd just found Lucinda, I'd called —"

He stopped and Sheryl said, "Who did you call?"

"My father. Then I called City Central..." He waited for her to make some comment, but she made none and he went on, "Why would he be so dumb, to use her phone? Why would he call? Is he some sort of sick bastard?"

"He could of called, not sure that he had killed Lucinda, hoping maybe she was still alive. He wanted to talk to her, not you, Idaho, or your other housemate." Sheryl put down her empty cup. "Can I have some more coffee? No, stay there. I'll get it —"

But Tom was already on his feet, reaching for the coffee pot. It was hard to tell whether he was nervous or genuinely helpful. "I'll get it ... Or could the guy have been calling Frenchy?"

"Who's Frenchy?" said Sheryl. "That your other housemate?"

"That's her," said Idaho. "She'd be on your report as Nancy Delarus. She's gone home to her parents, she couldn't stay here, she went all to pieces. I'll be moving out, too," she said and looked ready to go at any moment, as if a ghost had walked into the kitchen.

"Where is Frenchy? Nancy?" asked Sheryl.

"Her parents live in Pennant Hills."

"You have her number?"

"No, not her parents' number. She'd be at work now. She works at an accountancy firm, Foxglove, Berenger. She's a PA there."

Tom poured coffee into his own and Idaho's cups, sat down and said carefully, "One of Lucinda's boyfriends works there."

Sheryl said, just as carefully, "Are you suggesting something, Tom?"

"No-o. I just didn't know Frenchy worked there."

"You didn't really know her, Tom," said Idaho. "She and I never got around with your crowd. She works with this guy, Barry Something, and she introduced him to Lucinda."

Sheryl looked at her notebook. "Barry Mackaw, that it?"

"That's him," said Tom. "He occasionally drinks with our crowd down at The Sheaf at Double Bay."

"He's been checked, he had an alibi for the night of the murder. I've got it here."

"Okay," said Tom and drank some coffee. "He's off the list."

"You sound like a cop," said Sheryl with a smile.

"It rubs off, I guess. Or it's in the bloodstream."

"You never wanted to be a cop?"

"Only up till I turned ten or eleven. Then I knew I'd always be Scobie Malone's son, even if I got to be Commissioner."

"Lachlan Murdoch and James Packer have got famous fathers," said Idaho.

"They've also got billions. I could be overshadowed for that price." Then he changed the subject, asked Idaho when she would be moving out of the house.

"Next week or the week after, soon's I find a decent place. The rent's paid till the end of the month."

"Let me know if you want any help, to move, I mean." He stood up, making the kitchen smaller. "I've gotta be getting back. Can I call a cab?" He gestured at the phone on the bench. "Believe it or not, I don't have a mobile."

"You would have if your dad had billions," said Sheryl.

"No, I wouldn't. I'd have a girl tagging along beside me with it."

"You see, Idaho? He'd have a *girl* tagging along. They're all born chauvinists." Sheryl had succeeded in lightening the atmosphere, as if she was reluctant to leave Idaho alone in this house where, she had noted when they came in, the door to the murder room was closed. "I'll ride with you, Tom, then take the cab back to the office."

Tom made the call and five minutes later a horn was tooted outside the house. Idaho followed Tom and Sheryl to the front door, told Sheryl she would tell Sergeant Steeple her new address when she had one, then she leaned forward and kissed Tom on the cheek.

"Thanks for coming."

In the cab Sheryl said, "You've made a conquest there."

"Idaho? That wasn't the intention." Then he grinned. "My mother and my sisters think I'm a lecher. And all I am at heart is a Good Samaritan."

"Yeah," said Sheryl. "I've had some Good Samaritans at the gym, putting their hands in my pants to ease a pulled muscle."

"You women," said Tom, sounding an echo he didn't hear.

4

"Nigger," said Jack Aldwych, "I hope you don't mind me having you picked up? I sent Blackie with the Daimler —"

"A nice car," said Nigger Brown.

"Yeah. Luxury but unfuckingpretentious. Those were the words the salesman used. He knew me."

"Nice house, too," said Brown, looking around. "You've done all right, Jack. Rich, but unfuckingpretentious."

"You're a card, Nigger. You Abos always were cheeky, but I never blamed you. I used to give money to Aboriginal causes, so long's they were

197

tax deductible. I'm a charitable man, if it's tax deductible."

"The best sort, Jack."

They were in the Aldwych home in Harbord, a small seaside suburb just north of the harbour. The house was two-storeyed and occupied three sides of a large block; the fourth side backed on to a home for aged nuns. The nuns prayed for the soul of Mr Aldwych, prayers that fell on the deaf ears of both God and Mr Aldwych. Both floors of the house had verandahs that ran round all four sides; from there Aldwych could look down the hill to the lesser homes of the battlers. It was a crime-free area because the old retired crim wouldn't have it any other way. Or else.

"You must have been surprised when Blackie come to pick you up."

"Jack, what do you think? I never worked for you, you were big time, I was small time. Mini-time. I don't think you and me ever exchanged two words all the time we was working. Yeah, I was surprised. Scared, too, if you wanna know."

"No need to be Nigger. There was a time when I could have had your head taken off. You remember? Me and me boys were inside a bank, been there all night waiting for the bank staff to come on in the morning and open up the vault. Then you broke into that jewellery store next door and set off the alarm. Fucking police everywhere within minutes. I could of wept."

"I done eighteen months for that job, three months off for good behaviour. Thanks, Blackie."

Blackie Ovens, butler, handyman, standover man, had brought three light beers. He sat down opposite his boss, part of the household. He had once been burly, but most of the muscle had now drained out of him. He was seventy years old and all the rough, tough years were there in his face.

"All the time I was in the Bay I was shit-scared you was gunna have me done over. You never did, thanks. Cheers."

Aldwych raised his own glass. "Cheers. I was never vindictive, was I, Blackie?"

Blackie had trouble remembering. "Only now and again, boss. But never with Nigger here. We just put him on the list for future reference, was what you said. I remember that."

"And here we are in the future," said Aldwych. "I want you to do a job for me, Nigger. You still a good break-and-enter man?"

"I'm outa practice, Jack — I couldn't break-and-enter a tent. You're gunna laugh, but I been honest and straight for ten years or more now. The wife and kids think I'm Saint Francis of Assisi."

Blackie Ovens looked blank and Aldwych explained: "A do-gooder who let birds shit all over him. Bloody Italians, you can never understand them."

"I understand Sophia Loren," said Blackie.

"Get your mind above your navel, you're too old for that sorta talk."

Nigger Brown was retired from break-and-enter, but he couldn't help being intrigued: "What did you have in mind, Jack?"

"I want you to break into the Securities and Investment Commission and photocopy some papers for me. The ASIC offices are in King Street."

"Jack — government offices? You want me to break into *government* offices? I do that and they give me life, with my record. Frank Assisi would be in shit up to his neck."

"Nigger, I've had Blackie reconnoitre the place. We've got the layout, the alarm system —"

"Where'd you get all that?"

"Don't ask. It'll be a job that'll take you half an hour at the most. I'll pay you five figures —"

"Jack, how can I spend five figures, I'm doing life? The wife and the kids, they wouldn't touch it — the wife works for the parish church, thinks the Pope should be God. The kids ... Well, never mind about them. Five figures? What? Ten, twenty, fifty thou?"

"You see? You're adding up what you could do with it if you don't get caught. Nigger, I tell you, your talent, it'll be a breeze. Look up the record, who's ever broken into the Securities Commission? Anybody wants stuff outa there, they try to bribe someone who works there."

"Why don't you do that?"

"They're all too fucking honest. No, it's gotta be a break-in, Nigger, and you're the man."

"If I say no?"

"Nigger, you think I'd take it out on you?" Aldwych shook his head. "But accidents happen. You'd know that, running a tow-truck business."

5

Malone's phone rang: "Superintendent? This is the desk downstairs. There's a Mr Brown down here, says he wants to see you."

"Nigger Brown?"

A moment; then: "Yes, sir."

"I'll send someone down." Strangers, especially break-and-enter ones, were not allowed to roam freely in this building. He cut off the phone, then rang Clements: "Russ, Nigger Brown is downstairs, wants to see me. Send someone down for him, then you bring him around here. We'll see what he wants to tell us."

"You think our luck is turning?"

"I wouldn't know. But let's hope so."

He put down the phone, sat back, felt warm: he was still *involved*. The desk in front of him had not yet wrapped itself round him.

Five minutes later Clements brought Nigger Brown into the office: "I hope you don't mind me barging in like this, Mr Malone —"

"Nigger, you're always welcome. What can Inspector Clements and I do for you?"

Brown looked uncomfortable, more with himself than with the two police officers. He wore jeans, a work shirt and a light cardigan, as if he had come straight from a job. "I'm not a gig, you know that — I never informed on anyone. But ... Well, the wife, she's a down-on-your-knees Catholic, she's always telling me confession is good for the soul."

"One thing the Pope and I agree upon," said Malone.

"You a Catholic?"

"Sort of. The Vatican has its worries about me. What have you got to confess, Nigger?"

"I just been to see Jack Aldwych — remember him?"

"Vaguely."

Brown grinned. "Yeah, you would. Well, I didn't exactly go to see him. I was out at my office and he sent his standover man, Blackie Ovens, to pick me up. He give me to understand there was no argument, you know what I mean? So I went. I'd never had anything to do with Jack — we weren't in the same league, you know what I mean? And when I was in the game back then, I never worked for anyone else. A sorta small businessman."

"Get to the point," said Clements.

Brown took a deep breath. "He wants me to do a break-and-enter. The Securities Commission offices down in King Street."

The two detectives looked at each other; then Malone said, "What does he want from them?"

"He wants me to photocopy some papers from that Orlando firm, you know, the one Marilyn Hyx worked for."

"How does he expect you to get in there?" asked Clements. "I dunno, but I'd guess their security is as tight as ours."

Nigger Brown looked around, grinned. "I'm glad he didn't ask me to break in here."

"So are we," said Malone. "Get on with it, Nigger."

Brown seemed more relaxed now, as if, having taken the jump, he didn't find being an informant so soul-tightening. "He's gunna give me a layout of the system. I dunno how he got it, he says everyone who works there is too fucking honest — those were his words. But —"

"But?"

"Once when I was doing time I shared a cell with a Pom. He told me how he used to work back in England, we were sorta exchanging trade secrets, you know what I mean? He said there was a pub in South London, you could go there and buy the alarm system for every major office block or embassy, whatever you wanted, in London. I dunno if it's like that here in Sydney, it wasn't in my day, but since the world's gone electronic, there ain't any secrets any more."

"How true," said Malone and for a moment the three of them sat in remembrance of a world of secrets gone forever. "You're taking a risk, coming to us, Nigger. But we appreciate it. Were you tailed?"

Brown looked offended. "Mr Malone, I'm retired but I ain't forgotten what I knew back in the old days. You retire, you gunna forget how you worked?"

"Remains to be seen," said Malone, but knew the trade would always be with him.

"Blackie Ovens was gunna drive me back to Rooty Hill, but I got him to drop me off in town, said I wanted to do some shopping while I was there. I went into David Jones, hung about in there for a while, then come out and got a cab out here. I'd made my mind up soon's I left Jack Aldwych I was gunna talk to you."

"And we appreciate it," said Clements. "What does Jack want you to copy once you get into the offices?"

"Overseas bank transfers for Mrs Shipwood, Marilyn's boss, and a bloke named Sweden, Derek Sweden."

Malone looked at Clements again. "Why ain't we surprised?"

"When does Jack want you to do the job?" asked Clements.

"Sat'day night," said Brown. "They're public servants, he says, they never work Sat'day nights.

He's a cynical old bastard, I mean about honest people."

"Three nights away," Clements said to Malone. "I think we better talk to the Securities people. When do you have to see Jack again, Nigger?"

"Tomorrow, he'll have the system plan for me by then. Then I'm supposed to case the offices, so's I don't arrive there stone cold. I'm scared, just in case you haven't noticed. I do the job and get caught, I'm done for, they'll throw the book at me. I don't do the job, Jack will see I have an accident. Jesus, yest'day I was going along, happy as Larry —"

"Nigger," said Malone, "you don't have to worry. Play along with Jack Aldwych, we'll work something out."

"Like what?" He was totally depressed.

"Trust us. You've got Russ' card —"

"Yeah, it's in me wallet. How's it going on the Marilyn thing?"

"Progressing. You haven't thought of something else you can tell us?"

Brown shook his head. "Nup. But I'll keep racking the brain —"

"Do that, Nigger. What's your number?" Brown gave it and both detectives wrote it down. "We'll be in touch. Give us twenty-four hours. You want to get in touch with me or Inspector Clements, don't call us on your home phone — I don't think Jack could have it tapped, but just in case —"

"Jesus, has it got that bad? A civilian tapping into your phone?"

"Like you said, Nigger, no secrets any more. Have you got a mobile?"

"Who hasn't? That's the number I give you." Brown tapped his pocket, then stood up. "I'm glad I come to you. There was a day when I'd of never spilled to a cop, but things change, don't they? I'm all for law'n'order now."

"Thanks," said Malone. "It's voters like you keep us in a job."

Brown was feeling better; he flashed the big white smile. "Bullshit."

"We'll pay for a cab to take you to Central, Nigger, but you'll have to go home by train. If I gave you the cab fare all the way out to Rooty Hill, the State Treasurer would want a Royal Commission into it. They don't throw money away on law'n'order."

"Get outa here," said Clements, stood up and patted the smaller man on the back. "We'll look after you, Nigger. And thanks for coming."

"The wife ud be pleased. If I told her ..."

Clements escorted Nigger Brown out of the office and the building. Malone went round to Homicide's offices, was lucky and found John Kagal sitting in front of the blank screen of his computer.

"Leave it like that," said Malone. "The less you know, the better."

"I've been here too long, boss. I'm getting to be

as cynical as you and Russ." He looked around the room, at the desks, only two or three of them occupied, at the flow-charts on the wall like school blackboards, the history and geography of murder laid out in lists, diagrams and photographs. He sighed, then said, "Can I do something for you?"

"Your mate, Bob Anders. He still with the Securities Commission?"

"Still there, he's 2IC of the Sydney office."

"I want to talk to him. Ask him if he can see me and Russ tomorrow morning, say eleven o'clock."

"I ask what it's about? He's sure to ask me. Securities is built on questions, questions."

"It's about their alarm system."

Kagal raised an eyebrow. "This is to do with that guy I saw Russ taking around to you?"

"Questions, John, questions."

"I'm a cop." John Kagal could be a smartarse at times and there had been a time when Malone had waited, in vain, for him to fall on his face. But he was a good cop and would some day, Malone was sure, be Commissioner. One liked him while one was irritated by him. "It's to do with Orlando, right?"

"Right."

"I'll get on to Bob right away."

"Tell him not to let anyone but his boss know that Russ and I will be coming to see him. I don't want the alarm system going off too soon. We have a feller we have to protect."

Chapter Eight

❧

1

In Washington a general, with more gongs than a Buddhist temple, was declaring that the partners in democracy would pursue the war against terrorism to the ends of the earth and beyond ...

"Beyond?" said Lisa, switching off the television. "Into outer space?"

"Rhetoric is the first recruit in war," said Maureen.

She was majoring in aphorisms since she had joined the ABC as a researcher on *Four Corners*. Television had its own war, for ratings; but the ABC was a non-combatant, standing disdainfully on the sidelines. Or had been till the arrival twelve months ago of a new boss, a combatant if ever there was one. His name was never mentioned in the Malone household for fear Maureen would burst her brassiere. There is none so impure in temper as a purist, an aphorism Malone would never have dared to utter.

Maureen had invited herself to dinner and now she gave the reason: "Dad, we're going to do a piece on all the financial collapses, including Orlando and those other crashes, HIH and One.Tel. We've got word of a big collapse in America, some company named Enron, but it's too soon for us to make comparisons. The executive producer wants to get away from all the war news for a week or so —"

"Financial collapses are *good* news?" asked Lisa.

"Mum, good news is not good TV unless it's a sporting victory. A five-car pile-up on the M4, that's TV news."

"Are you on the story?" asked Malone.

"Dad, your darling daughter is the reporter. I've been promoted."

"Come near me for comment and I'll *de*mote you. Where do you start?"

"Tomorrow morning at the Securities Commission. I have an appointment with one of their senior men, a Mr Anders."

My darling daughter is going to prove a pain in the arse. "What time?"

"What *time*? Why?"

"Because I'm seeing him at eleven tomorrow morning and you can't see him till I've talked to him. Is it about Orlando in particular?"

"Ye-es. But you can't stop me talking to him —"

"Watch me."

"Da-ad —"

Any single-syllable word stretched to two or more syllables was a threat: another aphorism. "Look, Mo, go and talk to someone else, at least till Monday. I can't tell you why —"

"God, you're a drag! How do you put up with him, Mum?"

"I just do what I'm told," said Lisa. Malone rolled his eyes, a habit of Maureen's, and Lisa hit him on the arm. "Sometimes, that is. Mo, he wouldn't be asking this of you if it were not important. You keep forgetting he's on a murder — he couldn't care less about the collapse of Orlando. Right?" She looked at Malone.

"No, I care about the collapse, all those small investors doing their money. But yes, it's the murder I'm working on —"

"At the *Securities* Commission?" Maureen had been too long at *Four Corners*: they never took *yes* or *no* for an answer, not the first time. They were like cops: but Malone would never admit that, not to her.

Then there were three sharp raps on the knocker on the front door: Tom's signal. Glad of the interruption, Malone got up, went down the hall and opened the front door.

"Hi, Dad. Mo here? I called her at home, but her flatmate said she'd come over here for dinner —"

"She's here. Where've you been?"

Tom was glowing with health, as if he should

be lit for an alimentary canal commercial. "Cricket practice at the indoor nets. I tried Claire first, she's the lawyer, but she and Jason are out, I got the baby-sitter —"

"Why do you want a lawyer? You in trouble again?"

They had come down the hallway and into the dining room. Tom kissed his mother and sister, sat down at the table. "You finished dinner?"

"Have you eaten?" asked Lisa.

"I had a snack, but no dessert. Anything left?"

"Some lime pie. But, unless your father has already asked you, why are you here?"

Tom grinned at his sister. "They make you welcome, don't they? To think we came out of their loins —"

"Leave our loins out of it," said Malone. "What's your problem?"

"Do I have to have a problem to come and see you?"

"Your sister —"

Tom looked at his sister. "*Your sister?* He's in that sort of mood?"

"I'm afraid so," said Maureen and told him how she and their father were at cross-purposes.

"Don't say any more till I come back," said Lisa and went out to the kitchen.

Malone sat down at the table again, tried to sound more like a father than an interrogating cop. "You rolling your arm over as good as last season?"

Tom was another fast bowler; but not thick in the head. "I think I'm a yard or two faster than last year. I surprised a couple of the guys at the nets tonight, cracked 'em both under the ribs."

No remorse, just satisfaction: a typical fast bowler. Malone nodded approvingly. "Where are you playing Saturday? I'll come and watch."

Then Lisa came back with a big slice of lime pie and a cup of coffee. "All right, now fill us in on your problem."

Tom took his time, swallowing a mouthful of pie before he said, "I didn't want to tell you, Dad. It's just a wild — what was that we had at school about arrows?"

"*I shot an arrow into the air, it fell to earth I know not where*," said Maureen.

"This one's fallen right into this room," said Malone. "Go ahead, Robin Hood."

"He's a card, isn't he?" Tom said to his sister; then looked back at his father. "That guy Mackaw I told you about, Barry Mackaw. I was over at Pyrmont at lunchtime — hold it, Dad." He put up a hand as Malone was about to snap at him. "I just went over there to see how Idaho was getting on. She's there in that house on her own now, Frenchy's gone. She has the door shut on the room where Lucinda was done in. I thought I could help if Idaho was going to move out. She is, some time within the next week or two. Sheryl Dallen was there."

"Detective Dallen?"

Tom nodded. "She had some questions to ask about Lucinda's missing mobile — the Crime Scene guys didn't find it. But just after Idaho and I found her, someone made a call on Lucinda's mobile — it was on the Telstra record."

"Sheryl will tell Russ all that tomorrow — then maybe I'll hear it. What's your connection?"

"Dad, I didn't know ... It was Frenchy, Idaho and Lucinda's housemate, who introduced Mackaw to Lucinda. Frenchy works for Foxglove, Berenger."

"So?"

"So does Barry Mackaw. Who gave him an alibi, the night of the murder?"

"Jesus!" Malone raised his arms in exasperation.

"It's a perfectly reasonable question," said Maureen and Lisa nodded in agreement.

"It's a perfectly reasonable question if *I* ask it! It's not for him — he's out of the picture —"

"Answer the question," said Lisa.

"I don't bloody well know! That's in Russ' computer, not mine. For Crissake, Tom, why can't you stay out of it? I've tried hard enough to keep you out of it —"

Tom pushed the lime pie, only one mouthful eaten, away from him. The healthy light had gone out of him, he looked depressed. He was naturally cheerful, for him a glass was always half-full, not half-empty. But now the level had dropped.

"I can't stay out of it, Dad, much as I've tried — and Christ knows, I *have* tried! But I still can't get out of my mind how Lucinda looked when I found her. You may be used to sights like that. I'm not."

There was a heavy silence for a moment, then Lisa reached across and put her hand on his arm. Maureen leaned close to him and kissed his cheek. Malone knew he had lost his case.

"Righto," he said and even in his own ears his words sounded lame. "But you're pointing the finger — and if ever it got out that you were my son who was doing the pointing —"

"Dad has a point," said Lisa, then smiled, trying to lighten the mood. "There's an awful lot of pointing going on. Darling —" Her hand was still on Tom's arm. "Why are you so sure this Barry What'shisname might be the one who killed Lucinda?"

"I'm not sure," said Tom, almost savagely.

"No," said Malone, "and that's the bloody trouble. If you were not my son I could hand this over to Russ, let him deal with it and no questions asked."

"Why can't you do it without mentioning Tom?" said Maureen.

"Because do you think Russ isn't going to ask where I got it? Or guess? He's just fitting in as the new head of Homicide, he's got seven Assistant

Commissioners watching to report on him. And the bloody media — you vultures — never take your eyes off the Service. Or Force, whatever it's going to be called."

Nomenclature in the police organisation was a game of Scrabble. Cops believed there was a secret unit, locked in a doorless room, that did nothing but dream up new names for parts of the organisation or the organisation itself. Any public service is afraid of illegitimacy, its name must be protected, even if only by changing it.

"Righto, I'll talk to Russ first thing in the morning. And I'll call you, Mo, after I've talked to Bob Anders. Till then, both of you stay out of sight."

He sighed inwardly, at the burden of a cop who had kids with social consciences. And marvelled at cops and private eyes, shamuses, in fiction who had only alcoholism and malicious ex-wives to worry them.

"Finish your lime pie," Lisa told Tom, keeping things in perspective. "Help me clear the table, Mo."

Malone and Tom were left alone for a minute or two. "You understand, Dad?"

Malone nodded. "Yes, I do. Part of the trouble is, I'm in no-man's land at the moment. I'm on the outside looking in."

"You'll survive."

2

Clements took Malone's information with less umbrage and exasperation than Malone had expected. "Okay, I'll look into it. Or do you want me to pass it on to Rupe Steeple?"

"You check first. If we can keep Tom out of it, the longer the better —" He looked at Clements, waiting for a reaction.

"My thought entirely. Some day —"

"Some day what?"

"Some day Amanda is gunna be Tom's age. I'll be retired by then, but she could be taking up some cause and Romy and I'll be trying to tell her to pull her head in —"

"Good luck," said Malone and was satisfied. "Now the other thing is that Maureen is heading down to the Securities Commission to talk to Bob Anders. *Four Corners* is doing a piece on collapsed corporations. She's going to ask him about Orlando."

"She's bloody not!"

"That's what I told her. But you don't tell the ABC what it can and can't do, even if you've reared it and fed it and paid for its education. Don't ever let Amanda work for the ABC ... All I've managed is that Mo won't see Bob Anders till I tell her it's okay. In the meantime we wait for B.J. and Mrs Faulks."

They arrived at ten o'clock on the dot. Malone was back in his own office when Clements called him. He stood up, looked at his still paperless desk, wondered how long the luck would last, then went round to Clements' office.

Mrs Faulks had stepped right out of the Sunday social pages, where Claire and Maureen had once counted the miles and miles of smiles as vacuous as flickering neon tubes. She had a blankly pretty face, long blonde hair and a svelte, expensively dressed body; Lisa (Malone could hear her) would have said she had all the social appeal of lukewarm chardonnay. She was in her mid-thirties, Malone guessed, and would struggle never to be any older. Malone, looking at her and B.J. Shipwood, wondered whose toy was whose. And thanked God for his own simple love life.

"On the night in question we were at Terrigal," said Mrs Faulks, sounding as if she had had previous interrogations like this. Her voice didn't go with her appearance, it was thin and flat, the vowels twangy. "Admiring the view."

Of each other? Malone didn't put that question but asked another: "You can produce someone to corroborate that?"

"Superintendent, we were committing adultery," said B.J. "You don't produce witnesses for that, unless it's staged for an agreed divorce. Mr Faulks would never agree to a divorce."

Mrs Faulks looked offended at the mention of adultery, as if she had been accused of some bizarre sexual behaviour.

"Does Mr Faulks have a violent temper?" asked Clements.

"He's in the building trade," said Mrs Faulks. "Pussycats don't get far in that business."

"Has your husband ever discussed Orlando business with you?"

"He never discusses anything with me," said Mrs Faulks and sounded as if she didn't care.

"Did he ever mention Mrs Hyx to you, Marilyn Hyx?"

"No."

"Not even after she was murdered?" said Malone.

"No. I told you, he never discussed anything with me. That's why I spend time with Brandon. We discuss everything, don't we?"

He had enough sense of humour to smile. "Everything."

Clements asked a few more questions, but it was evident that B.J. had an alibi. He at last said they could go and they stood up, a well-dressed, good-looking couple who would grab the paparazzi's' flash if they ever appeared together at a fashion parade or a film premiere. If ever they did, the next flash would be Mr Faulks' violent temper.

"Good luck," said Malone. "Stay out of the limelight."

B.J. Shipwood smiled; he was that annoying article, someone who was likeable despite his conceit. "We'll be even more discreet from now on. Thanks."

Mrs Faulks was not quite as grateful: "None of this goes into a police report, does it?"

"We're discreet," said Clements and couldn't have looked more untruthful.

When the couple had gone, escorted out of Homicide and the building by one of the junior detectives, Malone said, "Why did you ask if Mr Faulks had a violent temper? You couldn't care less if he took B.J. apart."

"Nor Mrs Faulks," said Clements. "But we still don't know who tried to carve up B.J.'s mother. Whoever it was, he could also have done Mrs Hyx. They were both knife jobs."

"You're bowling a wide curve if you think Faulks might've done them."

"You got a better idea? Okay, maybe I am throwing balls in all directions, but Mr Faulks' temper is a strike against him."

"I still think Jack Aldwych knows something he hasn't told us."

"He'll keep. Let's go down and talk to Bob Anders. I like the heady feeling I get when I talk to these guys who talk about millions as if it were petty cash."

Malone had to smile. "You know, I'm just your sidekick now. Lead on, *boss*."

"Up yours," said Clements, but looked pleased, as if he was at last fitting into the frame as Homicide's boss.

Gail Lee drove them into the CBD, since parking there was like trying to land on the moon. The day was warm and dry and the tall buildings ahead of them as they drove into the city had the sharp outlines of etchings. Sun burst explosively on windows and shadow edged up the sides of lower buildings like slowly-rising paint. A 747 came in low from the north, heading for the airport to the south, and Malone closed his eyes and saw another scene: smoke and flame billowing out of other tall buildings.

"You okay?" Clements, beside Gail in the front seat, turned round.

"Just resting the eyes," said Malone and opened them again on a city that didn't appreciate its luck. And his and Clements' own luck: armies chased mass murderers, not cops.

Gail Lee dropped them in King Street and they went up in a lift to Bob Anders' office. He was waiting for them, rose to greet them with outstretched hand and a smile of real welcome. He was a tall, languid man with a dark moustache and hair cropped to a fuzz to disguise its thinness. He was gay but not gaily so; he had had the same partner for five years and had given up on the Mardi Gras. He had once worn an earring, but both ears now were ringless. All that distinguished him from the two heteros opposite him was that he wore a bracelet. Though not mates, the three of them were the best of acquaintances.

"Something up?" he said, coming straight to the point.

Clements gestured to Malone and the latter then told Anders what was planned for this office on Saturday night.

"They have everything they need to know about your alarm system and the bloke who's going to do the break-in is an expert. Or he was."

"Was?" Anders would never miss a trick; or a word.

"He thought he was retired till someone with more clout than him said he would be going to work again." Malone grinned as Anders raised an eyebrow in question. "No names, no pack drill. But the break-in expert has been to see us and we have to protect him."

"Have you seen the Orlando papers we sent you?" asked Clements.

Anders nodded. "There's enough there for us to bring in Mrs Shipwood and Mr Sweden for questioning. And maybe their accountants." He smiled, like a lion that had just come across a herd of crippled antelope. "These last six months, it's been like a picnic for us. Someone falls over and leaves a mess for us to investigate. It's more fun than the Spanish Inquisition."

"You look like a Spanish cardinal," said Malone.

"I tell myself that each morning when I'm shaving."

"How good are you fellers at changing your alarm system?"

"It can be done. We've had companies try that trick when word has leaked out that we were going to raid them. What do you want done? These days, you call in an electronics whizkid and in no time you're on another wavelength."

"We have to protect our man. If he can turn up here and the alarm system is different from what he's been given, he goes away, says he can't do the job and he's in the clear. What's the security in terms of guards, blokes who come around regularly?"

"You want their times?"

"So our feller won't be caught."

"No problem. I'll talk to my boss and we'll have the system changed by this evening, tomorrow morning at the latest. You won't want to know it?"

Both detectives grinned. "The less we know, the better. You run your shop, we'll run ours. All we've done is warn you about a shoplifter."

"You getting anywhere on the murder of that woman who collected all those papers?"

"Progressing." You never admitted getting nowhere, not even to the best of acquaintances. "When you're looking into the messes you mentioned, does all the greed you see upset you?"

"Does all the murder you see upset you?" asked Anders.

"Yes," said Malone, "but yours is cleaner."

"Not really. The poor buggers at the bottom, the shareholders and the staff of the companies, they still get murdered." Then Anders said, "Your daughter wants to see me about Orlando."

"She told you she was my daughter?"

"No. Scobie, I remember five years ago, when that guy was shooting gay-bashers —" Anders had been bashed himself; and saved by a man who had seen himself as a gay vigilante. The same man had also killed a youth trying to rape Maureen. "Names stick with me — I guess it's the same with you. There aren't too many Maureen Malones in this city. When she rang to make the appointment, I asked her if you were her dad. She said yes. Sort of reluctantly," he said and smiled.

"She's with the ABC. They're not related to anyone. We had a little argument last night. What'll you tell her?"

"I'll obfuscate. The government is giving us lessons."

"I think you're like my dad, a Commo."

"You think they didn't obfuscate? They were the masters. I'll call you this afternoon, let you know how things are going."

On their way out of the building Malone said, "When do we go to see Jack Aldwych?"

"Monday," said Clements. "We'll let him get over the shock of not getting what he wanted from ASIC. Let's get Nigger in the clear first."

Malone looked up and down King Street, a one-way narrow roadway thick with traffic from kerb to kerb. It was once a colourful thoroughfare sporting colourful characters, but asphalt and brick have obliterated the past; history, small history, goes down under the weight of progress. Malone, who occasionally peeped into the past, looked out now at the present.

People moved thickly, some with the stream, some against it, half of them with phones to their ears: shouts had given way to murmurs. Across the street a shaven-headed Hare Krishna youth, the sun bright on his yellow robe, silently banged his tambourine; beside him, oblivious to him, were two shaven-headed men in business suits, like lapsed disciples. A courier cyclist climbed the rise of the street, weaving in and out of the traffic like a fish in a rock-strewn stream. The sun shone on it all, benevolently.

"Do you think Sydney has changed since September 11?"

"No," said Clements, a realist. "Only out at the airport."

3

Foxglove, Berenger occupied five floors in a high-rise in George Street, the main street of the city. It had had naming rights to the building, but the full name of the firm was Foxglove, Berenger, Addlestein, Waterbury and Smith. Whether there had been dissension in the company or whether it had been decided the full name of the company would wrap itself round the building like a Crime Scene ribbon, the upshot was that the building was nameless, just a number. Except to financial journalists who, frustrated that no information ever came out of it, had christened it the Stifle Tower.

Sheryl Dallen and Gail Lee went up to the main floor, five storeys above street level, walked into a reception lobby as rich and discreet as that of a major Swiss bank and asked to see Miss Nancy Delarus.

"May I ask who's calling?" The receptionist looked as if she had been complexioned, coiffured, dressed, then varnished; including her voice. Bankrupts would have fled on encountering her, though they would have been called back by her employers. Bankrupts are a protected species with accountants.

Sheryl Dallen said nothing, just produced her badge.

The receptionist ruined her own effect by having to put on glasses to see what the badge said. "Oh, Police? Just a moment. Take a seat."

Instead of picking up her phone she rose and went towards a door, walking with a catwalk model's walk, as if she had two independent pelvises. She disappeared through the doorway and Sheryl said, "Can't we run her in for something? Anything."

Gail Lee smiled. "Sheryl love, look around you. We're in the castle of the kings of the world. Presidents and prime ministers come and go, but accountants go on forever. They're here when the economy is booming and they're here when it's going broke."

"Just like us," said Sheryl and felt better.

Then Nancy Delarus, Frenchy, came into the lobby, following the receptionist. She was puzzled and apprehensive, a small girl grown smaller. "You wanted to see *me*?"

"Could we go somewhere private?" asked Gail as two more clients came into the reception area.

Nancy Delarus looked at the receptionist, who nodded at another door. "There's no-one in the client room."

One wall of the client room was floor-to-ceiling smoked glass. The architect had meant it to be clear, to show the light of discovery; but the firm had been amused at his naiveté; smoke it was and no mirrors. Smoke and mirrors were used in the books and only if the client asked for that camouflage.

Nancy Delarus took a seat at the head of the big European beech table and Gail and Sheryl, like practised scouts, took seats on either side of her, round the corners of the table. She seemed disconcerted that she was going to have to switch her glances from side to side.

"Is this about Lucinda? Have you found who — who murdered her?" She had a small, throaty voice.

"No, not yet," said Sheryl. "What do we call you? Nancy or Frenchy?"

"Oh, Nancy!" She seemed uncomfortable here in this big room. "Frenchy — that's just what some of them call me, you know, socially. My hair style and my surname. But here —" She shook the gamine head. "No way, not Frenchy. This is a pretty, well, a conservative company."

"Okay, Nancy it is then," said Gail. "One of Lucinda's boyfriends works here, doesn't he? Barry Mackaw?"

"Yes, he's one of the bright ones. Some day, they say, he'll be a partner."

"What do you do? Are you an accountant?"

"Oh God, no!" Her voice came in little gasps. She wore a tan dress with a narrow yellow collar; no jewellery except for small gold earrings. She was attractive, but, Gail guessed, she would never have any confidence in herself. Gail also guessed that she would listen to Edith Piaf songs, seeing herself in them. "I'm an assistant, a, you know, general dogsbody."

"Do you work for Mr Mackaw?"

Nancy shook her head. She looked suddenly cautious, as if wondering where the questioning was going.

"You introduced him to Lucinda, that right?"

"Yes. He was pretty keen on her."

"Were you keen on him?" asked Sheryl.

There was no gasp this time; she looked at each of them shrewdly. "What is all this leading up to?"

"Where is Mr Mackaw at the moment? Is he in the building?"

"No, he's up at Tamworth, doing auditing on some rural companies."

Auditing, of late, had become a careless science. Books were being closed that had barely been opened. Where books hadn't been closed in time to hide discrepancies, shredding had been added as a required skill.

"You were interviewed by Sergeant Steeple and you told him you had seen Mr Mackaw on the night Lucinda was murdered."

Nancy was still cautious; like a better accountant. "Are you suspecting Barry of —" Her voice trailed off.

"We're not suspecting him, no," said Gail. "We're just retracing our steps. We've come to a dead end and we have to start all over again. It's a form of accounting."

But Nancy didn't smile. "So what are you asking me?"

Sheryl looked at her notebook. "You said you were both working back that night —"

"Yes, that's right."

"Both on the same floor?"

"No-o. He's on a floor above me. I saw him in the staff canteen, we had some coffee together —"

"When was that?"

"I'm not sure. Some time after five."

"That was the only time you saw him?"

"No-o. I worked till, I think it was 7.30, maybe just after. I met him on my way out — he came down to our floor to get something, I can't remember what he was after."

"Someone else was working on your floor at that time?"

"Ye-es. Three or four people, maybe five or six."

"Accountants work long hours," said Gail.

Nancy made no comment and Sheryl went on, "So you didn't see Mr Mackaw for, say, two or three hours, or two-and-a-half hours?"

"No-o. No, I guess not."

"Would anyone else have been working up on the same floor as Mr Mackaw? Another accountant or somebody?"

"I don't know. We tend to work just on our own floor, in separate sections. Look, what are you saying? That Barry might have —" She shook her head fiercely. "No! He's not like that — a murderer —"

"We haven't said anything," said Gail. "It's just as we said, we're starting all over again. You want us to find out who murdered Lucinda, don't you?"

"Of course!"

"Do you have Barry's phone number? His mobile?"

Nancy nodded, trying to get her emotions under control. "It's upstairs, in my bag."

"Do you know where he's working in Tamworth?"

"At Rubus, it's short for Rural Business. They own several properties and they're in cotton out around Moree."

"You're in different sections here," said Sheryl, "but you know where he's working? Have you been in touch with him?"

Nancy tapped fingers on the pale woodwork of the table. "Ye-es. I spoke to him last night."

"Nancy," said Gail gently, "have you got a thing for Barry? Are you in love with him?"

"I don't think that's any of your business! What's that got to —"

"You've answered the question," said Sheryl and stood up. "I'll be back, Gail. Ask Miss Delarus a few more questions."

She went out into the lobby area, aware of Nancy Delarus turning her head to stare after her, the look on the small face one of despair.

Out in the lobby, ignoring the questioning look of the varnished receptionist, she took out her mobile and called Clements.

"Boss, we have a problem —" She kept her voice low, seeing the ears prick up of the two clients still waiting to be seen.

"Put it to me," said Clements, who had just come back from the ASIC offices with Malone.

Sheryl explained the situation: "I think Miss Delarus has done her ovaries over Mr Mackaw — what's the matter?"

Clements was laughing. "Done her ovaries — I haven't heard that in years. I used to hear girls say it when I was your age —"

Sheryl humoured him by forcing a laugh; bosses had to be tolerated. "My mother uses it … Anyhow, Miss Delarus was Mackaw's alibi the night of the murder. Only trouble is, there's a two-hour gap, maybe a bit more, in the alibi." She detailed what Nancy Delarus had told her and Gail Lee. "Mr Mackaw is up in Tamworth, at the offices of a firm called Rubus. If we let Miss Delarus go, she'll call him and if he's the guy who was with Lucinda that night we may not see him again. Can we have him picked up for questioning by the Tamworth police?"

"Come back here, get travel vouchers for you and Gail and you two go up and bring him back here. In the meantime, I'll have Tamworth pick him up and hold him."

Sheryl clicked off her mobile with satisfaction, even smiled at the receptionist, and headed back to the client room. At Homicide Clements put down the phone and looked across at Malone.

"Bingo!" he said. "One down and one to go."

"This is bloody ridiculous," said Barry Mackaw.

He had been picked up late yesterday afternoon by Sheryl Dallen and Gail Lee, too late for them to bring him back to Sydney as the evening plane out of Tamworth had been fully booked. He had been held overnight at the local police station, while Sheryl and Gail had spent the night at a hotel. The expenses vouchers, they were sure, would merit their cost. Food has an extra taste when bought with government money.

Mackaw was now in an interview room at Homicide with Clements, Malone and Sheryl Dallen. Clements had invited Malone to sit in because — "Tom has pointed the finger at this guy. You can judge for yourself whether he's right. But let me do the talking, Superintendent, okay?"

"Your case, Inspector."

Also present was Roland Arbitz, a senior partner at Foxglove, Berenger. Mackaw had asked that he be called and Arbitz had come reluctantly, Gail had told Clements. He was a tall angular man whose face seemed to be made up of flat planes, an effect heightened by the square rimless glasses he wore. He had sparse grey-brown hair parted in the middle and what looked to Malone like square teeth. His voice was a hoarse whisper, as if it had spent years in the secret passages of accountancy.

"Miss Delarus, your alibi source," said Clements, "tells us she saw you just after five o'clock on that afternoon and then again around 7.30. That's quite a gap, Mr Mackaw."

"I was working upstairs, on another floor from Fren — from Miss Delarus." Mackaw, Malone had decided, was a very self-confident young man. He was good-looking in an unremarkable way, tall and slim and almost fastidiously well-dressed. The old picture of accountants as dry, desiccated creatures had long gone. "I don't believe either of us said we were together all that time."

"Then you can give us the name of someone who was working with you on that floor?"

Mackaw glanced at Arbitz, then said, "Well, no-o —"

Clements drawled it out. "No-o-o? Why not?"

For the first time Mackaw looked uncomfortable; so, Malone noted, did Mr Arbitz. "I was working alone."

Arbitz cleared his throat, whispered, "He was working for me."

"Doing what, sir?" asked Sheryl Dallen, notebook in hand like a weapon.

"Working on papers."

"Working on papers?" said Clements. "I'd of thought that was what accountants did all the time. We'd like to know a bit more than that, Mr Arbitz. Mr Mackaw."

Arbitz looked at Mackaw, then nodded; the latter said, "I was shredding papers."

Clements grinned at Malone, who grinned in reply. It was Sheryl who said, "That seems to happen a lot these days. A whole two hours of shredding paper? That must of made quite a heap."

"Why were you shredding lots of paper, Mr Mackaw? It's not the end of the financial year. We presume it's all been thrown out now, there's nothing to prove it ever existed. Wouldn't you agree, Mr Arbitz?"

"I can vouch for Mr Mackaw, that he was doing what he has just told you. Yes, the papers have been disposed of."

"You haven't told us why the missing papers were being shredded."

"I don't think I can tell you that. Client confidentiality."

Clements looked at Malone again and the latter spoke for the first time, "I thought only lawyers told us that one. Were they the papers of some company or client in trouble?"

The three detectives had to lean forward to hear the whisper: "Yes."

"Would you care to name the company or client so that we can check?" said Clements.

"You're joking!" Mackaw's voice was not a whisper.

"I don't think the superintendent or the

inspector go in for jokes like that," said Sheryl. "It was some client in deep shit, was it?"

Arbitz, if not Mackaw, looked shocked. Nicely put, thought Malone, and fired an arrow in the air: "Would it be Orlando?"

"Orlando?" Arbitz lifted his head, so that the planes of his glasses went blank.

"Yes, Orlando Development," said Clements, taking over the bowling. "We know you handle all their business, though we didn't know Mr Mackaw worked for them."

"I don't," said Mackaw.

Clements looked back at Arbitz, who reluctantly whispered, "He doesn't. We used him to shred the papers because he wasn't part of the team working for Orlando."

"Too many of whom might be honest?" said Malone, unable to keep his tongue quiet.

"You can be pretty insulting, Superintendent." This time Arbitz's voice rose above a whisper.

"Mr Arbitz, we're investigating the murder of a young woman. We don't pussyfoot around when we are given the bum's rush. Were you with Mr Mackaw the whole time he was shredding those papers?"

"Not the whole time, no."

"Most of the time?" asked Clements. "An hour, an hour and a half, two hours?"

"I can attest to Mr Mackaw's character —"

"Sure," said Malone, tongue loose again. "That's why you chose him to shred the papers."

"We don't have to listen to this, Barry —"

Arbitz made to rise, but Clements waved him down. "Don't let's get awkward, Mr Arbitz, or we'll start producing our own pieces of paper, unshredded. A warrant, for instance, to hold Mr Mackaw for further questioning. I think you might have enough problems with ASIC, you and your firm and Mr Mackaw."

"ASIC?" The hoarseness was back in Arbitz's whisper. "What do you know about ASIC?"

"Nothing," said Clements, the truth shining out of him as out of a busted lamp. "Now, how often did you see Mr Mackaw during that period we've mentioned on that night?"

"Once, maybe twice —" Arbitz seemed to have more on his mind than an alibi for Mackaw; shredded paper, maybe. "I went out for dinner —"

"Did you pop out for something to eat, Mr Mackaw?" said Sheryl. "A bite with Lucinda?"

"No, I didn't. I ate when I left the office, around nine, 9.15, something like that. I went to a café in Paddington, near where I live."

He's too glib, thought Malone. "Do you have a car?"

"Yeah."

"What sort?"

"A Beemer 328."

A 120,000-dollar job.

But Mackaw had read Malone's raised eyebrow. "It's second-hand. You're Tom Malone's father, aren't you?"

"What's that got to do with this?"

"Nothing, I guess." But his expression said otherwise.

"How long would it take you to drive from your offices over to Pyrmont, to Miss Rossiter's place?"

"I have no idea."

"You've never been to her place?"

"Just the once, we went by cab."

Too glib again. Malone looked at the young man and knew who had killed Lucinda Rossiter. But the case was not his and suddenly he wanted to walk away from it, against the grain of all the years he had spent in interview rooms like this. He stood up. "Let me know what you decide, Inspector."

Clements looked at him in surprise; but just nodded and said, "I'll do that, sir."

Malone went back to his own office in Crime Agency, met Greg Random at his door. "I've been looking for you —"

Malone explained where he had been. "Greg, do you ever get fed up with it all? Feel you need a shower, maybe even lose your memory and be glad you have?"

Random sat down, taking his time; everything he did was a deliberate act, making his own time through life and living. "What's upset you? The blood on the walls? Someone's dead eye staring at you? It happens, Scobie, it happens. I still remember the first dead'un I saw, when I was a probationary constable. A middle-aged woman with her throat cut — I think it was by her husband, but I don't remember. All I remember is *her*. It never got any better, even though I got used to it. To an extent."

"I'm not sure it's the blood on the walls. Or a dead eye staring at me. It's also the ones who do it, who do someone in, a girl, a bloke, anyone, and don't bloody-well care. Or no, maybe they care, but not so much as to say yes, they did it. I've just seen a bastard like that. His own neck is worth more than that of the girl he strangled."

"Scobie —" Random suddenly sounded paternal, even looked it. "Remember something called human nature? Is this the case over in Pyrmont? Saving your own neck is a natural response. People do it all the time."

"They don't all commit murder."

"Sometimes by remote control they do. This kid, you're sure he killed the girl?"

"Certain."

"Then let Russ handle it. He'll get the kid sooner or later. You've been promoted, up here in the heights we're supposed to understand human nature a little more."

"Do you?"

"No. But as —"

"No Welsh poets, please."

"No. Just an old Welsh saying: Power is an aphrodisiac, but Spanish fly is quicker."

"What's that got to do with human nature?"

"I thought you'd understand," said Random, smiled and went.

A minute later Clements came into Malone's office, slumped down in the chair opposite him. "I've had to let him go, but warned him he could be called in again, and soon."

"He could skedaddle."

"He won't. He's the sort who'll brazen it out, tell us we've got to prove he's our man. If he runs, he knows that brands him. He's not the first we've had like this."

"What do you know about human nature?"

Clements looked puzzled, shook his head. "Nothing. Who does? Maybe Jesus Christ did and look what human nature did to him."

"You should send an e-mail to the Ephesians. They're waiting to hear from you."

Chapter Nine

❦

1

"Jack —" It was 7.30 Sunday morning and Nigger Brown was on the phone. "I gotta see you —"

"Nigger, how'd it go?"

"A total fuck-up, Jack. That's why I gotta see you —"

"Okay, come over here soon's you like —"

"Jack, I'm not gunna come all the way over to Harbord in me tow-truck — it might be needed, bloody dills out for a Sunday drive —"

"Your tow-truck? Don't you have a car?"

"It's Sunday, Jack, the missus's got the car, she picks up the grandkids and takes 'em to Mass. You got the luxury car, you got Blackie to drive you, come out and I'll meet you at Blacktown —"

"Where? Blacktown? Nigger, that's the fucking Outback —"

"No, Jack, just this side of it. I'll meet you at McDonalds, nine o'clock."

"McDonalds?" But Nigger Brown had hung up.

Now they were in McDonalds, an egg-on-a-muffin in front of Brown, a carton of French fries in front of Aldwych. The large room was half-empty, but diners, or breakfasters, were arriving by the minute. Smiles never left the faces of the young people behind the counters; cheerfulness was part of the uniform. Nigger sometimes wondered if they were paid by the smile. But he liked the atmosphere and he was not a food snob. He wasn't a snob, period, as he would have told you.

Aldwych was in grey slacks, navy blazer and checked blue shirt; he looked like a banker slumming. Nigger Brown was in a tan polo shirt, white shorts and blue-and-white trainers. They looked like two strangers who had accidentally met at the same table. McDonalds could have made a commercial of them.

"Why here?" Aldwych looked around him. "Why'd we have to meet here, for Crissake?"

"Jack, I think you've become a snob. The old days we'd meet — well, not you and me, you and your mates — you'd meet in a pub or maybe a café. Not today. Pubs nowadays are all fucking poker machines and loud music, you can't hear yourself talk. Cafés, no more steak and chips, a cuppa tea. It's all bloody la-de-das with the *caffe latte* and their health salads. McDonalds is the hub of the world, Jack." He looked around him. "All sorts, people like you, guys like me, we all come here. You're outa touch, Jack."

"You gunna eat all them chips, mister?" A boy about seven, a fast food fossicker, stood by their table, long nose, beady eyes, a human bandicoot.

"No, I'm gunna take 'em home and start a potato farm. Piss off," said Aldwych.

The boy, evidently accustomed to knockbacks, moved on and Brown said, "That was pretty rough, Jack."

"There was an old comedian, W.C. Fields, you wouldn't remember him, he had a motto. Any man who hates kids can't be all bad. I agree with him."

"My grandkids, they'd kick you to death, they heard you say that."

"Proves my point, they don't allow freedom of expression. Now what happened last night?"

"Jack, whoever sold you that alarm system, they sold you the wrong one." He had no concern for whoever had sold Aldwych the plans; dealing with Jack Aldwych, it was every man for himself. "I got inna the building okay, no sweat, but when I got upstairs and had a look at the system —" He shook his head, a curl bouncing like a question mark trying to escape. "I'd of broke that system, the bells ud of started ringing like the bells of St Mary's, the wedding of the Pope —"

"The wedding of the Pope?"

"Catholic joke, Jack. Like I told you, I got into the building, no problem. But upstairs —" He shook his head again. "You want them papers, looks like you gotta go and ask for 'em."

"Yeah, that'd be dead easy." Aldwych munched on a French fry; though he still thought of them as chips. "Okay, you didn't get what I wanted. How much you gunna charge me? You're not expecting the full five figures?"

"Jack, I'm expecting nothing. I been clean now ten, twelve years, and I think that's the way I wanna stay. Tell you the truth, I dunno why you wanted me to do the job. You're worth — what? Christ knows. I don't care. Why are those papers so valuable?"

"Revenge, Nigger." He had thought about it, turned it over in his mind till it had become sweet-tasting. "I never liked being taken, not even when I had nothing."

"I never worried about something like that, revenge. Maybe it's the Abo in me, the Koori. It's hopeless, like throwing boomerangs at clouds. The boomerang comes back and chances are it clouts you."

Aldwych had to smile. "You're a miserable bugger."

Brown shook his head again. "No, Jack, just resigned. Almost happy." Then he corrected himself: "No, I *am* happy."

Aldwych looked around himself again; the restaurant was now full. He had the air of a general who had found himself on the wrong battlefield. Maybe Nigger was right, he had become a snob, something Shirl would never tolerate, if she had known. A youth went by: mohawk hairstyle, metal in his ears, eyebrow, nose, lower lip, tattoos from elbow to shoulder on his bare arms. Aldwych looked after him.

"What's that?"

"I dunno. A kid, almost happy, I dunno. What's worrying you? The haircut, the tattoos, the bits of iron stuck in him? I got a granddaughter, seventeen, she's got a fake diamond in her tongue —"

"In her *tongue*?"

"In her tongue. You couldn't meet a nicer, happier kid, if you can understand what she's saying." He grinned, a happy man's genuine smile. "It takes all sorts, Jack. You been rich too long. You've forgotten how to live with the battlers."

"I come all the way out here, out to the fucking Outback, for a lecture? I could have you knocked off, Nigger."

"Yeah, you could do that." Nigger Brown was surprised how unafraid he was. "But I think you're past that now, Jack. Nobodies like me, what'd be the point?"

Aldwych considered, then nodded. "You got a point. When did you become a philosopher?"

"Sitting in me tow-truck one day, looking at four dead kids in a pile-up. I knew 'em all."

Aldwych knew when to be silent; then at last he said, "What do I owe you? The chips?"

"They're on me. I owe you, that bank hold-up I fucked up years ago."

They stood up, still looking like strangers newly met in the hub of the world, and walked out of the restaurant. Some people nodded to Brown and looked curiously at the tall distinguished man with him.

"Probably a client," they told each other. "Nigger's giving him a quote, prob'ly, on his wrecked Rolls or Merc."

Out in the car park, standing by the Daimler with Blackie Ovens behind the wheel and nodding hello to Brown, Aldwych said, "Where do you live, Nigger?"

"Rooty Hill. Right next door to that woman was murdered, the one from Orlando. I found her."

"You didn't mention that the other day."

"You didn't ask me."

"You buggers can keep a secret."

"Forty thousand years experience, Jack. You whiteys're still learning." He put out his hand. "Good luck, Jack. Don't ask me any more favours."

Aldwych shook hands, feeling a sudden regard for the smaller, darker man. He looked around him again. "Blacktown? Why's it called Blacktown?"

"We were here first, Christ knows how many years ago. Right here, where you just ate French fries, my great-great-great-grandmother probably cooked yabbies. You think there's been progress?"

"Get outa here, Nigger," said Aldwych and got into his car. "Look after yourself."

"I been doing that," said Nigger Brown.

2

Derek Sweden had persuaded Rosalind to invite the Shipwoods to Sunday supper.

"Oh darling," she had said, "businesswomen are more boring than businessmen."

"I'm a businessman."

"No, you're not. You're a politician who's in business. There's a difference, darling." She still thought Roumanian, a process even her husband sometimes had difficulty with, despite his being a politician. "Why do we have to have them?"

"I want to study her husband, Harry. He was an economics lecturer. I just wonder if he put her up to all that's happened."

Out at Sylvania Waters the wife there had also shown reluctance. "You know I can't stand *her*. She's so damned superior, like all Hungarians."

"She's Roumanian," said Harry Shipwood.

"What's the difference?" She was not ignorant, just uneducated in Europe, an amorphous blob on the map, especially that bit down in the right-hand corner. She came of a generation when educationists had had very narrow vectors on history and geography. "We'll have to find an excuse —"

"Sweetheart," said Harry, "I want to study Derek Sweden. From what little you've told me, he could have been ahead of you in what's happened."

"He uses the same bank as us, the Shahriver, in those Caicos Islands. But he doesn't know that."

"You should swap cheque butts," he said, but smiled to show he didn't mean it.

When they went out to get into the Bentley, the surveillance officer got out of the unmarked police car. "Where to this evening, sir?"

"Circular Quay," said Harry Shipwood. "Parking there may be a problem."

"No problem at all, sir." He was a young man, bored stiff with this particular job. He was also already cynical: "We just tear up the parking tickets."

Harry gave him the address and the two cars drove into the city, the Bentley into the visitors' parking under The Wharf, where the Swedens lived, and the unmarked car into a No Parking zone.

"I'll be in the lobby, sir, if you have any trouble."

"Oh, I don't think there'll be any of that. He's an ex-Police Minister."

"You never know, sir."

And now the Shipwoods were upstairs in the Swedens' very large apartment. Rosalind had expected Harry Shipwood, a retired university lecturer (not even a professor), to come in unpressed corduroy slacks, a cardigan and perhaps even nylon socks and sandals. She didn't know that B.J., his son, was his occasional valet ("Dad, for Crissakes, why've you always got to look like a bloody beachcomber? You're not on *Survivor*.") Shipwood had trimmed his beard to a neat

Vandyke and had his hair cut. He was in beige slacks, a blazer, a cream shirt and (Rosalind couldn't believe it) a silk scarf at his throat. She didn't get as far as looking at his feet.

"Mr Shipwood, what a pleasure!"

"For both of us, Mrs Sweden." Cary Grant couldn't have been smoother. But neither was taken in by the other. He looked out at the harbour, as narrow here as the stretch of water in front of his own house. Except that back there he did not have a 60,000-ton cruise ship as the garden decoration. "What a beautiful view!"

"Do you have water views at Sylvia Waters?"

"Sylvania. On wet days, yes."

She looked at him coolly; then suddenly gave him a warm smile. She always appreciated a reliable foe. "You're not what I expected, Harry."

"I suspected that. You're not what I expected. With a name like Juliet, I thought you might see yourself as a tragic heroine. You'll never be that."

"A heroine, perhaps. But never tragic. And I'm Rosalind. Juliet is my sister, over there."

He gave her an equally warm smile, both connected to the same artificial source. "I know. I think I'm going to enjoy the evening. Just like back in the staff room at university."

"I went to your university. I think it was a Saturday."

"You and I should get together more often, Rosalind."

On the other side of the room Ophelia was talking to Natalie. The latter was, as usual, all in white, a contrast to the restored black hair.

"I'm admiring your hair," said Ophelia. "Who does it? Joh Bailey?"

"No, a hairdresser in Sutherland."

"Sutherland?" Ophelia looked at her escort. "Where's that, Mark?"

"I think it's on the edge of the map — just. That right, Mrs Shipwood?"

Mark Puzo was a State MP, a handsome man with two wives behind him and his eye out for a third, preferably one with money to supplement his parliamentary pension when it fell on him. Which might be at the next election. His principal political job for the Opposition party had been manufacturing lightning bolts, most of which had missed their mark. He was always careful around Ophelia, who could take the fork out of any lightning.

"Over in the east, Natalie — mind if I call you Natalie? Over here the map is a blank beyond Randwick racecourse. It's marked — Beyond lie dragons."

"I'm an immigrant," said Ophelia. "You must forgive my ignorance."

But Natalie Shipwood, now she was here, was not going to be put down by these people. "We always welcome refugees."

"Except lately," said Puzo. "But let's not mention that."

Then Juliet and Jack Aldwych Junior joined them. The gathering this evening was small, but Natalie would have felt more at home amongst the Taliban, that recent mysterious enemy that had just been discovered. Derek had arranged this, like the enemy he was.

Ophelia introduced her sister and her brother-in-law. "We're a close-knit family. You have family?"

Yes, but not close-knit. "A boy and a girl. Neither of them married."

"Her son is B.J. Shipwood," said Jack Junior.

The Bruna sisters looked at each other blankly.

"A pin-up boy," explained Puzo. "A rugby league player. But you Roumanians play rugby union, don't you? Another game."

"Not the women," said Juliet. "I'd never be any use in a scrum or whatever they call it."

"You kid yourself," said Jack Junior and smiled to show he meant it.

The chit-chat floated like shards of glass. Out on the balcony Sweden had managed to corner Harry Shipwood alone. Down below the Sunday crowds were starting to thin out as the evening cooled. Over past the international terminal and the cruise ship, beyond the grate of the Harbour Bridge, the sky was fiery, promising more dry weather, probably more bushfires.

"You think things will get worse?" said Sweden.

"What? The bushfires? Terrorism?"

"Those, of course. But I was thinking of Orlando." Sweden was a practised arsonist, he could start his own small fires.

"Derek, why ask me? I'm an innocent bystander." Harry Shipwood took a sip of his champagne. He had noticed it was Australian, not French, and guessed they were second-class visitors.

"You were an economist, a professor —" Flattery got you somewhere, sometimes. Not this time.

"Lecturer." Shipwood smiled. "I'm sure you knew that, Derek. I was lazy, never had enough ambition. But I must have been a good teacher. Some of my best pupils are now first-class crooks."

"Lecturer, then. But even now you must take an interest, especially in something so close to home."

"All I know is that you and Natalie, like good directors, looked after yourselves. You threw lifebelts over the blind side of the ship and when it went down, you two were — are — still floating."

"That's pretty insulting." Sweden tried to sound insulted, but he was too well insulated. "To Natalie, as well as me."

"Derek, economists deal in facts. Or are supposed to. I'm not passing judgement, just reporting. And only to you and Natalie."

"Has ASIC talked to you?"

"ASIC? To me?" Shipwood shook his head. "I'm retired, Derek. I doubt if ASIC knows I exist.

When did you ever see my fine Italian hand in anything that Natalie does?"

"You're Italian?"

"A figure of speech, Derek. It's more and more evident now in economics."

"That's true." Sweden knew now that he had made a mistake about Shipwood; the man was harmless, if cynical. But cynicism was now fashionable and not a chargeable offence. "Did the police come to see you about Marilyn Hyx?"

"I was a bystander there, too. They interviewed Natalie, but she is in the dark as much as I am about Marilyn's death. As much as you," he said and looked at Sweden over the top of his now-empty champagne glass.

"As a bystander, who do you think could have killed her?"

"I haven't a clue. Thanks —" As the Swedens' cook-maid brought him another glass of champagne. He waited till she had gone away, then he went on, "Marilyn had her secrets that none of us suspected — especially you and Natalie. She might have had secret enemies, for all we know."

"ASIC has a stack of papers she had in a strong-box."

"I know, Natalie told me. I've never sat on a board of directors, but don't you chaps lock the door when you want to discuss something amongst yourselves?"

"Marilyn was a trusted servant, as they say."

"Yes, I guess that's what we all thought. How's your arm? Natalie told me about it."

"Why do you ask?"

Shipwood sipped his drink, took his time. "He's still out there, the chap who tried to kill Natalie. I'm sincerely grateful to you, Derek, for what you did, saving her. That took guts."

"It was instinctive, Harry. It's a pity you or I weren't around to stop that guy killing Marilyn."

"True. And he's still out there, that's the worry."

"Have you made any guess at who he might be?"

"It's not in an economist's nature to make guesses."

"You could have fooled me," said Sweden and they smiled at each other, men who knew an audit when they saw it.

In the living room Natalie Shipwood and Jack Junior had found themselves together for a few moments.

"You look to have recovered well, Natalie. You've been through a lot."

"You think it's all over? I don't, Jack. How's your father?"

"I'm glad you asked. He's not happy. He hates losing money." This woman was a virtual stranger to him. But, said his wife, so were most women. "I think you and he should sit down, Natalie, just the two of you, and come to some arrangement."

"How much has he lost?"

"A million, two."

She laughed into her drink, spluttered a little, wiped her chin with a handkerchief. "Jack, I've lost much, much more than that."

His gaze was steady. "Dad doesn't think so."

"Oh?" She took another sip of her drink. "What do you think?"

"You and Derek, I'm sure, have lost nothing. Dad wants to meet you. He said to tell you he'll take a cheque on an overseas bank."

She made a good show of indignation. "He has a bloody hide! Tell him —"

Jack Junior took out a card, already scribbled on. "Here's his address —"

She looked at it. "Harbord? He thinks I'm going all the way over there to meet him —"

"I'd advise it, Natalie. Tomorrow morning, eleven o'clock. He'll be expecting you."

Then they were interrupted by Ophelia. "Supper's ready. You two look as if you're getting on beautifully. I always like it, don't you, Natalie, when young men pay proper respect to us mature women?"

"We're getting on beautifully," said Jack Junior. "Don't you think she looks like Elizabeth Taylor?"

"Of course!" Ophelia was an actor manqué; her favourite role would have been Lady Macbeth. "I should have seen the resemblance —"

"I've always envied her her love life," said Natalie, mollified a little by the flattery.

"That sort of thing is slow out at Sylvia Waters?"

3

Monday morning Nigger Brown rang Malone. "I'm on my mobile, in my tow-truck. I'm out on the Western Highway, a three-car smash. You wouldn't believe the bloody idiots running around loose. About Sat'day night —"

"Nigger, why are you calling me instead of Inspector Clements?"

"You're the boss, ain't you? Superintendent —"

"Righto, go ahead." Rank clung to him like paint.

"In and out like Flynn, Sat'day night. No worries. Yest'day morning I saw Jack Aldwych out at Blacktown —"

"Blacktown? What was he doing way out there?"

"Now don't you start, Mr Malone. Jack thought it was the bloody Outback. Anyhow, I told him getting into the ASIC place wasn't on. He wasn't too happy, but he accepted it. It's up to you now, Mr Malone. I done my bit."

"And we're grateful, Nigger. Take care."

"Oh, I'll do that, all right. Jesus, you should see the mess out here. Fucking idiots —"

"Nigger, without them you'd be out of business."

"Yeah, but it don't make it any better. I guess shit-cart workers felt the same."

"I'm sure they did, Nigger."

Malone hung up, sat back in his chair. He had had a relaxing weekend. He had played tennis Saturday afternoon; watched a video and made love, not at the same time, Saturday night. Sunday morning he had gone to Mass with Lisa, stayed awake during a sermon by a young priest who didn't believe that St Paul, one of Malone's know-alls, knew everything. The church had been half-full, its usual state. The Sunday after September 11 it had been packed, the twice-a-year Catholics, those who came only at Easter and Christmas, there to assure the Lord that they were hanging in there, if only by two threads. Now, with terrorism and hell's fire retreating, they would be there again at Christmas.

Con and Brigid Malone and Hans and Elisabeth Pretorius had come for Sunday lunch, couples from opposite sides of the social spectrum, who met here at their children's house once a month and enjoyed each other's company. Con was a retired communist and Hans a tired capitalist and between them they took today's world apart to the satisfaction of both. Brigid and Elisabeth turned deaf ears to their husbands and glowed in Lisa's stories of the grandchildren and the great-grandchild. A peaceful day where smoke and fire, bushfire and gunfire, were out of sight and out of mind. A weekend without mess, without idiots or swindlers or murderers.

Clements loomed in the doorway, looked around. "This office doesn't look lived-in."

"And there's a cypher at the desk. You sound like the Opposition Police Minister, the bloke who knows everything that's wrong and nothing that's right … Nigger Brown called me. I told him he should call you, but he's got something in his head about rank."

"It's the Abo in him. He thinks you're a tribal elder. What'd he have to say?"

Malone told him. "Now I think we should go over and talk to Jack Aldwych."

"That's why I'm here." Clements sat down, again working his backside into the seat of the chair. He's right, thought Malone: nothing in this office is lived-in. "We're getting nowhere with the Marilyn Hyx murder. Unless there's a clue hidden in those papers in the strong-box, one we haven't dug up yet."

Malone was surprised at his hesitancy in asking, "What about the Lucinda Rossiter case?"

"Relax. Tom's entirely in the clear there. He'll be called at the coroner's inquest, but that's all. Rupe Steeple is offering nothing that links Tom to the girl."

"What about the other bloke, Mackaw?"

"We think he's the one, me and the girls, Sheryl and Gail. We're keeping an eye on him, but the bugger's clever." He sprawled a little more comfortably in the chair. "We've got three more on our books, you'll get the reports today. A drive-by and two domestics. The drive-by, the dead guy's brother says they were terrorists did it. Jesus! The world is suddenly full of bloody terrorists!"

"Any idea who they were?"

"The brother, the dead guy, was a drug dealer. Whoever did him in, did it over drugs. Why should we care?"

Malone stood up. "Let's go over and see our old-time terrorist, our mate Jack."

"I'll say it for Jack, he never dealt in drugs."

They drove over to Harbord under a sky faintly tinged with yellow; the bushfires in the Blue Mountains and to the south were spreading. If Bing Crosby were still alive he would be singing of a Black Christmas. Images of the world over the past few weeks were wreathed in smoke.

Clements pulled the unmarked police car in behind the big green Bentley.

"Well, waddya know! You think Jack and Mrs Shipwood are in cahoots?"

"Not Jack. We may walk in on him strangling her."

Then the young officer approached them from the unmarked car on the opposite side of the road. Malone identified himself and Clements, then said, "You had anything to report?"

"No, sir. Our area commander is withdrawing the surveillance after today. We're short of men —"

Malone nodded, looked at the big green car. "In that Mrs Shipwood would be safe from tanks."

"I toddle along behind it, sir, like a go-cart."

"Who's in the house with her?"

"Mr Shipwood. He's pleasanter than she is."

"It's a husbandly trait," said Malone and somewhere in the far distance Lisa and Romy snorted.

Clements pressed the bell beside the big iron gates that fronted the house. Two huge Dobermans, thinking it was meal-time, came galloping round the corner of the house and down the short drive. They were barking and snarling at the two detectives when Blackie Ovens came out the front door and down to the gates.

"Oh, Mr Malone, Mr Clements. You wanted to see the boss? He's got a coupla visitors with him right now —"

"He's going to have a couple more, Blackie," said Malone. "Us. Now can you call off the man-eaters and let us in?"

Blackie Ovens barked at the dogs and they slunk away.

"He must of been a lion tamer," Clements told Malone. "How've you been, Blackie? How do you get on with those old nuns the other side of your back fence? They still praying for you?"

"Not for me. For the Old Man. I think they're praying for him to be — what's the word — canonised?"

"Cannonballed, more likely," said Malone. "Don't bother to announce us, Blackie. Let's just walk in, like the ignorant cops we are."

Blackie Ovens grinned at them. "He'll tear strips off of me after you've gone. But sometimes I like to annoy him, just to relieve the monotony."

"Monotony? You want to get back in the game?"

"Nah, nah. Just the monotony of getting old. I'll be seventy-one, a coupla months time. And me mum said I wouldn't last past thirty. She was a Catholic, a Tyke, like them old biddies over the back fence, praying for me holy soul every night and twice on Sundays."

"We'll pray for you," said Clements. "Or Mr Malone will."

"Thanks," said Blackie Ovens drily, aghast at the ignominy of cops talking to God about him.

4

"I suppose you," said Jack Aldwych, making no attempt to be polite, "are what they call the power behind the throne."

"Not at all," said Harry Shipwood. "I'm the husband making sure the little woman isn't shafted."

"All right, you two," said Natalie Shipwood, "with your blokey witticisms."

Then Aldwych had grinned at them both and waved his hand to chairs. "I think I'm gunna enjoy this."

Natalie arranged herself on her chair. Without moving her head she had taken in the room. It was high-ceilinged, a luxury of the past, and the furnishings were also from the past. Aldwych's dead wife, Shirl, had liked floral carpets, Dresdenware on the mantelpiece, Laura Ashley curtains on the windows, *nice* paintings on the walls; Aldwych, who had truly loved his wife, an honest love for an honest woman, had changed nothing after her death. Natalie Shipwood, who knew nothing of Shirley Aldwych, thought the old man opposite her looked out of place.

"You're early," said Aldwych. "Is that a sign you're nervous?"

"It was my suggestion," said Harry Shipwood. "Punctuality is the courtesy of kings. We weren't quite sure where Harbord was."

"Are you a snob?"

Shipwood smiled. "I don't think so, Mr Aldwych. Just honest and maybe not too good at geography. But if you want to know, I'm not really interested in social geography."

"You and me may have something in common, then. What about you, Natalie?"

"Can we get down to why we're here?" Small talk bored her, it was for small minds. Not that she would ever make the mistake of thinking this old criminal opposite her had a small mind. "I told your son yesterday I've lost virtually everything in the Orlando collapse —"

"Nat —"

She flinched: she hated being called Nat, like some old-fashioned bookie.

He had noticed the flinch and he repeated: "Nat, you and Derek Sweden unloaded a cartload of shares just before they went down the gurgler. My son, who's pretty smart, has done some due diligence on you and Mr Sweden, on what you sold." He reached into the pocket of the brown cashmere cardigan he wore, took out a paper and looked at it. Natalie Shipwood noticed that he read from it without the aid of glasses. "Over the last three months you — and I mean you, not you and Sweden — you took 12 million out of Orlando. That, plus what you've been milking for the past twelve months, adds up, my son reckons, to around 30 million." He looked up at her, eyes perfectly in focus. "Where is it, Nat?"

"Your son is dreaming," she said flatly, her own gaze steady.

Aldwych looked at Shipwood. "What do you know about this?"

"As I told Derek Sweden yesterday, I'm just a bystander in all this. I'm retired, Mr Aldwych. A loving husband, but retired."

Aldwych looked back at his prime target. "Nat —"

"Natalie."

His smile was that of a shark on an unwary swimmer. "Natalie. We're not sure the 30 million is all you took out of Orlando. Only the papers the Securities Commission have can tell us that. And I may be dead before they get around to going public."

"Mr Aldwych," said Harry Shipwood, "you are throwing millions around like poker chips. If you think my wife has that much money stashed away somewhere, why are you so concerned for what you say you've lost? My wife tells me it's a mere million, two hundred thousand."

"It's the principle of the thing," said Aldwych, still smiling. "I'm a man of principle. Ask any of the blokes I got rid of."

Shipwood coughed, holding back a laugh. "You sound like someone out of an old movie —"

Aldwych stared at him, the smile gone. "You sound like that's where you live, in some old movie —" Then he looked beyond Shipwood, at Blackie Ovens, Malone and Clements standing in the wide doorway. "Who let you in?"

"I did, boss —" Blackie Ovens didn't look in the least uncomfortable.

"We held a gun at his head," said Malone. "Hello, Jack. Can we join in? No, don't go, Mr and Mrs Shipwood. We may have some questions to ask."

Natalie Shipwood, he noted, was in her usual all-white; he wondered what she had worn to

Marilyn Hyx's funeral. Harry Shipwood was the surprise: the spade beard had been trimmed, his hair was neat, he wore a dark grey suit, white shirt with cutaway collar, a blue-and-green striped tie. The handyman had been left behind at Sylvania Waters.

The two detectives, uninvited, sat down and Malone gestured to the Shipwoods to resume their seats. "ASIC has informed us that there was an attempted break-in Saturday night at their King Street offices."

There was silence till Harry Shipwood murmured, "Interesting."

"Yes, isn't it? Any of you know anything about it?"

"Not a thing," said Jack Aldwych.

"It's not part of our investigations, we don't do break-ins, but we thought you'd like to know."

Jack Aldwych hadn't shifted in his chair; he smiled again and nodded his head in appreciation. "You haven't lost your touch, Scobie."

"Scobie?" Natalie Shipwood couldn't hide her surprise. "You two are friends?"

"Acquaintances," said Malone. "Russ has some questions, Jack."

"I thought one of you might," said Aldwych and turned his attention to Clements.

"Several questions," said Clements, taking over the bowling. "Jack, we take it Mr Leshner has been in touch with you?"

"Curtis Leshner?" Natalie Shipwood was even more surprised this time. "Why would he have been in touch with you?"

It was her husband who, relaxed, told her the reason. "It's the nature of the game, sweetheart."

"I'm glad you appreciate that," said Aldwych.

Clements was still looking at the old man. "Jack?"

"You know he has, Russ." He turned his head towards Natalie Shipwood in the way that people do with a throwaway line: "Any company I invest in, I have my mole."

Natalie Shipwood stared at him, but when she spoke it was as if she were speaking to herself: "God, how many other — *moles* are there in Orlando?"

"I should think there is only one, sweetheart," said her husband, still relaxed. "Mr Aldwych would know if there were any more."

"You bet your life I would," said Aldwych.

"The stirrer on your board, Mrs Shipwood," said Clements, "is Mr Faulks. We'd like to talk to him."

"Find him," said Natalie Shipwood unhelpfully.

"I think we have to be more helpful than that," said Shipwood. He's relaxed enough to be seen as only on the periphery; but he keeps putting his oar in, thought Malone. "He's a builder and developer, Inspector. He is running that development out at Rooty Hill, the one where Mrs Hyx lived. Hers was the first house out there that was sold. A sort of come-on for other Orlando customers."

Malone said nothing while Clements continued: "You seem to know more about Orlando than you told us last time we saw you."

"I've been discussing it with my wife since —" He gestured, a slow opening of his hand; not a nervous gesture. "Since the roof fell in, one might say."

"So Mr Faulks might have had some contact with Mrs Hyx outside of board meetings?" said Malone.

"It's possible," said Natalie Shipwood. "If he did, neither of them ever mentioned it to me."

"Has Mr Faulks lost much money in Orlando's collapse?"

"You'd have to ask him."

"He'd be interested in what's in those papers ASIC has?" said Clements.

"You'd have to ask him."

"I think we'll do that," said Malone and stood up.

"Why'd you come to see me?" Aldwych smiled at the two detectives, a host undisturbed by guests suddenly departing.

"Just to talk about old times, Jack," said Malone. "We'll be in touch again, Mrs Shipwood. You been satisfied with the police surveillance you've been getting?"

She said nothing; it was her husband who replied: "It has the neighbours on edge."

"Only those with a guilty conscience," said Malone and looked at Aldwych, who was smiling widely. "Tell 'em about it, Jack. You used to suffer from it."

"Never a guilty conscience," said Aldwych, still smiling. "The police surveillance, yeah. A pain in the arse."

"Exactly," said Harry Shipwood.

The two detectives were at the door, Blackie Ovens waiting to show them out, when Clements turned back, looked directly at Natalie Shipwood and said, "By the way, did you know your son is sleeping with *Mrs* Faulks?"

He didn't wait for an answer, pushed Malone ahead of him through the wide hall and out the front door. "Thanks, Blackie. Give our regards to the nuns. Where are the Dobermans?"

"Chained up."

"Let 'em loose when Mr and Mrs Shipwood come out."

"I might do that. Hooroo. Been nice seeing youse again. Like the old days, only friendlier."

Outside the big gates Malone said, "That was pretty shitty, wasn't it? Telling her B.J. is having it off with Mrs Faulks?"

Clements nodded. "I couldn't resist it. She's so bloody cold-blooded —"

"She won't be when she sees B.J." He saluted the surveillance cop with a wave of his hand, got into their own car. "Let's go and find Mr Faulks."

Clements rang his ex-girlfriend in the Telstra cellar, got the phone number of Faulks' development company. "Thanks, Rosie. I'll be in touch."

"Will you?" asked Malone as Clements clicked off his phone. "What'll Romy think?"

"I won't go near her. Rosie was a learner nymphomaniac when I knew her. She probably runs her own school now. Dangerous."

The women in one's life, the shadows that never altered in memory except that some grew paler. Two years ago an old girlfriend had come back into Malone's life: she had murdered her husband and had, in turn, been murdered by a person or persons unknown. Her case was still in the files, but Malone had turned his back on it. There were other women, and a son, in his life now and they had to be protected: against the past, his past.

Clements handed him the number he had scribbled down. "The Faulks office out in Alexandria."

Malone rang the number. "Mr Faulks not there? Where can I find him? My name is Cleary, Seamus Cleary — we have a project we'd like Mr Faulks to handle ... Thank you for his number, but we'd actually basically that is, like to talk to him, see him ... Rooty Hill? Yes, we know it. Thank you. Yes, tell him we're on our way. Cleary."

He clicked off the phone and Clements said, "Why does lying come so naturally to us now?"

"Experience, son. Head for Rooty Hill."

It took them an hour to get out to Rooty Hill; traffic has increased distance without any visible extension. The Faulks development was behind the street where Nigger Brown lived and Marilyn Hyx had lived. There were more Tuscan villas, looking for candle pines and a little lost amongst the stand-offish gumtrees. The street was already paved and kerbed and Clements pulled their car in under a signpost: Siena Avenue.

Faulks had obviously been told a possible client was on the way to see him. He came towards Malone as the latter got out of the car: "Mr Cleary?"

Malone looked over his shoulder, then, apparently puzzled, looked back at Faulks. "No. Superintendent Malone. This is Inspector Clements."

Garry Faulks was a dirt-under-the-fingernails developer; he did not fit the image of a director of what had been a multi-million-dollar company. He wore khaki shorts, a blue work shirt, thick work boots; on his head was a faded yellow towelling hat. Under the hat was a face that, twenty years ago, might have been handsome; now sun, grog and fortune had coarsened it. His belly was that of a man who relaxed heavily.

He hadn't been taken in by Malone's bluff. "You use that trick much? Using another name?"

"All the time. It saves us a lot of running around," said Malone and smiled to show he and Clements wanted to be friends with the native. "Where can we talk?"

"Come down to the office."

It was halfway down the block, a mobile office. There were a dozen houses on either side of the street, all in various stages of construction, Tuscan design run riot. The city was spreading west, heading for the Blue Mountains like a tide.

"Why so many Tuscan villas?" asked Malone.

"Fad. Next year it might be Swiss chalets or Dutch inns. I'm waiting for the day when we're building fucking igloos."

Faulks stepped up into the mobile office, suggested the man in there take a break. A young man, he looked curiously at Malone and Clements as he stepped down past them, but did no more than nod to them. But he had recognised them as cops: the recognition was in his face.

The office had an air-conditioner run off a generator somewhere. Faulks waved the two detectives to two chairs, perched himself, heaving his belly up, on a desk. "Now what's this all about? Orlando?"

"Partly that." Malone let Clements do the talking; it was his case. "Partly about the murder of Mrs Hyx in the next street. You built and sold her her house?"

"Yeah, hers was the first. She came to me one day after a board meeting and said she wanted it. I said okay, it was a good advertisement for me and Orlando."

"Did you call on her after she'd moved in?"

"Yeah. Why?"

"Just as the builder or as a director of Orlando?"

Faulks studied them both for a long moment. "Look, what's your point? I mean why are you here, all the way out from Police Headquarters or wherever you come from?"

"Homicide," said Clements. "We're working police. Headquarters is just the board of directors."

"The point is," said Malone, "as a director of Orlando did you know what was going on, the last few months? Did you go and call on Mrs Hyx to see if she could tell you anything?"

The air-conditioner spluttered; without looking at it, Faulks whacked it with an open hand and it started up again. "I might of."

"Might have what?"

"Yeah, I suspected something was whiffy with Orlando. I couldn't get anything out of Mrs Shipwood, so I thought I'd try Marilyn."

"And what did she tell you?"

"Fuck-all." Faulks was beginning to lose his temper; his face was a round barometer, the mercury going up. He slid off the desk, stood up straight, hauled his shorts up his belly. "What the fuck are you getting at?"

"When she told you nothing, did you lose your temper, Mr Faulks? We've been told you have a very short fuse."

"Who told you that?"

"Oh, half a dozen people. You deny it? The short temper?"

Faulks seemed to calm down, one could see the effort. Then he said, "Look, I *liked* Marilyn. She was a very attractive woman, for her age —"

For her age: the male qualifier, as Lisa would say.

"We got on well together. I took her out a coupla times —"

Malone and Clements were surprised, but they were beyond showing it.

"Did anyone know that? Your fellow directors? Mrs Shipwood?" Malone paused before he said, "Your wife?"

"No, no-one. Marilyn was — well, discreet. We both were."

"Did you pick her up at her house? Drive her home?" How had Nigger Brown and his wife missed them?

"No, never. We'd meet in Parramatta, have dinner, that sorta thing. The only time I went to her house, I walked there from here, one Sat'day morning. Look, I'd of never harmed Marilyn —" The temper went out of his face. All at once he looked sad, another man. "If you wanna know, I cried when I heard what had happened to her. The guys here wondered what had happened to me."

"Did your wife notice anything?"

"What's she got to do with it?" The face reddened again; or pinked.

"We just try to cover all angles, Mr Faulks," said Malone. "We're investigating a murder."

Faulks had a quick mind: "Christ, you don't think my wife might of —" He shook his head. "Nah, she didn't know a thing about Marilyn. And she wouldn't of done anything like murder — Christ, no. She'd just ask for half our property and go for a walk."

"You have trouble, Mr Faulks," said Malone and stood up. "Thanks for your time. We may be in touch again."

"Look — what I told you about Marilyn? Does that go in the record?"

"No. We'll let her rest in peace, as they say."

He and Clements left the mobile office and walked up the street. Workmen, clambering up and down roof frames like oversized kids on playground equipment, stopped suddenly and watched them. Then they went back to work; hammers clacked-clacked-clacked. A cement truck spun its bowl slowly, oozing out grey dough. Life went on, as they say.

When they reached their car Malone leaned on the roof and looked across at Clements. "I think Mrs Hyx was a pretty complex woman, what d'you reckon?"

Clements nodded. "More so than a lot I've known."

"She was a trusted private secretary, yet she was going to shaft the woman who trusted her.

She slept with young B.J. and it looks as if she got into bed with Mr Faulks. Yet the last two weeks of her life, Nigger told us, she went to Mass every morning and she had a vision, the Virgin Mary paying her a visit. Was she a sinner looking for grace before she did the dirty on her boss? Or was she making it up?"

"I wouldn't know, mate. Sin never worried me. I left that to you Catholics."

"We indulge in it, son, so that we can get moral about it . . . In that strong-box, did Marilyn leave a will?"

Clements' memory was as good as that of a computer. "No."

"Well, we'd better find out if she left one and where. In the meantime, while we're out here let's go around to her place and see what's happening. If the house has been put up for sale and who's selling it. We might even find Mr Hicks out front, spruiking the sale."

But there was no Mr Hicks and no FOR SALE sign outside the house when they pulled up in front of it. They got out of their car, stood for a moment looking at the house.

"What's in the garage, I wonder?" said Malone.

"I don't think people leave their wills in their garage."

Then a woman came out of the Brown house, hurried across to them. "Can I help you?"

274

"Mrs Brown. I'm Superintendent Malone and this is Inspector Clements."

"Oh yes." She was small and plump; hidden somewhere in her was a girl who had once been pretty. "My husband told me about you."

"We were just acquaintances," said Malone. "A long time ago."

She was grateful. "Thanks for putting it like that. Cyril —"

"Who?"

"Cyril, my husband and me, we've been keeping an eye on Mrs Hyx's house. Once a week Cyril takes her car for a run, just to keep it up to scratch, he says. He's a car man, a wonder since he sees so many of 'em smashed to bits."

"Is it in the garage?" asked Clements.

"Sure. You wanna look?" She produced a bunch of keys from an apron pocket; she had come prepared. "It's a Volvo, she bought it when she moved in here."

She opened the garage doors. A pale blue Volvo stood there, looking as if it had just been wheeled out of a display window. "Cyril washed it the other day and polished it. I think he's got his eye on it, if it comes up for sale."

"Did the local police find anything in it? In the glove-box or the boot?"

She shook her head. "I wouldn't know. Cyril was the one talked to them —"

Clements had been going through the car. He straightened up, came out of the garage to where Malone and Mrs Brown stood in the yellow sunlight. He sniffed, there was smoke in the air, but made no comment on it.

"Nothing. The local Crime Scene fellers look like they cleaned it out."

"Mrs Brown," said Malone, "your husband —" He caught himself just before *Nigger* slipped out. "Cyril, he said Mrs Hyx had a vision just before she was murdered. Did she describe it to you?"

"Not really. I think she was embarrassed to mention it. The Virgin Mary, you know, the Mother of Christ —"

"I'm a Catholic, Mrs Brown. But like your husband, I found it a bit hard to believe. The Madonna of Rooty Hill —"

"I know. We laugh about it, but — I dunno. She might of. Do you believe in visions?"

"I'm afraid not, Mrs Brown. Maybe it's the cop, not the Catholic, in me." He looked sideways at Clements. "Inspector Clements is an unbeliever in every way."

"Especially in visions," said Clements.

Mrs Brown might be devout, but she wasn't without a sense of humour. "I told our parish priest about it and he hoped it hadn't happened. Said he had enough trouble coping with the Archbishop, let alone having the Vatican land on him. Imagine!"

"Where did Marilyn see the vision? She tell you?"

"Out in the back garden at night, late."

"I'd move," said Malone and grinned.

"Go on!" She laughed and hit him gently on the arm. He could see how happy Nigger, *Cyril*, would be, coming home from a gore-smeared smash on the freeway, to her sympathetic arms. "I'll tell Cyril you were here."

"Take care, Mrs Brown."

Against murder, freeway smashes, visions, everything.

Chapter Ten

❦

1

Mick Kelray was depressed. Then, when he opened the letter and saw the heading:

FAIRBROTHER, MILSON & GUDERSEN

SOLICITORS

it seemed that his heart stopped. Then he read on and when he had finished the short letter he was, to his surprise, weeping.

"What's the matter, love?" Phoebe had wheeled herself in from the kitchen.

He held up the letter. "It's from some solicitors. Marilyn has left us her estate. Everything, it looks like."

Phoebe said nothing, sat shocked and motionless in the wheelchair. She was still in her nightgown and dressing-gown, in which, to him, she always looked smaller and frailer. Then she blinked, shook her head and looked at him. "Why would she remember us? Like that?"

He dried his eyes, took hold of her limp hand and told her of his visit to her sister.

"Why didn't you tell me, Mick? We never had secrets from each other."

"I didn't want you worrying. Love, we're broke, skint. I been wondering how to tell you. She told me what her bitch of a boss had done. We're not the only ones, hundreds like us, maybe thousands, I dunno, we've done the lot. All we've got is this house and our pension. But now . . ."

She took her hand out of his, turned her head away for a moment, then looked back at him. She was not wearing her glasses and her eyes seemed frightened. "Mick, what else did she say when you saw her?"

"What d'you mean?"

"She say anything about you and me?"

"Only that she was sorry you'd had a barney, stayed apart all these years. That was all."

"Mick, I've had a secret I never told you —"

He reached for her hand again. "What?"

"She was in love with you."

"No!" He involuntarily tried to take his hand out of hers, but she clung to it. "I never give her a second look —"

"I didn't say you did. But she was in love with you. I never told you, but that was why we quarrelled. She was young, full of herself, everything was hers, she thought. She'd tried to take you away from me if she could of —" She was suddenly very composed; and that surprised him. "It was here in this house, she'd come to tea one day when you were working overtime — I told her to get out and never come back —" For a moment the composure broke; she heaved a deep sigh, letting emotion out of her. "I wish it had never happened. Maybe she did, too."

He could think of nothing to say. There was a faint recollection of Marilyn in those days: a bit of a wild thing, boyfriends in a queue. But never a pass at him, none that he could remember.

"Don't worry about it, love," said Phoebe and squeezed his hand.

"I can't help it — I been worrying for the past month. Keeping my mouth shut, not wanting to worry you —"

"I meant, don't worry about why Marilyn and I quarrelled. It's over, Mick." She squeezed his hand again. "We'll get by, love. Things aren't as bad as —"

"As what?"

She smiled and he leaned forward and kissed her: he had always loved her smile. Then she said, "As they are in *The Bold and the Beautiful*."

"Christ, I should hope not!"

Then they both laughed and she said, "Ring the solicitors and make an appointment. We'll see what she's left us. Maybe some things my mum and dad had, that she wants to pass on to us."

"Love, we can't go by car, not into the city.

Parking is bloody hopeless — I'll go on me own, by bus —"

"No, we go together." She was gathering herself together: Herself, him, the future. "Spend some money, Mick — we may never be able to do it again. Get one of those taxis that take wheelchairs. Let's be bold and beautiful, just once."

"Christ, I love you!" he said and wept again.

When he rang the solicitors they told him Miz Gudersen would see him at 3.30 that afternoon. He hung up and said, "Miz Gudersen will see us this arvo."

"*Miz*? Whatever happened to Miss and Missus? Anyone call me Miz Kelray, I'd run over 'em in my wheelchair."

Kelray got his only suit out of the wardrobe, brushed, sponged and pressed it. He ironed a white shirt and found a tie that had no stains on it; it was a Waterside Workers' Federation tie and he couldn't remember why or when he had worn it; certainly not when on strike. He pressed a green blouse for Phoebe and brushed and pressed the jacket and skirt she wore. Then he cleaned both his and her shoes. He felt neither bold nor beautiful, but it was worth a try.

At three o'clock the taxi called for them and Phoebe, in her wheelchair, was lifted into the raised rear section of the taxi. The driver was Italian, voluble and sympathetic. He chattered at them both while he drove them into the city —

"Phillip Street, that right? Where all them lawyers hang out, with their funny wigs and things. I got a kid at university, he doing law. Snotty little bastard, knows everything, he lucky I don't kick him outa the house. He'll finish up a judge, but I'll be dead by then. We all will be, won't we, eventually?"

"Eventually," said Mick Kelray: *but not today*. He turned round and grinned at Phoebe, sitting up like the Queen Mum in the back of the taxi.

"Wave to the peasants, love," he said and she smiled at him and did.

"Could you come back and pick us up at 4.30?" he asked when they arrived outside the building that housed Fairbrother, Milson & Gudersen. "Getting a cab like yours is not easy, mate."

"No worries, mate. I'll be here, 4.30, or as close as I can get to it. Hope you not gunna get bad news in there."

"No worries, mate," said Mick Kelray.

Ms Gudersen came out of her office to greet the Kelrays. She was an attractive woman in her mid-thirties; her dark curly hair was drawn back in a chignon and she was (Phoebe had heard the expression) power-suited. But she was pleasant and welcoming and she had good news:

"Your sister, Mrs Kelray, has left you all her estate. It has to go through probate, but you will inherit her house at Rooty Hill, her car and all her stocks and shares, plus a sizeable balance in her bank account. Oh, and she also left a brooch, which I gather has sentimental value for you both?"

"My mother's," said Phoebe.

Mick Kelray looked at her, worried for her; but she was holding up well. He was surprised at how at ease he felt here in these unaccustomed surroundings. The wood panelling, the glass-fronted bookcase with its shelves of law books, the big desk behind which Miz Gudersen sat: this was the solid life he'd read about. It gave him comfort, something he hadn't expected.

"I don't wanna sound — well, *greedy*. But what's the estate worth?"

Ms Gudersen looked at a paper on her desk. "The house at Rooty Hill is valued, in round figures, at $350,000. The stocks and shares are, again in round figures, $300,000. The car — well, about $40,000. The bank balance $17,000. That's —" She did a quick mental calculation; Kelray was impressed that she hadn't reached for a calculator, the crutch of the young. "It's just over $700,000."

"Holy Jesus!" said Mick Kelray and put his hand on Phoebe's.

"He gets excited," said Phoebe. "Men do, about money."

"Some women, too," said Ms Gudersen, surrounded by lawyers' fees. "But I hope you're happy about the will?"

Phoebe nodded; she was still calm. "I am. I'm just —" She stopped and looked at Mick. Then she looked back at the lawyer. "I'm sorry I spent so long separated from my sister."

All of a sudden Mick Kelray had a thought: "When did she make the will? When's it dated?"

Ms Gudersen looked at the date. "September 7th."

"Jesus —"

"What's the matter?" said Phoebe.

"She must have had a premonition someone was gunna kill her."

2

Maureen and Tom were in the beer garden of The Sheaf hotel in Double Bay. It was not yet crowded, but at least half the tables were occupied. Maureen had a vodka, lime and soda in front of her and Tom had a beer in hand when Idaho Breslin stopped by their table.

"Hello," she said a little hesitantly. "Mind if I sit down a moment? Or am I interrupting something?"

Tom looked blank for a moment, then he looked at Maureen and laughed. "This is my sister Maureen. She goes for more intellectual types than me, ABC guys, even the odd newspaper guy. Idaho Breslin, Mo."

Idaho was embarrassed, looked at Maureen. "Sorry. He has girls all over him —"

"Don't we know it?" said Maureen. "You like a drink?"

"No, I have to meet some friends." She looked at Tom. "I'm off to Melbourne. I've landed a part in a TV soap, it means six months work. I play a cop ... I wanted to get out of Sydney, get as far away as I could —"

"It's a good idea," said Tom and raised his glass to her. "Good luck. If I come to Melbourne, maybe we can have dinner or something?"

"Yes," she said, "We were just getting to know each other —"

Maureen, the born investigator, watched her brother and this big, attractive girl sitting miles apart at the small table, Tom suddenly wary, Idaho (what a name!) trying to compress the distance between them. *She's in love with him; or wants to be.*

"I haven't seen you here before," said Idaho.

Maureen looked around her, then back at Idaho. "I've just found out I can't stand crowds. I'm a journo, people are my source, my material, but I prefer to take them in small doses."

"You could've fooled me," said her brother.

"We women could fool you any time we wanted," said Maureen, then smiled at both of them to show she didn't mean it. Or not much.

"I understand what you mean," said Idaho. "I sometimes wonder why I wanted to be an actor —"

Maureen remarked her voice. In the chatter around them Idaho could be heard clearly. Like her father Maureen was a fan of Late Late Movies and she remembered Barbara Stanwyck, who had the sort of voice that could be heard through the tangled wires of noise. Idaho's was like that, though less rough than Stanwyck's.

Then Idaho looked up and said, "Oh hello, Barry —"

Maureen looked up at the slim blond man who had paused by their table. He looked at Tom first, then at the two girls. "Haven't seen you here lately —"

"No," said Idaho. "I just haven't felt like it, not since ... This is Tom's sister. Barry Mackaw."

Tom had told her of Mackaw. The journalist, the investigator, in her took over: "Sit down for a moment, Barry. Idaho is off to Melbourne."

Mackaw hesitated, then sat down. He was wearing a dark blue shirt and bone-coloured slacks; on his wrist was a heavy gold watch. Maureen was taking inventory of him, but he wouldn't have known.

"Like a drink? Buy him a drink, Tom." She was suddenly provocative and felt Tom kick her under the table.

"No, thanks. I got to meet some of the guys." Then Mackaw, as if aware that he was trapped, if only for a few moments, looked, *stared*, at Tom. "Your old man questioned me, I suppose he told you?"

Tom's gaze was just as steady. "No, he didn't. He never talks business with us, does he, Mo?"

"Never," said Maureen. "It's a rule in our house, our mum applies it. But since you brought it up, Barry, what'd he question you about?"

"Stop it, Mo," said Tom. "She's a journo, Barry. Watch her."

"Oh, I don't mind," said Mackaw and settled more comfortably on his chair. "I understand they questioned you, too. Maybe not your dad, but the cops. And Idaho. Everybody who knew Lucinda. Did you know her?" he asked Maureen. It was more than a question, it was a hardball thrown at her. *You won't get the better of me, journo.*

"No, I didn't. Idaho here is the first of Tom's friends I've met. And you." She gave him a smile sickly sweet. Hardball questions at Maureen always bounced back. Out of the corner of her eye she saw Tom grin.

"We're not friends," said Mackaw. "Acquaintances, right?"

"Best of acquaintances," said Tom. "Bosom strangers."

"Well, we won't be that much longer —"

Maureen, sharp-eyed, thought she saw Mackaw take a deep breath, like a man taking a high dive. He has to have the last word, she thought.

"— I'm leaving for the States next week. The firm are transferring me to New York."

"Lucky you," said Idaho. "For how long?"

"Two years. It's a lucky break — well, not so lucky. I've earned it."

"Yeah, you must have," said Tom. "Well, good luck. Don't get involved with any of those New York girls. I see 'em on *Sex and the City*. You wouldn't wanna be married to any of 'em."

"Not like us, eh?" said Maureen and smiled at Idaho, who smiled back.

Mackaw stood up. "Well, good luck in Melbourne, Idaho." He made it sound as if she were heading for Antarctica. "Nice meeting you, Maureen."

He went off and Maureen thought: he's so bloody sure of himself. Then she said, "What do you think of him, Idaho?"

"I don't know what Lucinda ever saw in him. But we're a myopic lot sometimes, aren't we, us girls? Well, I better be going." She stood up and Tom, a gentleman, stood up with her. "Goodbye, Tom. Look after yourself. If you come to Melbourne —"

"Sure," he said and kissed her on the cheek.

She left them, walking away into faint memory, unless one saw her in the future in the soap opera. Tom stared after her, then sat down.

Maureen said, "Give her encouragement and she'd fall in love with you."

"I got a hint of it."

"You're sure of yourself, bro."

He grinned. "Not really. When it happens, I want to be really sure."

He took out his mobile phone.

"Who are you calling?"

"Dad."

3

"Tom called me last night," said Malone. "Barry Mackaw is being transferred to New York. Next week."

"I wonder if he applied for the transfer?" said Clements. "Or whether Foxglove etcetera are getting him out of the way because of the Orlando paper shredding?"

"Maybe a bit of both. Have you wondered why he killed that girl?"

"Haven't you?" Clements shrugged. "Maybe she was strong-arming him, maybe she wasn't sure who put her up the duff. She put the word on Tom, didn't she?"

Malone nodded. "It could've been anyone's. Or it could've been Mackaw's and that wasn't in his scheme of things. Can you hold him?"

"No. I've had John and Gail and Sheryl going through everything again, and all we've got is we know he did it and we haven't got a skerrick of proof."

They were in Malone's office, Clements seemingly more comfortable in his chair now. Malone was slowly becoming accustomed to his desk, though it was still relatively free of paper. Reports came in every day, the tides of crime, but he was just on the mailing list, they were not his cases. His new cards, like final notices, had arrived sooner than he had expected: SUPERINTENDENT SCOBIE MALONE. He had crossed the boundary, there was no going back.

"What have you come up with on the Hyx case?"

"Nothing. We're at a standstill there. There were two more jobs last night, a domestic and a buggered-up hold-up at a service station. Both out west, but the locals haven't called us in on them, not yet. I just wish they would, give us something where we're not up against a blank wall."

"Have you checked everyone at Orlando? Someone who might've had it in for Mrs Hyx?"

"Everyone. If anyone has it in for anyone, it's for Mrs Shipwood. We've checked the board — our two main suspects are Sweden and Faulks, but I don't think it's either of them. Sweden would have the best reasons, if Marilyn was going to dob him in. But with a knife? He'd either shoot her or have a hitman ... The rest of the directors?" He shook his head. "Yes-men. They turn up, listen to what the chairperson has to say, touch the forelock, draw their money and go home. From what I read, the country's full of them."

"Spoken like a true shareholder."

"Maybe I should look up my stars, see if there's any good luck for me the next coupla weeks."

"What'll they tell you? Astrology charts are for the under-thirty-fives. I looked up my dad's chart last Sunday — he's eighty and this Wednesday a tall dark stranger's going to come into his life and love is on the horizon. I read it out to Mum ... Yes?"

Sheryl Dallen had appeared in the doorway. "Excuse me for interrupting, sir —"

Sir, not boss: the boundary was receding.

"There's a Mr Kelray wants to talk to us. John and I saw him last week about the Rossiter case. I left him my card — he's just called. He'll be here in half an hour."

"Thanks, Sheryl," said Clements. When she had gone he looked back at Malone. "You want to sit in on it?"

"So long as I keep my mouth shut?"

"Yes," said Clements, the boss.

4

Mick Kelray had agonised over whether he should call that nice girl from Homicide. He had not always been a law-abiding man, not down on the wharves; down there it had been, too often, us and them. He had brought home stuff that had fallen out of busted crates or off the backs of trucks; it wasn't stealing, just tidying up. He had busted the head of a strike scab or two; that wasn't assault, just wounds in a small war. He had seen blokes, scum, who helped the drug smugglers, but he had never dobbed them in; he was not public-spirited, let the public look after itself. But now he was tempted to dob in someone ...

"What d'you reckon, love?" He had never before asked her for advice on conscience.

"You think he might have had something to do with that poor girl's murder?"

"I dunno. He might of. He might have had nothing to do with killing her, and I'd be dobbing him in —"

She was, always had been, more public-spirited than he. Isolated in her wheelchair, on a thin tributary of the mainstream, she was all for law and order. "Mick, think of that girl —"

"I never knew her, Phoebe. I only knew the other one, the one with the funny name. Idaho or Iowa or Utah, some State in America. The dead one might of got what was coming to her —"

"Mick."

He had said the wrong thing. "Sorry. You're right, she didn't deserve to be strangled —"

"Mick, our luck has turned. Except —" She paused a moment and he thought she was going to cry; then she went on: "Except for Marilyn's death."

"That was what turned our luck."

"I know. But I try not to think about it. We'd like to know who killed her. That girl's parents, they'd like to know who killed her."

He nodded, but was still reluctant. "I dunno —"

"Are we gunna move out to Rooty Hill or stay here?"

"Love, I've seen her house, you'll like it. It's like all the kids say — it's *fantastic*. We can put one of them lift things in on the stairs. There's a lot of land, I might even take up gardening —"

She laughed, loving him till it hurt. "You couldn't grow a weed —"

"I can try," he said, laughing with her. "We'll have no trouble selling this place — yuppies will jump at it —"

"There aren't yuppies any more. They're upwardly mobile or something —" She was a student of the social scale, educated by TV. "When are you gunna take me out there to see it?"

"Tomorrow. But first, what about me seeing the police? You think I oughta give 'em a call, tell 'em about that young bloke?"

"I think you should, Mick."

So he had called Detective Dallen and now it was the next morning and here he was at Homicide with her, her boss and Superintendent Malone, Con Malone's son.

"Well, before I start, I better explain something. Youse are on that Orlando Development thing? No, I don't mean it going down the drain. I mean the murder of Marilyn Hyx."

Malone could feel the lift of excitement all round and he murmured, "Connections."

"Yes, Mr Kelray," said Clements. "That's why you're here?"

"Well, no, not exactly. But — well, the wife is Marilyn Hyx's sister. We've just found out everything she owned, she's left to us. I'd been to see her, not telling the wife, and I had that on my mind the night I saw this young bloke come outa the house where the girl, I've forgotten her name, was murdered."

"Rossiter," said Sheryl Dallen. "Lucinda Rossiter."

"Yeah, that was it. I didn't know her, not to talk to her, but I used to nod and say hullo to one of the girls lived with her. Miss Breslin, Idaho or Utah or something."

"What did you see that night?" asked Clements.

Mick Kelray looked around him. This was new territory to him, police territory. Out beyond the glass partition of Clements' office he could see the desks and the computers and the big board, which he didn't know was called the flow-chart, with photos on it and lines drawn. Several detectives, men and women, were at the desks, some of them staring at their computer screens. This, he guessed, was what he had once read was called the business of policing. And now he was part of it, if only for half an hour.

"I was out at my car, doing something to it, I've forgotten what, and this young bloke come running out of Number 22, the girls' place. He came up towards me, didn't seem to see me at first. Then he saw me, turned around and skedaddled down the street."

"Would you know him if you saw him again?"

"I think so. I got a good eye for faces —" He looked at Malone. "Your old man, Con, he'll tell you that. You stand in a picket line a day, a week, and you read faces. Yeah, I'd know him, no worries."

"Why didn't you mention this when we came to see you?" said Sheryl Dallen. "Sergeant Kagal and I?"

"I told you," he said carefully. "I had other things on me mind. You saw the wife that day — she's on me mind all the time —"

"We understand that," said Sheryl, all at once sympathetic again, and he looked at her gratefully.

"Well, we'll bring him in, put him in a line-up and you can identify him," said Clements.

"You know who he is?" said Kelray.

Clements nodded. "We just have to have him identified. You'll help us wrap up the case. But don't discuss it with anyone, okay? That's important."

"Not even with the wife?"

Malone and Clements, married men, looked at each other; then Malone said with a grin, "Righto, discuss it with your wife." Then he went on, "Mr Kelray, you said you'd been to see Mrs Hyx. Did she say anything to you about the way things were for her at Orlando? If she felt threatened?"

He frowned, trying to remember. He was getting old, too bloody old for memory games. "No, I can't remember her saying anything like that. She told me how her boss had salted away money overseas somewhere, she didn't say where — she said she didn't think her boss' family knew how much there was. But no, she didn't say anything about anyone threatening her."

"Did she look or sound worried?"

"Not that I remember. But she must of been — I found out yest'day, from the solicitors, she made her will just before she'd seen me or around then. Her and my wife hadn't spoken for twenty years and she seemed more concerned about that. The wife feels the same way. Lost years, my wife calls it ... Well, when d'you want me to have a look at this bloke?"

"This afternoon?" said Clements. "We'll have to round up other guys to stand in the line-up."

"Well —" Mick Kelray looked uncomfortable. "This afternoon I promised to take the wife out to look at Marilyn's house. We're gunna put ours on the market and move out there. She's looking forward to it —"

Clements glanced at Malone, then looked back at Kelray: "We're married men, Mr Kelray, we understand. No comment, Detective Dallen —"

"Haven't said a word, boss," said Sheryl Dallen and winked at Mick Kelray.

The mood had been lightened. Clements said,

"We'll pick up our suspect and have him at Bay Street station tomorrow morning for a line-up. We'll send a car for you at 9.30, that okay?"

"When you go out there, to Rooty Hill," said Malone, "do you have a key to the house?"

"No, I forgot about that —" Mick Kelray shook his head at his forgetfulness.

"Go next door, the house on the right. There's a Mrs Brown there, she was a friend of your sister-in-law. A good neighbour. She'll let you in, she has a key. We hope you like the house, Mr Kelray."

"What room was she — was she murdered in?"

"The living room —" Malone shook his head. "Dead in the living room ... Sorry, Mr Kelray."

"It's okay. I'll tell the wife it happened outside somewhere ...I better tell you now. When I give the nod tomorrow morning against that young bloke, I'm not gunna feel too good."

"Mr Kelray," said Malone gently, "all you'll be doing is helping us. We have to prepare all the evidence for the prosecution. After that it's up to the judge and the jury. No-one ever convicts another man on his own. At least not in our system."

"Yeah, I guess so." Kelray hesitated, then he put out his hand and shook hands all round. "The thing I gotta keep in mind is that young girl dead —"

"That's the way we look at it," said Clements. "The victim."

Sheryl Dallen escorted Kelray out of the building while Malone and Clements sat and looked at each other. "One down, one to go. I think I might look up my astrology chart."

"For a tall dark stranger. Try your luck."

That evening Malone went home, had dinner, sat with Lisa and watched television. They surfed through seven cookery shows, three quiz shows, four survival shows ("Wouldn't it be nice if none of them survived?" said Lisa) and watched two cops solve a multiple murder case in less than an hour. Lisa made them tea and toast, then they went to bed.

She lay in the crook of his arm, one leg thrown over his, the pretzel of love. "Are you still uninterested?"

"No. Tomorrow morning we'll wrap this one up and though it's Russ' case, I'll get satisfaction from it."

"I'm glad." She raised her leg a little higher on his. "It's just struck me, I've never slept with a superintendent before."

"I've never slept with a superintendent's wife. You come here often?"

"All the time. Where's your loving hand?"

"On its way."

5

Next morning Malone went over to the Bay Street station. It was on the edge of Darling Harbour, opposite an amusement park, overshadowed by new tall apartment buildings. He should not have gone and he didn't tell Clements he was going. This was not his territory nor was the Rossiter murder his case.

Rupe Steeple obviously saw it that way: "Why are you here, sir?"

Respect the rank: "Sergeant, I'm not here for the Rossiter line-up. I want to see Mr Kelray on another matter. The Orlando case, the murder of Marilyn Hyx."

"Kelray is involved in *that*?"

"Only on the edge, peripherally, as they say. Mrs Hyx was his wife's sister."

"It's a small world."

"We're all connected, Rupe."

"Yeah," said Steeple, a sketch of a grin on his mouth. "You're on the periphery of this one, as they say."

"At the very edge. You got Barry Mackaw inside?"

"We're about to do the line-up now. Finding young blokes this hour of the morning for the line-up ain't easy. Mackaw wasn't too bloody happy when my guys picked him up."

"He won't be too happy when Kelray gives him the nod."

"You're sure of him?"

"Dead sure, Rupe. You can start writing out the ticket now."

There were seven young men in the identification parade. It was organised by a senior sergeant, an officer not connected with the case; that was the protocol, to ensure impartiality. Malone stood well back so that Mackaw would not see him. Mackaw was Number 4 in the line-up of men around his own age and height. Three blonds, three with darker hair, all with the fashionable just-out-of-bed hairstyle: Malone wondered where they had been found. Mackaw stood confidently in place, as if the other six were under suspicion and he was there only to make up the numbers.

But Mick Kelray was in no doubt. He walked up and down the line twice, taking his time; then came out and said something to the senior sergeant, who nodded to Steeple. Then he saw Malone and came across to him.

"Not here, Mick. Outside." Malone led the way out of the station, not wanting to see Mackaw brought out, not wanting to be seen. That case was over, bar the trial.

Out in the early morning sunshine, traffic edging by like thick metal sludge, Kelray said, "He's the one, Superintendent, no worries. Like I said, I remember faces. Soon's he looked at me, he knew he was done. He remembered my face."

"Thanks Mick — mind if I call you Mick?"

"That's what I been all me life. Go ahead." Mick Kelray seemed a new man this morning. "What can I do for you?"

"Mick, when you saw Mrs Hyx, Marilyn, did she mention to you that she'd been overseas at any time?"

"Yeah, early in the piece, when we were getting to know one another again, she said she'd had a coupla trips. To America and to England and Europe. Organised tours, I think they were."

"She ever mention going to the Caribbean?"

"Where's that? Oh, the West Indies, around there? No. Come to think of it, there'd of been souvenirs, I guess, if she'd been there. I dunno what there'd of been, bongo drums, I dunno. When the wife and me were out at her house yest'day we had a good look-around. There was souvenirs all over the place —"

Relatives, the original forensic team: sharper-eyed than police.

"— pictures, some things from Disneyland, a mug with a coat-of-arms on it, things like that. Nothing that looked like it come from the Caribbean."

"Righto, Mick. And thanks." He nodded back into the station. "For everything."

"Glad to be of help. Oh, we met that Mrs Brown and her husband. Looks like they'll be good neighbours. Not swingers, not like we're surrounded with in Pyrmont."

"No, Mick, definitely not swingers."

"Well, hooroo. Give my regards to your old man. Salt of the earth, a real union man. The old days —"

He went off to the police car that was waiting to take him back to swinging Pyrmont, to the narrow terrace house soon to be sold, to Phoebe waiting to be wheeled into their new life, no matter how short it might be for her.

Rupe Steeple came out. "Well, he's been charged. He's already called his lawyer, but he knows he's done like a dinner. He'll probably be out on bail tomorrow morning, but it's all over for him. Thanks, Scobie."

"For what?"

Again the sketch of a grin. "For the connection. Give my regards to your son."

Malone drove back to Strawberry Hills, went up to his office and rang Tom at his investment bank: "They arrested Barry Mackaw this morning and charged him."

There was silence for a moment at the other end of the line, then Tom said, "Good, the bastard deserved it. You have anything to do with it?"

"No. Russ and Sergeant Steeple. I was just on the sideline, the periphery."

"Bull. Thanks, Dad," said Tom and hung up.

Malone sat back, looked at the phone with satisfaction for a long moment; then he picked it up again and rang Bob Anders at ASIC:

"Bob, in all that paper on Orlando, is there anything that tells you when the first money was transferred overseas to any bank, say Switzerland or in the Caribbean?"

"Scobie, I can't tell you that. This is confidential evidence —"

"What if I give you other confidential evidence? Look into Foxglove, Berenger — they've been shredding paper, Orlando paper."

"Scobie —"

"Bob, you owe me. I don't care a stuff about Orlando, but I do care about the woman who was murdered. That's what I'm trying to trace — who murdered her."

There was silence, then Anders said, "Okay, but if you have to use the information, you don't say where you got it —"

"Not a word."

"I'll be back to you."

In the Good Old Days it would probably have taken a day or two for the information to surface. It hurt Malone to think it, but computers have their advantages. Bob Anders was back on the line in ten minutes:

"The first transfer went to Zurich just over three years ago, July 1998. Then, apparently, it was decided the Shahriver Bank in the Turks and Caicos was a less conspicuous haven. Little did they know," he said. "We've had those banks there and in the Caymans targeted for months."

"Glad to hear it," said Malone. "Go on."

"An account was opened at the Shahriver in December 1998 and the Swiss money was transferred."

"Someone would have had to go there to open the account?"

"I should think so, the size of it. In all, in the past two, nearly three years, Mrs Shipwood has deposited just on 30 million in the Shahriver Bank. Didn't they have a branch here in Sydney?"

"Once upon a time — they came up in another case. But they closed down, I guess they thought we'd made them too conspicuous. Thanks, Bob. Take care."

"You, too, Scobie. Good luck."

Malone put down the phone, stared at it, debating whether to pick it up and call Clements. Then the old domain called; he was still more at home in Homicide than here in Crime Agency. He stood up, but Greg Random was blocking his doorway.

"Going out? You do more gallivanting than any superintendent I know."

"Just round to see Russ. They wrapped up that Pyrmont case this morning. The kid who did it was picked out of a line-up."

"Good. That was the one your son was involved in?"

"Not *involved* in. He and the dead girl's housemate found the body."

"You're on the defensive."

"Wouldn't you be?"

"My girls, all three of them, they go to places I keep expecting to be raided and they keep telling me there's nothing to worry about. Maybe cops should be celibate, like priests."

"I suggested that once to Lisa."

"What happened?"

"She took off her nightgown."

"We're the weaker sex, you know that? Show us some cleavage and we dive in fully clothed … How's the Orlando thing going?"

"I'm on my way to talk to Russ about it now. You want to sit in?"

"No, thanks. The less I know about boardroom shenanigans, the better I feel."

He left, fading away in his ghost-like way, and Malone went round to Homicide. Clements was at his desk, sifting through paperwork as if it were garbage. "G'day. Homesick?"

"That's about the strength of it." Malone sank down on to the couch beneath the window, into the dip scooped into it by Clements' backside in the past. "I saw Mick Kelray this morning."

"Interfering again? When will you learn?"

"Simmer down." As Clements had often told him. "I didn't interfere in that line-up for that kid Mackaw. They've charged him incidentally."

"I know. Rupe Steeple's already been on to me. He wasn't happy about you putting in an appearance down there at Bay Street."

"Righto, everyone's unhappy. But the Rossiter case and Tom's part in it is not why I'm here. I talked to Kelray about Marilyn Hyx —"

Clements brushed aside the papers in front of him, leaned forward with his elbows on the desk. "Mate, I don't like saying this. But when are you gunna learn — on our cases, Homicide, you talk to me before you go gallivanting off on your own initiative. That's not the way the system works and you should know it as well as anyone. You didn't come in off the street yesterday."

"All right, I'm just an apprentice superintendent. But be patient with me —"

"I'm trying. Hard." Clements leaned back as if he were exhausted.

Malone told him of his conversation with Mick Kelray. "When I got back here I called Bob Anders. If you want to know, he ticked me off, too, for straying off my patch —"

"Like I said, you'll learn."

"He listened to me and he got back to me. Our gal Natalie deposited just on 30 million in the Turks and Caicos Islands over the past two to three years. Bob says someone would have had to go there to open an account that size. I want you to get the girls to get in touch with Immigration and all the overseas airlines, see if anyone connected with Orlando headed in the direction of the Caribbean during that period. Mrs Shipwood, any of her family, any of the directors —"

"It's a wild shot —"

"I shot an arrow into the air ... Never mind. Get the girls on to it."

"Never mind the girls. I'll get Andy on it." Clements stood up, gestured out through the half-glass wall that separated him from the main office.

A moment later Andy Graham appeared in the doorway. "Yes, boss?"

Boss: the old, familiar term, now an echo.

"Andy, the superintendent has something we want you to work on —"

Graham sat down in the chair opposite Clements, turned to Malone, who, on the couch, was below his level. "Hi, sir, what can I do for you?"

He was big and clumsy, crashing his way through the office and life like a good-tempered buffalo. Some of his colleagues thought of him as that; but Malone had always seen him as Homicide's bloodhound, still as eager as a novice after ten years in the squad. They should send him out after Osama bin Laden, thought Malone, he would bring him in within days. "Andy, it'll be tedious, but this is what we want —"

Graham listened without interrupting; then he said, "No problem. It may take a bit of time, but you'll get what you want. The list, Orlando's board, all that, it's in the computer, boss?"

"Everything's there," said Clements. "All we want is what you'll find in Immigration's and the airlines' computers."

"No worries," said Andy Graham and galloped off, hitting the door jamb as he went out, bouncing off it and plunging on.

"He exhausts me," said Malone, "but I wouldn't trade him for a dozen computers. You and Romy coming for dinner tonight?"

"I've got a bottle of Grange '92, fell off the back of a truck. I'll bring it and maybe we can have a celebratory drink in advance. I'm really looking forward to nailing Mrs Shipwood. Did Bob Anders tell you about the bonuses she and Sweden paid themselves two months before the wheels fell off? Three million each. She may not have done in Marilyn Hyx, but I want her nailed to the wall, anyhow."

"I'll supply the hammer."

Chapter Eleven

❧

1

"If I'd known you were bringing such an expensive wine," said Lisa, "I'd have made something more exotic than steak-and-kidney pie. Pheasant or venison, a real European dish. Made us feel at home, yes, Romy?"

"Dumplings and sauerkraut," said Clements. "Steak-and-kidney pie was invented for a Grange."

"Where'd you get it?"

"Don't ask," said Malone. "He says it fell off the back of a truck."

"I'll tell you where he got it," said Romy. "It came into the morgue one day with a body. No relatives or friends claimed *him* — he still hasn't been identified. So I claimed the wine, otherwise it would have finished up in the Minister's office."

"You're lucky Maureen isn't here," said Malone. "*Four Corners* would make a show out of that. How are things at the morgue? Busy?"

They were at the Malone dinner table; steak-and-kidney pie and three veg. before them. There was an air of friendship and common interest between the four of them; the men, longtime friends and workmates, had had the good fortune to marry two women who had become equally strong friends. Compatibility in such terrain is an oil not easily found.

"Is this going to be gory," said Lisa, chewing on a piece of kidney.

"No," said Romy. "I leave all that behind me when I take off my gloves … Yes, we're busy. I was complaining today that we had no room left in the body storage room, when one of my assistants asked how it must have been in New York the day after September 11, did they have enough body storage rooms. That shut me up."

"That's what assistants are for," said Malone. "They breed them to tell bosses home truths."

"We're running out of blood at the blood bank," said Lisa.

"Who's getting gory now?" said Clements. "What would our kids think, listening to us? What do bus drivers and council workers talk about over steak-and-kidney pie?"

"Whatever they talk about, they don't wash it down with Grange Hermitage at God knows what this cost," said Malone and raised his glass. "Here's to the dead who die with a bottle of the best in their kit."

They drank to their dead anonymous donor. Then Romy said, "How are you settling into your new job? Being a boss with more responsibility?"

Malone was aware of Clements gazing steadily at his glass, like a judge deciding on the colour of the wine. "I think I have less responsibility now than I had before. I've got less than Russ has at the moment."

"Are you enjoying it, Russ?" asked Lisa.

There's collusion here, thought Malone. Like Russ and me swapping the bowling in an interrogation.

"I remember reading somewhere, something about anyone can hold the helm when the sea is calm," said Clements, avoiding Malone's eye. "You two have had better education than Scobie and me. Maybe you'll know who said, it."

"It sounds obvious enough to have been said by a man," said Romy. "Probably some Greek philosopher. They had the obvious answers to everything."

"Unlike German philosophers, from what she tells me," said Clements. "A miserable lot."

Malone said, "I wonder why there have been so few women philosophers?"

"Too busy housekeeping for male philosophers," said Lisa, and looked at Romy. "They live in a world all their own, don't they?"

Later, while the two women were out in the kitchen stacking the dishes, housekeeping for the philosophers, Malone said, "We're fantastically lucky, aren't we?"

"Fantastically, mate. Incredibly. At the end of the day or any other time. It's just struck me — Mrs Shipwood, I haven't once heard her say *at the end of the day*. She still thinks she has time, that everything's not over."

"Not for her, maybe. But all the other poor buggers … When we saw her out at Jack Aldwych's place, she didn't look scared. She'd got over that anthrax fright."

"Do you think she knows who did it?"

"Your guess is as good as mine. Do you reckon Jack might have sent it? Or Garry Faulks? It would have been no trouble getting the ecstasy tablets — you can buy 'em now like aspirin. Is anyone investigating it?"

Clements shrugged. "Bay Street say they are still looking into it, but I think it's just routine. It scared the shit outa the Federals, though — they've had Canberra on their necks. Any Middle Easterner who's six-foot-six and has a beard had better look out he's not nabbed as Osama bin Laden. Whoever sent that anthrax didn't think about how wide the scare would go."

"If it was Jack, do you think he'd care?"

"No. And I'm not gunna ask him. I think it was a one-off and it's not gunna lead us to who killed Marilyn Hyx."

"I'm still wondering what sort of woman she was."

"Give up, mate, we'll never fully understand them. All those philosophers fumbled it."

Then the two women came into the living room, sat down and Lisa said, "We've been discussing plans. You two are due for long service leave next year, am I right?"

Both men were cautious: "Ye-es."

"So we are taking you both to Holland and Germany to educate you in culture, cuisine and sophisticated behaviour."

Malone's pocket asked, "Who's paying?"

"We are, it's on us."

"You've saved that much out of housekeeping? I've been paying you too much."

"I knew we should of married a coupla homebody chicks," said Clements.

"Like Rosie, the learner nympho?" said Malone.

"He hasn't told me about her," said Romy, looking unworried. "I wondered how he knew so much for an unsophisticated Aussie."

"It was a top subject at the Police Academy."

When the Clements had gone, Lisa went back into the kitchen and Malone followed her. "What have you and Romy been discussing? It wasn't just a trip to Europe."

"You don't want to go?"

"Yes, I do. And I'm sure Russ wants to go, too. He's never been out of Australia, except to New

Zealand. But you and Romy were talking about something else —"

"You want a cuppa and some toast? No?" She was setting the table for breakfast. Everything in her life was ordered, but she never gave the impression of being a fusspot. "All right, yes, we were discussing something else. You two. We've been worried neither of you is happy in his new job."

Malone leaned his backside against the sink, took his time. "Yeah, but I think we've both hoped you wouldn't notice. I'm a bit lost in — in the upper echelons. It's not hands-on, the way it's been for so long."

"And Russ?"

"He's not a boss, but I'd never tell him that. He's an organiser, what I think the army calls an adjutant, but he doesn't like calling the shots."

"He seems to be all right so far."

"That's because he's got a good team under him. If the team was swapped tomorrow, he'd be lost."

"Then he depended too long on you?"

"Maybe. But don't ever mention it to him. I depended on him for years."

"I'm going to tell you something now and if you mention it to Russ, I'll lock the bedroom door with you on the outside —"

He grinned. "How long would that last?"

She approached him, kissed him. "No, I wouldn't do that. But ... Romy wants to retire, but she doesn't want to tell Russ till he's settled in in his new job."

"Why? I thought she liked her work?"

"She's suddenly tired of looking at corpses, ones that have been murdered. She said it all came to a head, *in* her head, when she and Russ were standing on opposite sides of that girl who was murdered over at Pyrmont. I didn't ask her, but I wondered if the fact that Tom was there, knew the girl, had something to do with it ... She said it had happened before, she and Russ at a murder scene, but the last time was twelve months ago. Then that night at Pyrmont — you were there —"

"I didn't notice anything, I mean between them —" But he had been more concerned for Tom.

"Neither did Russ, she says. It was just *her*. She saw herself and Russ standing over Amanda — their own daughter lying there on that bed —"

There had been times when those sort of images had plagued him: Claire, Maureen, Tom looking at him with sightless eyes. "What'll she do?"

"She says she'll teach, a day or two a week. She's already talked to Sydney University. But she'll not teach about murder victims. What she's not sure of is how will Russ take it."

"Christ, I think you two underestimate him! He'll understand. Jesus, do you think we're not sometimes turned sick by what we see? You think *I* sometimes don't see —"

"Don't say it," Lisa said and put a finger to his lips.

"No, I won't ... Romy doesn't need to worry. Russ will understand."

"Whatever made you policemen in the first place?"

"It's too far back to remember. Maybe I just thought law and order wasn't a bad way to live. I didn't join to look at murder victims."

"I know that," she said and kissed him again.

2

Next morning Malone went to a meeting of senior officers on law and order; or more specifically, the rising crime rate. It was the first time he had been to such a meeting since his promotion and several senior officers from other areas came up to congratulate him.

"Welcome to the higher altitude," said one of them. "You having trouble breathing?"

"It's heady," said Malone and the other officer, a chief superintendent, grinned, winked and passed on.

That morning the media had been banging loud drums, talkback hosts were demanding more police:

"As if recruits are standing on street corners waiting to join," said Greg Random as he and

Malone took their seats. "Have you noticed a rush of Asians to join up?"

"Watch it," said Malone.

"I'm not a racist, but … Ah, the hell with it."

Assistant Commissioner Charlie Hassett, Commander of Crime Agency, presided with his usual subtle approach: "We're gunna have racism rearing its ugly head — we're gunna hear a lot about Middle Eastern appearance. I'm not sure how they tell the difference between Italians, Greeks, Spaniards, Turks and Arabs, unless they've got their worry beads. But you can bet we're gunna hear a lot of it. Middle Eastern appearance. So be careful, see your men aren't branded as racists. There are a lot of dinki-di Aussies, big bronzed Anzacs, still creating shit in our community —"

"How true," said Malone to Random. "How many directors of Middle Eastern appearance are with companies going down the gurgler?"

"You said something, Superintendent Malone?" asked Hassett.

"No, sir. Just agreeing with everything you said."

"That's a change — for the Irish. To continue —"

After the meeting Malone went back to his office to find Clements waiting for him. The big man could not conceal his excitement, suddenly he was enjoying his new job:

"Andy has come back with the goods. He found someone who booked out on Qantas for LA in

December 1998, booked through to Miami and on to Nassau in the Bahamas."

"Who?"

"The closest connection. Harry Shipwood."

3

"You're bloody stupid," said Harry Shipwood. "Why've you got to fool around with Mrs Faulks? Her husband is your mother's worst enemy."

"He wasn't when I first started taking her out," said B.J.

"When was that?" asked his mother.

"About twelve months ago. It hasn't been regular, it's been on and off."

"You've been sleeping with her?"

"Mum —" said Chloe. "What do you think he's been doing? Holding hands, talking about the footy?"

"Don't you put your oar in," said her mother.

"Well, it's got to stop," said Harry Shipwood. "Are you in love with her?"

Chloe laughed, choking on her muesli. "God, they're so naive, the two of them!"

"You knew about it?" said Harry.

"Of course I did. He brought her here one night when you and Mum were down in Melbourne." She was the only one not yet dressed, still in her nightgown and dressing-gown. Harry and B.J.

were dressed for whatever they had planned to do about the house today. Natalie was dressed for battle, for another day at the office in her battle whites, only the jewellery was not yet donned.

The four of them were at breakfast in the small room off the kitchen. It was the only room in the house not all-white. The designer had insisted — "One must start the day on a bright note. With all due respect, Mrs Shipwood, white ain't bright. You must be lifted to face the day!" So they sat between yellow walls; blue curtains on the big window; yellow and blue tablecloth; yellow and blue crockery. The colour scheme was no help this morning.

The Shipwoods had a daily maid, a Colombian girl, but she did not arrive till 9.30. Natalie had always wanted their breakfast to be private; it was, she told herself, when they were *family*. The room looked out on the lawns and, down below them, the jetty and their cruiser. They all, in his or her own way, admired the view. This morning, however, the view was depressing. The sky was light sepia at the bottom, rising to yellow; they had had to close the windows against the smell of smoke. The bushfires were getting out of control, ringing the far reaches of the city. Things were also getting out of control here in the breakfast room.

Natalie was furious: "God, how many other women have you had here while Dad and I've been away?"

"None," said B.J. sullenly. "That night here with Dorothy was the only time."

"Where was Mr Faulks?" asked Harry.

"Down in Melbourne with you. It was the night of the Business Council dinner."

"Why didn't she come with him?"

"She told him she wasn't well, she had her periods or something —"

Chloe choked again on her muesli.

"Jesus!" It was a long time since they had seen Harry so angry; if ever. "If he'd known, he'd have thought we were conniving with you. Who else have you been involved with, what other women from Orlando? Any of the girls there?"

B.J. sat silent. Chloe looked at him, pushed away her cereal bowl and reached for some toast in the blue-and-yellow rack. Then she said, "You'd better tell them about Marilyn."

The sudden silence was tangible, one could feel it as a presence. Then Natalie said in a very tight voice, "Marilyn? Marilyn Hyx?"

B.J. just stared at his plate of Weet-Bix; he had once featured in a TV commercial for the cereal. His mother waited for an answer, then she turned to Chloe: "Our Marilyn?"

"Yes," said Chloe, biting into her toast. She was the least ruffled of the four of them, as if she had been waiting for this morning to arrive and was relieved now it was here. "It took me a long time to understand why he went for older women. I tried to talk him into seeing some of my girlfriends, one or two of 'em were hot for him —"

"Shut *up*." B.J. didn't raise his voice, but it grated like a shout.

"Why?" said Natalie. "Why Marilyn, Brandon?"

He raised his head. "I *liked* her. You did, once. And you, too." He looked at his father. "I'm not kinky because I like older women. I just felt comfortable with Marilyn. It was never going to get outa hand — it was all over by the time — by the time she was murdered."

Chloe put down her half-eaten piece of toast; still unruffled, she said, "You knew about it, didn't you, Dad? She must've told you."

Harry Shipwood was sitting very still; when he spoke his voice was as quiet as B.J.'s had been: "She told me nothing."

Natalie said, "Told you what? When?"

"I think we've had enough discussion this morning," said Harry. "We don't want to be arguing when Ramona gets here."

"Forget Ramona. I asked you — told you what? When?"

Harry stared at Chloe. "Why couldn't you keep your mouth shut?"

"I've kept it shut all this time," said Chloe, still calm. "You're my father, I didn't want to believe what I saw you doing the morning after Marilyn was murdered —"

"What did you see?" Natalie was leaning forward.

"He was burning a shirt."

"It was just an old shirt," said Harry. "I'd spilled some paint on it —"

"No, Dad. It was the shirt you were wearing the night before, when you went out. You and Mum went to some do in Parramatta — it was the blue shirt with the small check, one I liked —"

"You didn't come to that affair," said Natalie. "You came as far as the door, then left me there on my own. You said you were going to the Leagues Club or somewhere. I was there on my own for an hour and a half, then you came back —" She turned again to her daughter. "I didn't notice anything on his shirt."

"I don't know where it was — it could've been on his sleeve. All I saw the next morning was him burning the shirt. Then I found his blood-stained handkerchief — it was beside the ashcan, as if he'd dropped it and didn't know —"

"You're accusing him of killing Marilyn," said B.J. quietly. Then suddenly he erupted: "Jesus, why, Dad? Why kill her over some fucking money? Christ Almighty you used to sneer at people always chasing money —"

"That was an act —" Natalie was quiet, but one could see the tension in her. "He knew and approved everything we did. Went overseas to set up the accounts ... But to kill for it —" She shut her eyes and for a moment looked as if she were about to faint.

Chloe reached across the table to her. "Mum —"

Natalie opened her eyes. "No, I'm all right. Why, Harry? Why?"

"I did it for you," he said quietly, sitting very still in his chair. All at once he looked sad, not at all angry. "She was going to smear you all over the media, the talkback jocks, everyone. I love you, sweetheart, that was why."

"Oh Christ," said B.J. and suddenly, to the others' surprise, began to weep. Then he stood up, kicking back his chair so that it fell over, and went quickly out of the room.

"What's the matter with him?" Natalie turned to stare after the disappearing B.J.

"You really don't get it, do you?" said Chloe and sat back. It was almost as if she had become the parent, the one to keep control. "You two have really fucked up our lives. All Brandon ever wanted to be was Mummy's boy —"

"Oh, for Crissake!" Harry pushed his chair away from the table, looked for a moment as if he, too, was going to run out of the room.

"It's true, Dad. But Mum was too busy making money — and you never had any time for him —"

"He's been selfish, all his life —"

"You haven't been? You and Mum?"

"What about yourself?"

"Sure, I've been like that, I admit it. It was the easiest way to get along in this dysfunctional family. Take care of yourself, look after Number One —" She stood up, still calm, taking her time.

"Where are you going?" Natalie looked up at her.

"Up to hold Brandy's hand. Mother him, if you like to call it that —"

Then she was gone, unhurriedly, and husband and wife, father and mother, were left staring at each other over the breakfast table.

Natalie was struggling to hold herself together; she was falling apart, as if all the plastic surgery was splitting at the seams. The black hair looked incongruous above the aged face; there was no gold to shine this morning on the suddenly wrinkled neck and the bony wrists. "Harry, why didn't you tell me?"

"Before, sweetheart? Or after?"

"Before —" She was stumbling for words. "Yes, before."

"Natalie, how could I have told you *before*? I didn't know what I was going to do, I hadn't planned it. That night we went out to Parramatta, to that charity do, as soon as I picked up my name tag at the door I knew I couldn't go in and face those that I knew would be there —"

Her mind was blank, she couldn't remember who had been there or why.

"— the fat man Leshner was there and Faulks and his missus. One or two others from Orlando.

You and I, we both knew there were rumours of what was happening — someone was leaking it, but we didn't know who it was or to whom —"

"Why did you think it was Marilyn?" She was gradually stiffening herself; her hands, that had been opening and closing, were now still. "We trusted her —"

"*You* trusted her. I was never sure —" That was not true. It was that he had become unsure of everyone at Orlando.

"When you went out there to see her … *Why* did you go to see her? Had you planned to?"

"No, it was spur of the moment. Just that we were out there, the Back of Beyond —"

"Don't joke, Harry … Did she tell you she was planning to expose us?"

"Not in so many words, no. She got angry, said she had things that would tell the world we were thieves — she even said something about a vision, whatever the hell she meant by that —"

"Harry, you probably worked her up into that state —"

"Sweetheart, stop trying to find excuses for her. She hadn't kept all those papers, those records, to start a bonfire." He turned his head, gestured out at the smoke-tinged sky. "Or a bushfire. After it happened I went through the house — I thought I'd be panic-stricken, but I wasn't — I can't explain it —"

"How did it happen?"

"I really don't know. Honestly. There was a knife on the coffee table between us, she'd been slicing an apple or something when I got there, she was watching TV, they were re-running what happened in New York ... I just lost my temper and —" He stopped suddenly, looked down at his hand, which had picked up a table knife. He stared at it, then threw it on the table. "She was going to ruin you, Natalie. No two ways about it. I did it for you, no other reason. I'm sorry, if that's what you want."

"Oh Harry!" Her cry was like that of a trapped animal, suddenly freed but too wounded to limp away.

4

When Malone and Clements got out of their car the two old comedians, if that was what they were, were sitting on the bench in front of the Shipwood residence. The yellow light made them look older, as if a patina of years was settling on them.

"Last time you were here, we thought you were estate agents," said the taller man, rubbing the top of his bald head. "That was a laugh. You're coppers, aren't you?"

"Police, yes," said Malone. "You know any police jokes?"

"Not today. Dan and I have decided there's little to joke about today. The world is going down the toilet." He gestured at the folded newspaper between them. "Dan has never liked toilet jokes."

"Too much crap," said Dan Ovenden and coughed a laugh that had no merriment in it. "The Shipwoods are in the crap, aren't they?"

"What've you heard?" asked Clements.

"Just rumours," said the taller man. "We didn't lose anything in their company — we're cautious investors, aren't we, Dan?"

"He wouldn't invest in Buckingham Palace if it was on the market."

"We know people who did do their money in Orlando," said the taller man. "People who live around here. You going to arrest them? When you bring 'em out, we'll give you a standing ovation, won't we, Dan?"

"I'll put me teeth back in and whistle." They couldn't forgo the gags.

"We'd rather you didn't," said Malone. "That is, if we do arrest them."

"Don't deny us our little pleasures," said Dan Ovenden and his eyes seemed to glimmer behind his gold-rimmed glasses. "There's not much to applaud these days."

"Very true," said Malone and followed Clements up the short driveway to the front door of the Shipwood house. The garage doors were closed, no Bentley or other cars on display.

Clements looked at the house. "You think they'd like to be in Tuscany now?"

"More likely Majorca or the Bahamas."

Then the door opened before Clements could lift Gog or Magog, the knockers. "Oh. Are Mr and Mrs Shipwood in?"

The woman was dark-haired, dark-eyed, twenty kilos past pretty. "Yes, they here —"

She went to push past them, but Clements blocked her. "You are —"

"Ramona — the maid —" She hung back against the door jamb. "They told me to go home — there's trouble —"

"What sorta trouble?"

"Mr Shipwood, he down on the boat — got a gun —"

"Shit!" said Clements and pushed past her into the house.

Ramona looked at Malone; she had come all this way looking for a peaceful life, but there were still guns. "Please — can I go?"

"Go home, Ramona. We'll straighten this out."

"I hope so. I don't wanna lose my job —" First things first. She pushed past Malone and almost ran down the driveway to a small, shabby car in the street. The two old men stood up as she ran past them, but she ignored them, got to her car, fumbled for keys, opened the door and fell in.

Malone went into the house, heard voices and followed the sound into the big living room. B.J. and Chloe stood by the open French doors, holding hands, and Clements was on his mobile.

"Yes, *now*! Get the SPG — the bloke has a gun …
Okay, we'll just keep watch till you get here." He
clicked off his phone and looked at Malone, shaking
his head. "Sutherland are sending back-up —"

B.J. let go his sister's hand and turned round.
"You said SPG? The guys with the body gear and
guns? Jesus, why do we want them?"

"Your father's got a gun — it's a procedure
we've gotta go with —"

Malone went to the French doors, looked down
towards the water. Natalie Shipwood stood on the
end of the jetty, talking and gesticulating at Harry
Shipwood, who sat in the well of the cruiser,
looking down at her and seeming to be saying
nothing.

"You said he has a gun — what sort? A .22,
something like that?"

"No, a Walther," said B.J. "We keep it on the
boat."

"A Walther? Where's the ammo?"

"There's ammo on board. Yes, I think Dad has
loaded it. Can't you go down and reason with
him? He won't talk to me or my sister."

"He doesn't look as if he's talking to Mum,"
said Chloe.

Malone turned to Clements, who said, "No, you
can't go down there. There's a negotiator on the
way — we have to wait for him —"

"Jesus!" Chloe, who had been standing very
still, staring down towards the jetty, suddenly

swung round. "Fucking procedure! My father's down there — he might kill our mother, kill himself, and you say we have to wait on some fucking negotiator! I'll go down there myself —"

"No!" B.J. grabbed her hand again. "He's not gunna listen to you — or me. But Christ —" He turned back to Clements. "Why do we need the SPG? I've seen 'em on TV — swarming all over the fucking place —"

"They prevent a lot of carnage," said Malone. "How many times have you seen them let fly? Just them being there may quieten your dad. I've seen it happen, twice — the bloke with the gun sees what's surrounding him and he weighs his chances —"

"Some of them put the gun to their own head —" said Chloe, then put her hand over her mouth before it destroyed her any further.

Malone stepped past her and out on to the brick path that bordered the top end of the lawns. "Mrs Shipwood! Natalie!"

She turned and looked up towards him, didn't seem to recognise him, then turned back to say something to her husband. Then he stood up in the well of the boat and shouted, "Superintendent Malone? Come on down. Just you, no-one else."

"Yes," said B.J. "Go down and talk to him."

"No," said Clements, moving out to stand beside Malone. "We wait for the negotiator."

"How long?"

"I dunno. Sutherland said they'd be here in ten minutes, but whether they've got a negotiator on staff, I dunno ... Anyhow, you're not going down there. I'm in charge, mate. Keep that in mind."

"Holy Christ!" said B.J. "Arguing about who's in charge!"

"Shut up, B.J.," said Clements. "I dunno what happened before we got here, but you four Shipwoods created this situation. Not us. We just have to clean it up. And we'll do it my way, understand?"

Across the water a woman was hosing a garden that bordered her lawns; bands of colour ran down like molten metal. A man was wheeled out in a wheelchair to sit in the sun, but he immediately started coughing, pointed up at the sky and was wheeled back into his house, the woman behind his chair arguing with him. A small cruiser went down the waterway, its wake slipping away from it like oil to slap against the boats moored along the jetties and landing stages. A man and woman on board, both wearing yachting caps, waved and Natalie Shipwood raised a stiff arm and waved back.

"What caused all this?" asked Clements.

B.J. and Chloe looked at each other, then B.J. said, "Dad told us he killed Marilyn Hyx. That's why you're here, isn't it?"

"Yes," said Clements, showing no reaction, not looking at Malone. "That's why we're here. And that's why we need to wait for the negotiator. To get your dad up here without him doing any harm to himself or anyone else. Has he threatened your mother?"

"No, he wouldn't do that," said B.J. "He said he killed Marilyn because he wanted to protect Mum."

Then Malone said, "Here she comes."

Natalie Shipwood was coming back up the lawn, walking stiffly, as if afraid her legs would buckle beneath her. Harry Shipwood was still standing in the well of the boat, looking up towards the house. Chloe suddenly let go of her brother's hand and went quickly out to put her arm round her mother's shoulders.

The two detectives stepped forward to meet them. Natalie stopped, leaning on her daughter, and stared at the two men. For a moment it seemed she was not going to speak to them, was going to walk right by them, then she said, her voice not much louder than a husky whisper, "He wants to talk to you Superintendent. Please go down to him —"

"I can't, Mrs Shipwood —"

Then faraway there was the sound of sirens, that thin scream of warning. Natalie turned her head towards the west. Down on the boat Harry Shipwood was also looking west. Then he turned and shouted at the house: "Malone! Superintendent, come down here before they get here!"

"Please, Mr Malone, go down —" This pleading Natalie Shipwood was almost unrecognisable. "I'm afraid he'll shoot himself — the gun is loaded —"

The sirens were getting closer, but it would be a minute or two before the reinforcements were here, would be spreading out around the house. Malone looked at Clements: "It's worth the risk — if he sees the SPG blokes, he may —"

"Go down," said Clements. "I'll take the responsibility. Have you got your gun?"

"No, I didn't bring it. We weren't expecting this —"

"Better take mine —"

"No!" Chloe let go of her mother, stepped towards Malone. "Please — he won't shoot you. But if he sees you with a gun —"

"I'll be okay," Malone told Clements. "Just keep me covered."

"From here with a Glock?" But Clements nodded. "Okay, but don't get too close to him. No heroics."

As Malone began to walk down over the lawn the sirens abruptly died away; the world was suddenly silent. He walked steadily but unhurriedly, raising his arms above his head as he stepped onto the jetty. He had been in this sort of situation before and he could feel the tightening in his belly; his bladder suddenly seemed full, ready to burst. Don't let me piss myself, he said to no-one in particular: you didn't ask God to control your bladder.

"Stop there, Superintendent. Have you got a gun?"

"No, Harry." He opened his jacket. "Put your gun down."

Harry Shipwood smiled, a tired smile. "Not yet. Those sirens — are more police on the way?"

"Yes. And the State Protection Group."

"Those guys with flak jackets and riot guns? Jesus, who do they think I am — Mr bin Laden? I'm not a terrorist, you can see that ... Step up here with me, Superintendent. Come aboard, as they say —" He backed away to let Malone clamber up into the well of the cruiser. "Okay, Superintendent —"

"Scobie. Let's cut out the rank, Harry."

"Whatever you want." He was holding the gun loosely, but pointed at Malone. Then his hand stiffened, the gun coming up; Malone felt his belly tighten till it hurt, waiting for the bullet. But Shipwood was looking past him, up at the house. "Holy Jesus!"

Malone, now on board the boat, looked back. Clements and the Shipwood family were still in the doorway of the living room, but they were surrounded now by police. SPG men were spread across the top end of the lawns, kneeling, guns aimed, making no attempt to take cover. It was a show of force designed to make Harry Shipwood realise the hopelessness of his situation.

"Doesn't look good, Harry. What's the point?"

"Sit down, Scobie. No, you sit there, between

me and the army." He sat down in one of the chairs bolted to the deck and Malone sat opposite him. "The neighbours must be loving this."

On both sides of the waterway people were coming out of their houses; on the opposite bank a couple brought out deck chairs and sat down to watch the show. A police officer on a loud-hailer was telling everyone to go back inside, but only a few obeyed the order. The man in the wheelchair was now outside again, not complaining this time about the atmosphere.

"We should've put on a regatta," said Harry Shipwood, then settled down as if Malone were the only man in sight and was to get all his attention. "You ever read philosophy, Scobie?"

"Never read it, no. But in police work we have to practise it every day. Like now."

"Good point." He looked up towards the house again, then back at Malone. "Philosophers are like proverb-makers, they all contradict each other."

"I've said the same thing. My wife wonders why there have not been more women philosophers —" Keep 'em talking: he remembered a lecture on negotiation. "What philosophers are you contradicting right now?"

"Oh, dozens, probably … When Natalie first started to make good, I read Nietzsche — you heard of him?"

"No."

"An arrogant bastard, preached the superiority of the masters. The Nazis thought a lot of him..." He was taking his time, as if he had loads of time. "I didn't worship money when I was at the university — I taught the theory of it, but didn't worship it. Then when Natalie started to make it, lots of it, I thought that's for us. Superiority of the masters, the ones with money. Greed was just taking over, remember? It was no longer a social sin. We started to salt it away — you know about that?"

"The Shahriver Bank in the Caicos? Yes, we know about it. ASIC are going to try and bring it all back here."

Shipwood smiled. "Good luck to 'em ... We thought it was a lot of the ready, but it'd just be joke money to a billionaire like Bill Gates or one or two of our homegrown ones. It's turned into a joke, a sour one —" Then he looked up towards the house again. "How patient are those buggers?"

Malone didn't look over his shoulder, but he knew to whom Shipwood was referring. "Very patient. I've seen them lay a siege for twelve or fifteen hours."

"Well —" Shipwood remained staring up at the house a few more moments, then he looked back at Malone. "I was saying ... A sour joke. We had all that money overseas, but we could never bring it back, not all of it, to enjoy it here. And here —"

He nodded up towards the house. "Here, I found, was the only place I wanted to be."

"It's all over, Harry."

"Yeah ... We've lost our kids, too, Natalie and I. You have kids?"

"Three. Still friends with me and my wife."

"No trouble?"

"No," said Malone and made it sound truthful. "Your kids, B.J. and Chloe, they want you to put the gun down. They're on your side, Harry, they want you alive."

"Sure. And they'll visit me in jail every week for the next fifteen years." He looked at the gun. "I don't really have a choice, Scobie."

"Where'd you get that?" *Keep him talking.* "A Walther isn't too common."

"Any sort of gun is common these days, Scobie. You're a cop, you should know that ... James Bond used one of these in his early films, a Walther PPK. And they were very popular with the IRA at one time. I've never used it, not even to take potshots at fish or birds. I've carried it on the boat for — I dunno. Protection. Against what? Against them?" He nodded up towards the SPG. Then he leaned back, stroked the Vandyke beard. "You can't help me?"

"Harry, I don't know the circumstances of why you killed Marilyn Hyx. All I can do is help you stay alive. That's something."

"Not enough, Scobie."

Then he reached behind him, produced a mobile phone. Keeping an eye on Malone, he punched some numbers. Then: "Sweetheart?"

Malone turned his head to look up at the house. Natalie Shipwood, still in the doorway, had a mobile to her ear.

Then he looked back at Shipwood, who was shaking his head. "No, sweetheart. It's all over. I love you."

He clicked off the phone, dropped it behind him again. Malone sat very still, wondering if he could jump across the short space between them and take the gun from Shipwood. The latter sat very still, as if he, too, was making a decision.

Then he looked at Malone, for a moment had trouble focussing his gaze. "Nietzsche said something else. About the melancholy of all things completed."

And put the gun in his mouth and pulled the trigger.

Chapter Twelve

❧

1

"You should be disciplined. You did the wrong thing," said Assistant Commissioner Charlie Hassett.

"I admit that, sir," said Malone and kept a straight face. "But a dozen professional negotiators wouldn't have got through to Harry Shipwood. His mind was dead before I went down to talk to him."

"That's true, sir," said Clements. "I authorised him to do it, I was in charge, when Shipwood said he would only talk to Superintendent Malone."

Hassett looked at Greg Random. "They stick together like shit to a blanket, don't they?"

"They're great negotiators," said Random. "For each other."

"You buggers drive me up the wall. Okay, how's the rest of this mess?"

"Mrs Shipwood has half a dozen charges against her," said Clements. "They'll let her out on bail, then we sit and wait for another year or so."

"And Mr Sweden?"

"Lilywhite — or that's how he's made it look. He's got everything covered. ASIC will have a hard job nailing him."

"Unless Jack Aldwych gets him," said Malone softly.

"Pardon?" said Hassett, whose ears would have made him at home in any branch of the animal kingdom. "You said something about Jack Aldwych."

"Sweden and Mrs Shipwood owe Jack money. That's how he looks at the collapse of Orlando."

"They owe everybody money, from what I've read. Has Aldwych threatened them?"

"We're not sure —" said Clements.

Hassett looked at Random. "They're negotiating again. Get 'em outa here." The three of them were at his office door when he looked up and grinned at them. "Give my regards to Jack. I love to hear of reformed characters."

That was the day after the suicide of Harry Shipwood. Malone was sent on trauma leave and recovered more quickly than he or the doctors expected. The weeks were rolled over on the calendar; weeks turned into months; 2001 turned into 2002, a number that pens still stumbled on. The images of September 11 began to fade but would never be erased. The war against terrorism went on, but now was just skirmishes in Afghanistan, a country a lot of people still had trouble finding on the map.

Osama bin Laden was still just a shadow, still unbombed, still not caught. The bushfires finally petered out, with millions of dollars' worth of damage but, fortunately, no lives lost. The skies cleared of smoke, above New York, above the outskirts of Sydney, and people, as they have forever, began to think of other things.

Natalie Shipwood, everything, including herself, collapsed, sits in her house at Sylvania Waters, wanting to die but afraid to. The Bentley is gone, Ramona has found a job elsewhere. Natalie still dresses all in white, but the black hair is grey now and all the jewellery is gone. There is no resemblance to Elizabeth Taylor, not at any distance.

B.J. Shipwood is now in England playing for a rugby league club there. He lives in Leeds with a blonde model, a Scandinavian girl of his own age who mothers him.

Chloe Shipwood works in Hong Kong as house model for a dress manufacturer, but is thinking of moving on. To where, she is not sure. Just somewhere where the Shipwood name won't mean anything. She thought of changing it, but so far hasn't. She has had several offers of marriage or other arrangements while in Hong Kong, but has declined them all. She will come home, she thinks, for her mother's trial, due in September.

Derek and Rosalind Sweden, teflon-coated, still sail on the waters of Sydney society, which forgives everything if the price is right and the hospitality lavish. Sweden is no longer on the board of the Business Ethics Council, having resigned for health reasons and to pursue other interests, as the saying goes. There is no longer any board of directors for Orlando Development, so he no longer has any conflict of interest. The money that was in the Shahriver Bank is now invested in European equities in the name of a trust in Bucharest. The Roumanian government recently gave him the Star of Queen Marie, second class. Rosalind wears it on occasions when decorations are worn.

Jack Aldwych still sits in his house on the hill at Harbord, reminiscing with Blackie Ovens about the Good Old Days. Age has slowed him and if he has mellowed, it is only because it is now too much effort to think of revenge and other useless pursuits. He has never read Nietzsche, wouldn't have a clue who he was, but he is suffering from the melancholy of all things completed.

Mick and Phoebe Kelray are now in the house at Rooty Hill, happy as a newly married couple might be; almost. Phoebe's arteriosclerosis has got no worse, but the doctors tell Mick it is only a matter of time. A stair lift has been installed and Phoebe, laughing like a child, rides up and down it, like a child. Mick laughs till he cries.

They are becoming close friends with Nigger and Josie Brown. The latter two are happy, except when Nigger drives out to the freeway with his tow-truck. He sits there, looking for a moment at the mess of lives in the wrecks, swearing at the fucking idiots there are on the roads, and he never tells Josie what he thinks in those moments.

The Malone children, and the grandchild, go their own ways, but always connected to their parents.

Malone and Lisa, Clements and Romy, are now in Europe on the men's long service leave. If sophistication was supposed to coat the men during the tour, so far it isn't apparent. Neither of them is enjoying the food any more than that at home: true-blue Aussies, they compare every meal to those back in Sydney. They do appreciate the architecture of times past; they are not dumb nor blind and they walk through art galleries and admire Rembrandt and Hals and Turner. They sit at open-air cafés and watch the passing parade, especially the women, but make no comment to their wives. Lisa and Romy watch the slow conversion with silent amusement.

Malone and Lisa were in bed in an inn in the Black Forest; they were leaving for home tomorrow. "Are you glad you came?" she asked.

"Yes. No regrets at all. I may even contribute towards what it cost you. Within reason."

"Of course, within reason. I've added up all the tipping I've done. You can repay that."

"You were too generous. Fifteen and twenty per cent!"

"Kiss me. Where's your loving hand?"

"Here in the forest —"

Then his mobile rang. It was the bloody kids, back home in Sydney, wanting to know if Mum and Dad were enjoying themselves.

THE END

Kirribilli
June 2001–December 2002

About the Author

Jon Cleary is one of the statesmen of Australian storytelling. He was born in Erskineville, Sydney, in 1917, and has been a self-supporting professional writer since the 1940s, working in films and television in the United States and Britain. Seven of his books have been made into feature films and three have been adapted for television. A number of his recent Scobie Malone stories have been optioned for a television series. His most famous novel, *The Sundowners*, has sold more than three million copies, and his work has been translated and published in 14 countries. He has collected a number of literary prizes including the coveted Edgar Award, the Australian Literary

Society's Church Medal for Best Australian Novel, and the Award for Lifelong Contribution to Crime, Mystery and Detective Genres at the 1995 inaugural Ned Kelly Awards.

In Scobie Malone, Jon Cleary has found the perfect device both to apply his characteristic dry humour and at the same time deal with contemporary issues. In fact, no one writes about life in Sydney today better than Cleary. A lifetime of meticulous research gives him the edge on many crime writers who set their books in particular cities; Cleary's are not only page-turning mysteries, but fascinating snapshots of modern society.